DESIRE BY
STARLIGHT

Acclaim for Radclyffe's Fiction

2010 Prism award winner and ForeWord Review Book of the Year Award finalist *Secrets in the Stone* is "so powerfully [written] that the worlds of these three women shimmer between reality and dreams... A strong, must read novel that will linger in the minds of readers long after the last page is turned."—*Just About Write*

Lambda Literary Award winner *Stolen Moments* "is a collection of steamy stories about women who just couldn't wait. It's sex when desire overrides reason, and it's incredibly hot!"—*On Our Backs*

Lambda Literary Award winner *Distant Shores, Silent Thunder* "weaves an intricate tapestry about passion and commitment between lovers. The story explores the fragile nature of trust and the sanctuary provided by loving relationships."—*Sapphic Reader*

Lambda Literary and Benjamin Franklin Award Finalist *The Lonely Hearts Club* "is an ensemble piece that follows the lives [and loves] of three women, with a plot as carefully woven as a fine piece of cloth."—*Midwest Book Review*

ForeWord's Book of the Year finalist *Night Call* features "gripping medical drama, characters drawn with depth and compassion, and incredibly hot [love] scenes."—*Just About Write*

Lambda Literary Award Finalist *Justice Served* delivers a "crisply written, fast-paced story with twists and turns and keeps us guessing until the final explosive ending."—*Independent Gay Writer*

Lambda Literary Award finalist *Turn Back Time* "is filled with wonderful love scenes, which are both tender and hot."—*MegaScene*

Lambda Literary Award finalist *When Dreams Tremble*'s "focus on character development is meticulous and comprehensive, filled with angst, regret, and longing, building to the ultimate climax."—*Just About Write*

Applause for L.L. Raand's *The Midnight Hunt*

"*The Midnight Hunt* has a gripping story to tell, and while there are also some truly erotic sex scenes, the story always takes precedent. This is a great read which is not easily put down nor easily forgotten."
—*Just About Write*

"Thrilling and sensual drama with protagonists who are as alluring as they are complex."—Nell Stark, author of the paranormal romances *everafter* and *nevermore*

"An engaging cast of characters and a flow that never skips a beat. Its rich eroticism and tension-packed plot will have readers enthralled. It's a book with a delicious bite."—Winter Pennington, author of *Witch Wolf* and *Raven's Mask*, the Kassandra Lyall Preternatural Investigator paranormal romance novels

"'Night's been crazy and it isn't even a full moon.' Who needs the full moon when you have the whole of planet Earth? L.L. Raand has created a Midnight otherworld with razor-cut precision. Sharp political intrigue, furious action, and at its core a compelling romance with creatures from your darkest dreams. The curtain rises on a thrilling new paranormal series."—Gill McKnight, author of *Goldenseal* and *Ambereye*, the Garoul paranormal romance series

"L.L. Raand's vision of a world where Weres, Vampires, and more co-exist with humans is fascinating and richly detailed, and the story she tells is not only original but deeply erotic. A satisfying read in every sense of the word."—Meghan O'Brien, author of the paranormal romance *Wild*

By Radclyffe

Romances

Innocent Hearts

Promising Hearts

Love's Melody Lost

Love's Tender Warriors

Tomorrow's Promise

Love's Masquerade

shadowland

Passion's Bright Fury

Fated Love

Turn Back Time

When Dreams Tremble

The Lonely Hearts Club

Night Call

Secrets in the Stone

Desire by Starlight

Erotica

Erotic Interludes: *Change Of Pace*
(A Short Story Collection)

Radical Encounters
(An Erotic Short Story Collection)

Stacia Seaman and Radclyffe, eds.:

Erotic Interludes 2: *Stolen Moments*

Erotic Interludes 3: *Lessons in Love*

Erotic Interludes 4: *Extreme Passions*

Erotic Interludes 5: *Road Games*

Romantic Interludes 1: *Discovery*

Romantic Interludes 2: *Secrets*

The Provincetown Tales

Safe Harbor	Storms of Change
Beyond the Breakwater	Winds of Fortune
Distant Shores, Silent Thunder	Returning Tides

Honor Series

Above All, Honor

Honor Bound

Love & Honor

Honor Guards

Honor Reclaimed

Honor Under Siege

Word of Honor

Justice Series

A Matter of Trust (prequel)

Shield of Justice

In Pursuit of Justice

Justice in the Shadows

Justice Served

Justice for All

First Responders Novels
Trauma Alert

Writing as L.L. Raand

Midnight Hunters
The Midnight Hunt

Desire by
Starlight

by

RADCLY*f*FE

2010

DESIRE BY STARLIGHT

ISBN 10: 1-60282-188-7
ISBN 13: 978-1-60282-188-0

This Trade Paperback Original Is Published By
Bold Strokes Books, Inc.
P.O. Box 249
Valley Falls, NY 12185

First Edition: November 2010

CREDITS
EDITORS: RUTH STERNGLANTZ AND STACIA SEAMAN
PRODUCTION DESIGN: STACIA SEAMAN
COVER DESIGN BY SHERI (GRAPHICARTIST2020@HOTMAIL.COM)

Acknowledgments

"Write what you know" is a time-honored convention, but as most authors soon discover, if we only wrote what we have actually experienced, how dull our books would be. The beauty of fiction lies in the art of discovery, for the author and the reader, as we create and experience new worlds, new thoughts, new sensations—or revisit cherished ones. Within the pages, real or virtual, we dream, we dare, we revisit past joys, conquer old fears, and step beyond the confines of the here and now. What we know becomes what we hope to know, and that expectation keeps us coming back time and again.

If there's any shine on this story, the credit goes to my first readers: Connie, Diane, Eva, Jenny, Kelly, Paula, Sandy, and Tina, who read and reread various versions while I worked on fine points.

Ruth Sternglantz edited with her usual wisdom and thoroughness, and Stacia Seaman, as always, made me look good. Somehow, once again, amazing Sheri created a cover the first time out that captured perfectly my vision of this book.

And to Lee goes the credit for creating my freedom to be. *Amo te.*

Radclyffe
November 2010

Chapter One

Women loved Cassandra Hart—even her press releases said so. Jenna's quick peek at the seemingly endless line of fans snaking up to the signing table at the Barnes & Noble in Hoboken, New Jersey, indicated quite a few men loved her too. True, the jostling, eager readers had come to see Cassandra Hart, *New York Times* best-selling romance author, and not Jenna Hardy, but that was just fine with her. She loved being Cassandra Hart, especially on nights like this one. Tonight she'd wowed a sell-out crowd, and the satisfaction was nearly as good as sex.

No matter how many successes she had, she still suffered a few pangs of anxiety before every book launch, but this event had been standing room only. She'd chosen a steamy scene from her newest romance featuring sexy federal agents and renegade mercenaries, and the applause when she'd finished had vibrated through her with the electrifying charge of an orgasm. Riding high, her pulse racing and her body tingling, she'd let the question-and-answer period go overtime and now her signing was running late too. Her publicist, agent, and good friend Alice Smith signaled vigorously from the back of the room and the message was unmistakable. *Stop signing! Time to wrap this up!*

Pretending not to see Alice's semaphore-like arm motions, Jenna accepted the next book, already opened to the page she usually signed, from the store assistant. She smiled up at a youngish blonde in blue jeans and a tight long-sleeved T-shirt that announced *EMTs Do It Better.*

"Hello," Jenna said, meeting the woman's gleaming blue eyes. "Thank you so much for coming. How are you tonight?"

"I'm wonderful! I just love your books, Ms. Hart." The blonde's dazzling smile widened. "And I *really* love Cyn Reynolds. She could arrest me any day."

"I'm with you," Jenna said, laughing at the frequent comment about one of her recurring characters. "I'm so glad you could come tonight."

Jenna loved talking with her readers. Writing was such a solitary experience, something she did alone hour after hour in a silent room, and she often wondered if it really mattered to anyone what she was doing. But hearing the excitement in this woman's voice, she was reminded of one of the most important reasons that she wrote. For a few brief moments her words connected her to other human beings, and she was no longer alone. "To whom would you like me to sign this?"

"Oh, could you sign it to me—oh, I'm Sally—and could you say—Happy birthday, from Cassandra. And"—the blonde hesitated, blushing—"could I get my picture with you?"

"Of course." Jenna rose, ignoring Alice's frown and pointed look at her wristwatch. Readers like Sally made her life possible, so she took her time with every one, asking their name, writing a personal message in their book, thanking them for their support. She waited until Sally came around the table to stand beside her, then lightly clasped her waist and smiled as the store assistant, using Sally's camera, took their picture. Then she sat down, took the next hardback passed to her, and greeted another reader.

A faint cloud of Obsession accompanied the firm press of a hand against her shoulder.

"You need to pull the plug on this," Alice murmured in her ear. "You have an early flight in the morning, double bookings in the afternoon and evening, and you look completely exhausted. I told you that signing last night was a bad idea."

"I'm all right." Jenna pressed a hand to her midsection, hunger pangs reminding her she hadn't eaten after rushing from the airport to the hotel, hurriedly changing, and grabbing a cab over to the bookstore. Her flight from Washington, DC, where she had given a reading at a small bookstore in Dupont Circle, had been delayed, and she'd barely gotten any sleep. She was still glad she'd squeezed in the extra event, despite Alice's protests. She hadn't sold very many books, but the audience members—largely gay and lesbian— were among her staunchest supporters. She frequently reminded Alice that a great deal of her success lay in being accessible to those who bought her books. Unlike many best-selling authors, she still did small independent bookstore events even though Alice nagged her to conserve her time and energy for the national tours. Feeling Alice's glare on the back of her neck like an angry wasp, she tried to stretch out the cramps in her lower back without Alice noticing. "How many more in line?"

"More than you can handle."

"Just a little while longer." Jenna tuned out Alice's long-suffering sigh and focused on an elderly gentleman in a three-piece suit who looked only moderately uncomfortable surrounded by the primarily female crowd. "Hi, so nice to see you."

He held out her newest title, whose cover featured two camo-clad women in a tight clinch against a backdrop of strafer tracings. "I'd like to get this for my wife. Her name is Joan."

"Wonderful," Jenna said. "Shall I say it's from you?"

He looked momentarily abashed, then smiled broadly. "Yes please. Could you say, 'Love from Martin'—and then your name, of course."

Jenna wrote the message and signed *Cassandra Hart* with her trademark flourish. "Here you are."

As she handed the book back, she caught sight of the glossy promotional photograph on the back cover of a woman standing on a bridge high above the Hudson, chestnut hair stylishly windblown and wide-set green eyes just the tiniest bit provocative. Like always, she experienced a moment of confusion. Was that really her? Cassandra Hart looked confident, sexy, and a little bit sinful. Jenna had worked hard to create that image, to become that woman, and if she had to get by on a couple hours' sleep and airport food a few months a year to ensure she remained that woman, she would. Gladly.

"I'm sorry," the store manager announced to the remaining fans in a pleasant voice, "but we're going to have to end our event for the evening. We will have signed copies of Cassandra's newest book at the registers for those of you in line who would like to purchase one, but they will not be personalized. We're so sorry, but Ms. Hart is finished signing for the night."

Jenna knew better than to argue. If she did, Alice was likely to drag her bodily from the store. She pushed back from the table and was about to stand when a willowy redhead in a beige linen suit and open-collared emerald green shirt the exact color of her eyes stopped in front of the table and leaned down, one hand braced on the tabletop in an unexpectedly intimate pose.

"I'm sure you've had a very long day," the redhead said, "and I won't keep you. I just wanted to tell you that my fifteen-year-old niece thinks you are the most astonishing author on the planet. It means a lot that she can feel good about herself because of what you write. So—thank you."

"You're welcome." Jenna settled back into her chair and grabbed a book from the box the assistant was refilling. She opened it to the title page. "What's your niece's name?"

"Meg."

The redhead's voice was low and melodious and her emerald eyes so intense they might have been the actual gemstones.

"Have you read this one?" Jenna asked, her pen poised over the page.

"Not yet."

The woman leaned closer, her expression so magnetic everyone else in the room faded to sepia. "I have a confession to make."

"Really?" Jenna searched for a sign the redhead's intent matched her seductive tone. Oh yes indeed, there was an invitation in that hot gaze, if she wanted to play. "And what deep dark secrets are you hiding?"

"I don't really read romances. I prefer thrillers."

"Somehow I don't find that particularly surprising." Jenna had the urge to lean away precisely because she *wanted* to move forward, deeper into the redhead's space. She wasn't used to being captivated by a woman. That was *her* role. In fact, her Number One Rule was to never go to bed with a woman she couldn't control.

"I heard your reading tonight," the woman went on, "and if the rest of the book is as good as the sex, I think I could be missing something."

"Perhaps if you gave it a try," Jenna said, "you might be converted."

An arched brow winged upward. "Try what? The sex or the book?"

Jenna hesitated, considering. She was hungry, she was tired, and after three weeks on the road, she still had another four weeks ahead of her. She should grab a quick shower and a few hours' sleep. But she loved the pace, she loved the excitement, and she loved the unexpected. This redhead was definitely unexpected, she was too charged to sleep, and she hadn't had sex for months. She plucked a bookmark off the stack remaining on the table, turned it over, and wrote the name of her hotel along with her room number. She slid it into the book after writing on the title page: *Dear Meg, Celebrate your life and all the wonderful things to come. Love, Cassandra Hart.* Handing the closed book to the redhead, she said, "The evening's activities are up to you. Keep the bookmark."

"Oh, I've already made up my mind."

"Don't tell me. I like surprises."

The woman laughed, pulled the bookmark free and slid it into her jacket pocket, and sauntered away. Watching her go, Jenna finally rose from the table and smiled at the thought of what other surprises the night might bring.

"You don't have time for that." Alice drew Jenna away from the table with one hand on her elbow. "It's almost eleven and you need to be at the airport by six."

Jenna regarded the woman to whom she attributed much of her success. At forty, Alice looked a decade younger. Her milk chocolate eyes and sharply contrasting silver-blond hair added to the allure of a sensuous smile. An inch or two shorter than Jenna's five-eight, she was voluptuous where Jenna could barely boast curves. Many an editor and publisher had looked at Alice and seen a throwback to the pinup starlets of an earlier age. They underestimated her barracuda instincts when negotiating contracts, much to Jenna's benefit. She and Alice were very close friends, but business always came first for Alice. Jenna didn't mind. She felt the same.

"When have I ever been late for a flight?" Jenna draped her navy silk blazer over her arm. June had turned the corner into summer and she hadn't needed to wear it over her white silk tee.

"I'm the one who makes your schedule, remember?" Alice spoke quietly so those nearby would not hear. "We can't afford for you to burn out, especially not for something as trivial as a quickie—"

"If you were getting a little something a little more regularly," Jenna teased, "you would appreciate the benefits of physical therapy."

"Then I'll schedule you a *massage* in Chicago."

"Wonderful." Jenna skirted around the table to put an end to the conversation. She glanced back over her shoulder and flashed Alice a grin. "Make sure you sign me up for the full body package."

❖

Jenna finally dragged herself into her hotel room just before midnight and immediately kicked off her low heels and shed the navy pants that matched her blazer. While dialing room service, she powered up her laptop and checked her e-mail. Her editor had sent the galleys for her next novel, the story of a returning soldier who fell in love with the widow of one of her fallen comrades, and she downloaded that while ordering shrimp cocktail and a salad.

"How soon can you bring that?" Forty-five minutes. Plenty of time for a shower. "That's great. Thanks."

She deposited her underwear into a laundry bag, folded her suit into her suitcase to deliver to the hotel dry cleaners as soon as she reached her next destination, and padded nude toward the bathroom. Her eyes stung with fatigue and the turned-down bed called to her invitingly as she passed, but she wanted to get to the galleys tonight.

And she really should eat something. She'd noticed when getting dressed earlier that her waistband was loose and she was dropping weight she really couldn't afford to do without. Always on the thin side, despite having what her stepmother Darlene called a trucker's appetite, she had trouble maintaining her weight when her schedule was so hectic she often forgot meals. She could review the galleys while she ate—multitasking was her forte, after all. Besides, there was always the possibility she might have company if the bookmark message did its job.

Smiling at the memory of the sexy redhead from the bookstore, Jenna stepped under the warm water, tilted her head back, and let the spray wash away some of the weariness. Beneath the exhaustion, she was still soaring with the evening's success. That charge kept her going, gave her more satisfaction than anything else she'd ever known, and she never wanted the high to end. The breakneck pace of her life, like a train hurtling forward, carried her far beyond the past she wanted to forget.

She'd discovered by accident when she was ten or eleven that the voices of the characters she created in her imagination drowned out the sounds of Darlene's harsh criticism, muffled the loud curses outside her window of drunks wandering home through the trailer park in the small hours of the night, and muted the insidious none-too-subtle putdowns of the kids in school. Never had she dreamed then that her escape into those fictional worlds would someday provide her freedom from a life she abhorred.

Fifteen minutes later, clean and relatively refreshed, Jenna wrapped herself in the plush white robe offered by the hotel and sat down at the desk to answer e-mail while awaiting her late-night supper. Before she made it through her unread mail, the bell outside her suite chimed. A quick glance at the clock sent her heart racing. Too soon to be room service.

She opened the door to the length of the security chain. "Yes?"

"Ms. Hart?" a female voice inquired.

"Yes?" Jenna's pulse kicked higher.

"I thought I should return this to you." Her bookmark emerged through the three-inch opening, held between well-manicured, tapered fingers.

Heat flared in the pit of her stomach, and Jenna tilted her head to see out into the hall. The redhead smiled back.

"What's your name?" Jenna asked.

"Brin MacIntyre."

"I just ordered room service. Are you hungry?"

"Eternally."

Laughing, Jenna closed the door, slid the security chain free, and opened it. "I thought you said you didn't read romances?"

Again, the red-gold brow winged upward as Brin stepped inside. "I don't follow."

"I believe you're quoting one of my books with that line."

"Is it getting me anywhere?"

"Oh yes."

Jenna slid the chain back on, wrapped her arms around Brin's neck, and kissed her. The kiss started out languid and soft, just a slow exploration. Brin was a very good kisser. With a tug from Brin, the tie on Jenna's robe came loose and warm hands clasped Jenna's waist. Her breasts tightened and her nipples hardened. The arousal was automatic, pleasant, welcomed.

Leaning back from the kiss, Jenna assessed her partner. Brin's eyes were glinting hotly, her mouth a sensuous curve. She looked as confident as her kiss suggested she was. Jenna wanted more of those hard kisses and demanding hands, just as soon as she was sure Brin agreed to her Number One Rule. She was in charge.

"I want to take you to bed," Jenna said. "First I want that beautiful mouth of yours"—she brushed her thumb over Brin's lower lip and moaned softly when Brin gently bit her—"on me until I come. Then I intend to make you come, more than once."

"No complaint from me," Brin murmured without hesitation.

"You should know, too, I'll be leaving at five in the morning."

"Then we shouldn't waste any time." Brin walked Jenna backwards to the open bed, gently eased the robe from Jenna's shoulders, and guided her down. Holding Jenna's gaze, Brin unbuckled her belt and pulled her shirt from her pants. She had just opened the last button, exposing small breasts beneath a pale silk bra, when the doorbell rang again.

"Damn, that's room service," Jenna moaned, already so wet, so ready for that first searing caress she hurt.

Brin smiled and crossed to the door. Without opening it, she said, "Leave it in the hall."

"Very well," a voice from outside responded.

Within seconds, Brin eased into bed, braced herself on her forearms, and settled her hips between Jenna's thighs. The pressure against Jenna's clitoris made her stomach tighten.

"God, you feel good," Jenna whispered.

"I'm going to make you feel a whole lot better very, very soon."

❖

Gard Davis studied the corpse.

The elderly woman lay on her back beneath a handmade quilt in a handsomely crafted bed that Gard was willing to bet had been in this woman's family for over a hundred years. Although her skin was tinged with the faint blue of death, she was still beautiful. Her thick white hair flowed softly around a delicately sculpted face that, despite the decades, remained poignantly elegant. Gard saw no evidence of struggle, pain, or anything amiss, but she went through the prescribed steps because the deceased, and her family, deserved her best. She felt for a pulse in the carotid and radial arteries, and found none. She placed her stethoscope on the chest and listened for breath sounds or a heartbeat, but the torso remained motionless and deeply silent. Straightening, she arranged the covers until only the woman's face showed against the soft linen pillowslip.

"What do you think?" asked Rob Richards.

"I think Elizabeth Hardy was a very lucky woman."

"Huh?" Rob's broad, open face puckered with confusion as he surveyed the dead woman. He was reliable and loyal, and unfailingly literal.

"What is she, ninety-four? Ninety-five? She died in her sleep." Gard shook her head. "She's lived all her life on this farm. As near as I can tell, she loved it. I hope I die in my sleep in my own bed when I'm her age."

Gard couldn't imagine dying with the sense of peace Elizabeth Hardy seemed to have attained. She was already thirty-three and had spent most of the last decade rootless. She didn't see happiness in her future, not after losing her family, her lover, her social status, and pretty much everything that had defined her—or what she'd thought had defined her. With an irritated shake of her head, she turned to the paperwork she needed to fill out.

"You can go ahead and get the gurney, Rob. We'll take her over to Simpson's funeral parlor."

"Shouldn't we call someone?"

"I know she doesn't have any family around here, and I don't want to leave the body in the house. It's going to hit ninety tomorrow. We'll let Mark Simpson do what needs to be done while we call the sheriff and have her track down the family, if there is any. Then I'll call them."

"Okay, Gard. I'll be back in a couple minutes."

"No rush," Gard told her assistant. Elizabeth Hardy was in no hurry, and neither was she. She had farm calls to make in the morning, but one thing she had plenty of now was time.

CHAPTER TWO

J enna fumbled in the near dark on the bedside table for her jauntily jingling cell phone. She recognized the personalized ringtone. Alice. A garish rainbow collage, reflections from the neon signs and passing cars on the street below, shot through the open drapes and slashed across the ceiling. The first thin fingers of gold hinted at the coming dawn.

"It's the middle of the night, Alice." Jenna's voice sounded scratchy and worn in the otherwise quiet room. They hadn't slept, and her brain was hazy from the nonstop sex. When she wasn't on the brink of orgasm, in the throes of orgasm, or breathlessly struggling to recover from an orgasm, she'd been busy repaying the favor. Brin was extraordinarily talented and Jenna did not want to be outdone. Satisfying her bedmates wasn't so much a matter of pride as it was a matter of giving as good as she got, or better. She didn't want to be beholden, not even in the bedroom.

"This is your wake-up call, sweet thing."

"I've got fifteen more minutes." Brin's mouth teased between her legs and Jenna laced her fingers through the thick, damp hair at the back of Brin's neck, tugging slightly to signal her to wait.

"I hope you got some sleep," Alice said briskly. "The plane lands at eleven and we've got just enough time to collect our bags and stop at the hotel before the one p.m. Borders signing."

"I know." Jenna tried to shift away and Brin followed, ignoring her silent command. Brin continued with the maddening cycle of licking and sucking that had kept Jenna on the edge of coming for what felt like a century—driving her to the peak and then, just as she started to crest, easing the pressure until Jenna crashed back down again, whimpering and cursing while Brin laughed. Jenna's thighs tightened and she started to climb faster.

"Did you fall back to sleep?" Alice asked.

"No. I'm here." Jenna struggled to keep her voice even and calm but her toes were curling with the first whispers of release humming through her blood. So close now. So close.

"Jenna?" Alice said suspiciously. "Tell me you didn't work all night."

Jenna bit her lip and yanked on Brin's hair. She didn't care if it hurt—Brin knew she was torturing her, and she was *not* going to come with Alice Smith on the other end of the line. Brin finally relented and chuckled softly, her breath dancing over Jenna's twitching clitoris. Jenna arched off the bed at the electric shock of pleasure. God she wanted to come.

Drawing in a breath, she said, "Alice Ann. Stop harassing me. I'll see you in the lobby." She disconnected and threw her cell phone onto the floor. "Oh my God. I was two seconds away from coming all over you with my agent listening."

"Don't wait any longer on my account," Brin murmured and drew Jenna back into the warm haven of her mouth.

Jenna closed her eyes, her body on autopilot while she mentally reviewed what she needed to do before heading to the airport. She was prepared for Borders and she wasn't reading until tonight at Wald—

"Oh!"

The sharp edge of orgasm penetrated her consciousness and pleasure swamped her synapses. The climax was raw, hard, blinding after the long delay, and she lost herself for a few seconds until she could refocus on what mattered. The galleys…she needed to proof them on the plane. She'd have just enough time.

❖

At 5:15 a.m. Gard stored her emergency colic kit and med box in the back of her Ford F150, locked the cap down, and climbed behind the wheel. Bursts of pinks and purples flamed over the Green Mountains, and though she'd seen dawn break thousands of times before, she paused to watch. The pyrotechnic brilliance had eluded description by the finest poets and painters and songwriters for centuries, and as she sat absorbing the splendor, the tight place in the center of her chest eased a fraction. She knew the ache for what it was. A core of loneliness she'd learned to live with and could usually ignore. Still, simple pleasures like this helped assuage the distant pain that never left.

Frantic barking finally drew her gaze from the spectacle and across the hard-packed expanse of the paddock beside her two-story white Greek revival farmhouse to the open doors of a red wood barn three times the size of her house. Her yellow Lab raced toward the truck at breakneck speed, and she barely managed to lean across the front seat and shove the door open before the four-legged rocket propelled itself into the front seat.

"Beam," Gard chided and reached over to close the door. "When have I ever left without you?"

Sunbeam graced her with a wide doggy smile before planting her paws on the armrest and sticking her head out the open window.

"Hold on." Gard shifted into gear and headed down the drive to the rutted dirt road that bordered her thirty acres to Route 7, a two-lane blacktop road and the closest thing to a highway to be found in the county. Her farm backed up against the Green Mountain National Forest and her nearest neighbors were a mile away. At night she couldn't see their lights or hear any sound other than coyotes howling, owls hooting, and the sonorous rumble of bullfrogs in the small pond out behind her house. A far cry from the never-ending bustle of Manhattan. She reached over and stroked Beam's back. The solid, warm body under her palm and the quick splash of a wet tongue over her forearm banished the familiar melancholy.

She had been looking forward to a morning of routine calls until John McFarland had called at 4 a.m. to say one of his broodmares was colicking. She was headed there now and hoped the situation wasn't so far advanced she'd need to operate. Anticipating an easy day, she'd told Rob to take the day off since they'd been up half the night seeing to Elizabeth Hardy. Rob's stint in the Navy Medical Corps made him an excellent surgical assistant and she primarily used him on the afternoons when she performed surgeries in her clinic. He rarely went out on field calls with her unless she expected to need help with a seriously ill large animal. The owners usually provided ample assistance. Sometimes they wanted to provide more help than she actually needed, but she had learned very quickly upon setting up practice in the countryside that the best way to keep her clients happy was to let them give her advice on everything from the proper way to birth a calf to the appropriate treatment for founder. Once in a while they actually listened to her advice. John McFarland, fortunately, was a savvy farmer who knew when to ask for help.

Just as she was about to turn onto the long gravel drive to the farm, her cell phone rang.

"Davis," she said.

"Gard, it's—"

"Hi, Rina," Gard said to the county sheriff.

"I don't know if it's a good thing or not we talk so often you know my voice." Rina laughed.

Rina had a nice laugh, deep and mellow like aged scotch. Gard imagined Rina's blue eyes and short wavy brown hair, her quick smile, her small tight body. Rina had been flirting in a friendly, test-the-waters kind of way for the last few months, but Gard hadn't given her any openings to take it further. She liked Rina, and she wasn't interested in complicating a good relationship for casual sex. Since even casual demanded more intimacy than she could do, that didn't leave much. Which was one reason she was celibate. She didn't want to think about the other reasons.

"Pretty early for a social call," Gard said, chasing away the dark memories.

"Believe me, I really wish it were. You busy?"

"In the truck."

"Damn, I forgot how early you start." Rina's voice dropped. "Although I rather like morning people."

"I'm your woman, then."

"So you keep promising." When she next spoke, her tone was more serious. "I've got the information on Elizabeth Hardy's next of kin. At least I'm pretty sure I do."

"Hold on." Gard kept a small clipboard with a pad of paper and an old-fashioned wooden pencil stuck to her dashboard with a suction cup for taking messages on the fly. Sliding the pencil from the clasp, she said, "Go ahead."

"I tracked down a Frank Hardy who seems to be the grandson of Elizabeth Hardy's cousin on her father's side, once or twice removed. He's dead, there's no wife listed, but there is a daughter, Jenna. At least I think she's his daughter. I got lost in the interdepartmental computer archives trying to track birth records and can't verify that until the records room at the courthouse in Harrisburg opens at eight and I can talk to an actual person. Looks like they lived somewhere out near Lancaster, PA. You want her number or do you want to wait?"

Gard thought about it. Based on her comparison of Elizabeth Hardy's body temperature to the ambient temperature inside the old farmhouse, which was a good ten degrees cooler than outside, she had deduced that the elderly woman had died approximately twenty-four hours before. She did not like to delay informing the next of kin for a protracted period of time. Somehow leaving the dead in limbo, unmourned, bothered her.

"Give it to me. I'll call after I finish at McFarland's. I'll contact you after I talk to her and let you know if she's the right person."

Rina rattled off a number and Gard scratched it down.

"Will there be an autopsy?" Rina asked.

"Not unless the family insists. I didn't find anything suspicious about her death."

"Okay then. If I don't hear from you, I'll call the courthouse and keep chasing the records."

"Thanks." Gard clipped the pen back on the dash. "Sorry to drag you out of bed so early for this."

"You can make it up to me with breakfast," Rina said.

Gard hesitated. Nothing wrong with having breakfast with a woman she considered a friend and colleague. Rina was smart enough not to read more into it. "After I get things settled at McFarland's, I'll make that call to Jenna—what's her last name?"

After a few seconds of silence, Rina said, "Looks to be Hardy. Either she's not married or she kept her own name. Must run in the family. Elizabeth Hardy was married about fifty years ago but resumed her maiden name when her husband died."

"After I talk to her, I'll call you and we'll see where things stand with breakfast. I'm already behind and I haven't started yet."

"Fair enough. But I expect a rain check at the very least."

"You've got it, and thanks again."

"No problem," Rina said. "I appreciate you doing the hard work."

"Comes with the fancy title. Talk to you later." Gard could have passed off notification of next of kin to the sheriff, but she was the county corner and she would do what needed to be done.

❖

Jenna stepped out of the elevator into the hotel lobby at exactly the appointed time of 5:30 a.m. and winced when a din of voices hammered at the headache bequeathed by her night without sleep. A bellman in a brass-buttoned navy jacket emerged from the jostling group of men in business suits congregated in front of the reception counter and hurried toward her.

"May I get your luggage, ma'am?" he asked.

"Thank you." She gratefully relinquished her bags, scanned the crowd, and spied Alice at the registration desk, undoubtedly taking care of their bill. In her blood-red fitted jacket, tailored skirt, and heels, Alice stood out from the men in regulation blue and gray like an exotic bird among pigeons. Even after ten years of friendship, she still got a jolt of pleasure when she saw her. Alice was beautiful—beautiful and indispensible.

Even though she was still annoyed by Alice's ill-timed phone call, she had to admit she was lucky to have someone who took care of all the details. Hell, Alice not only managed her career, she managed her life. All Jenna needed to do was concentrate on her writing and the personal appearances Alice scheduled. The only area where Alice *didn't* take care of her needs was in the bedroom. Had things been just a little different, she might have done that as well.

Jenna studied Alice from across the lobby as she waited for the bellman to load her bags into the limo Alice had arranged to take them to the airport. Alice was everything she found appealing in a woman—aggressive, competent, confident. When she'd pitched her first novel to Alice at a book fair almost ten years earlier, she'd been young, unagented, and naïve. She'd felt a spark of attraction, of connection, the moment she'd sat down across from the older, sophisticated woman, and she'd known from the glint of interest in Alice's eyes that Alice felt the pull too. But three minutes into Jenna's pitch, Alice had said, "You've got a winner and I can sell it for you," and that was the end of anything sexual between them.

For Alice, business trumped lust and, Jenna suspected, possibly even love. She wasn't certain about that, because she'd never seen Alice in a serious relationship. Alice never lacked for female companionship, but like Jenna, she never dated anyone exclusively and rarely for very long. They were similar that way, which was probably why they got along so well. Most of the time.

Watching frown lines form between Alice's eyebrows as she crossed the lobby to her, Jenna did not think this morning was going to be one of their more amicable moments.

"Jesus," Alice said in a low voice, "you look like hell."

Jenna knew that wasn't true. She looked fine unless someone looked closely. Under careful scrutiny, the light makeup she'd applied would not completely cover the circles beneath her eyes or disguise the gaunt hollows in her cheeks.

"Don't start," Jenna said. "I'm fine. Let's go."

"I *know* you didn't get any sleep, damn it. You at least have to eat." Alice glanced at her watch. "We'll get breakfast at the airport. I'd rather clear security—"

"Great," Jenna said quickly, because she really wasn't hungry.

Exhaustion tended to blunt her other senses. At least all of them except the senses Brin MacIntyre had taken care of quite thoroughly the night before. She wondered how long she could survive on adrenaline and endorphins. She smiled to herself. If she managed to find a Brin MacIntyre in every city on her tour, she just might make it after all.

"What's so funny?" Alice held the heavy glass door open for Jenna to pass.

"Nothing. I was just thinking about the rest of the tour."

"It's going really well, you know," Alice said as they waited under the canopy while the limo driver and the doorman loaded Alice's luggage into the trunk of the spacious Town Car. "There's been a lot of buzz after every event and the sales numbers look excellent. This book is going to get you a Golden Quill."

Jenna snorted. The prestigious award was a coveted prize for any romance writer, but despite her growing popularity, she wasn't a contender for that award yet. At the pace she was going, in five years, she would be. "That would be great, but I'll be happy just to see the book do well."

"I had a long conversation last night with Edith Reynolds," Alice said, referring to a well-known New York editor. "She agrees with me—you're ready to break out and bring a crossover audience with you. She's interested in small-town contemporaries with a little heat, and you're perfect for that. She wants to bring out three in one season."

"Three? In what...the next year?"

"You've handled that many before," Alice pointed out.

"Sure, but not when I had two others already scheduled." Jenna shook her head. "If I'm going to start a new series, you know it has to come out strong. I can't take the chance of being rushed."

"We can't say no to this. If I have to, I'll get you an extension on one of the others." Alice made a soothing noise and rested her palm low on Jenna's back, guiding her into the rear of the car. "I have faith in you, sweetheart."

Jenna's headache went seismic. Opportunities like this didn't come along every day. She wrote faster than almost anyone working in her genre, and she wanted to stay out ahead. She had to stay out ahead. Talented new authors cropped up every day. "You know I'll do what needs to be done. But damn it, Alice—it better be iron-clad."

"You know it will be."

Jenna gazed out the window of the limo on the way to the airport, too tired to carry on a pointless conversation. Alice knew what she was doing. For some reason, Jenna's stomach objected to the stop-and-go motion of the limo in the crowded airport traffic and she struggled to ignore the rising nausea. By the time the vehicle pulled to a stop in front of American Airlines, she feared she was seriously in danger of vomiting. She brushed the back of her hand over her forehead and realized she was sweating.

"Are you all right?" Alice asked.

"Yes. I guess I probably do need some breakfast." Jenna remembered the room service cart that she'd never brought into her room. When had her last meal been? Lunch in DC the day before, or had it been breakfast?

Cool fingers cradled her jaw and Alice's worried eyes swam into view.

"Sweetheart, you really don't look well."

"I'm fine," Jenna said, a little breathless. Outside the limo, a redcap was efficiently stacking their luggage onto a cart. "Let's get the check-in taken care of. Some coffee and a bagel will fix me right up."

"All right. But tonight you're getting a solid eight hours if I have to tuck you in myself."

"Promise." Embarrassed by Alice's concern, Jenna quickly pushed across the seat and followed Alice out. The instant she stood, a wave of dizziness cut her legs out from under her and she collapsed.

CHAPTER THREE

Has she been rolling?" Gard leaned on the stall gate, observing the bay mare. Her neck glistened with sweat and she shifted restlessly, intermittently pawing the ground with her front hooves. Despite being agitated, she was also listless. Her abdomen was not grossly distended, but she definitely displayed signs of intestinal colic. While not often fatal, the disease was still the number one natural killer of horses and could go from a medical problem to a surgical emergency within hours. By then it was often too late.

"Nope—she looked like she wanted to but I walked her a bit and she calmed down some." John McFarland was about Gard's height—five-ten or so, and had probably once had the same coal black hair as she did. His was still thick, but gray now, and where her eyes were charcoal verging on midnight, his were light blue. He resembled most farmers Gard knew—weather-lined skin putting his age anywhere between forty and sixty, clear direct gaze, work-roughened hands. His tone was typically laconic, but his concern was evident in the furrows across his brow and the tight line of his mouth. A fifth-generation farmer, he knew his way around all the common ailments likely to affect his stock, but Gard went through the list of questions that needed to be asked so she didn't overlook anything.

"When did you first notice she wasn't right?"

"Right before I called you. She was fine last night. Can't be more than a few hours, whatever's going on."

"Teeth okay? No problems with worms?"

He shook his head.

"Change in her feed?"

Again, a negative jerk of the head.

"How old is the foal now?" Gard asked. "Two months?"

"Just about that," McFarland said.

Gard hadn't attended the foaling, which was normal for uncomplicated deliveries. A seasoned farmer could handle normal births and even some complicated ones without veterinarian assistance. Sometimes she wasn't called in until situations had turned desperate, but that was the job. She hadn't grown up among the independent, self-sufficient people she now counted as her friends and neighbors, but when she'd moved into their midst, she'd instinctively recognized that here, unlike the circles she was used to, wealth, power, and position did not earn respect. Only honesty and competence did, and she worked hard to deserve it. "Nothing unusual with the birth?"

"This one was her second, and easy. Can't say as I've noticed anything out of the ordinary with her."

"Hold her head so I can get a listen."

They eased carefully into the stall so as not to startle her, and while John held the lead shank, Gard listened to her abdomen. "Pretty quiet. Heart rate's good, though. Let's get a tube down and empty her stomach."

Gard opened her kit and pulled out a thick coil of rubber tubing to pass through the mare's nose into her stomach as well as a long plastic sleeve for the rectal exam. When the intestines failed to function because of mechanical obstruction or surrounding inflammation, gas and fluid built up in the stomach. If it wasn't evacuated, the stomach could rupture, which always led to death.

"Ready?"

McFarland nodded, gripping the rope attached to the halter close to the side of the mare's head.

Gard slid the lubricated nasogastric tube into the horse's nostril and gently advanced it until bilious fluid and air came rushing out.

She nudged a bucket over with her foot to catch the drainage. "Not a whole lot."

McFarland grunted. The relatively small volume of accumulated fluid in the stomach indicated that whatever was wrong had not progressed very far, which was an excellent sign. Once the evacuation was complete, Gard removed the tube and went to work at the other end of the mare. After she stripped down to her T-shirt, she slipped a long plastic glove over her right arm to well above her elbow. She squeezed some lubricant into her palm and carefully eased her hand into the horse's rectum. She went slowly, knowing the mare was in pain. She didn't want to get kicked and she didn't want to risk damaging the fragile colon. When she was nearly at the extent of her reach, she encountered a sizable amount of manure and carefully loosened the mass, extracting as much as she could. Inverting the glove and tying it off, she set the specimen next to her kit to examine in the lab for parasites or unusual foreign materials.

"I don't feel anything twisted. Might be she's just impacted," Gard said. "There's quite a lot up there. I'll put some water with a little mineral oil down the tube and see if that doesn't loosen her up. That and some Banamine for the pain may do it."

"I'll keep an eye on her the next couple of hours," McFarland said.

"Call me if she gets worse," Gard said after she administered the medications.

"Thanks, Doc."

Gard gathered up her equipment and hauled the tackle boxes back out to her truck. After storing them away, she climbed into the cab, where Beam greeted her as if she'd been gone for a week. She pulled out a billing form from a plastic file box she kept on the floor on the passenger side and quickly filled in the appropriate spaces so her office manager could send the bill. Then she fished around in the glove box for her cell phone and checked the number Rina Gold had given her.

Time to call Jenna Hardy.

❖

Jenna came to amidst a cacophony of voices that were way too loud, a glaring white light that was way too bright, and a murderous headache that made her want to vomit. With a moan, she draped her forearm over her eyes.

"Jenna?" Alice asked. "Sweetheart, are you awake?"

"God, I wish I weren't. What the hell happened?"

"You…fainted."

Jenna lifted her arm enough to open her eyes and peered up at Alice. "Fainted? I never faint. Are you sure?"

"Believe me, I'm very sure. You scared the living hell out of me."

"Where am I?"

"At the first aid station at the airport."

"How long have I been here?"

"Just a few minutes. The ambulance is on its way."

Jenna pushed herself up on her elbows, suddenly much more awake. "Ambulance? What for? I'm fine." She stared around the barren cubicle. A single molded plastic chair, a two-drawer metal cabinet with a steel tray of wooden tongue depressors and a box of latex gloves on top, and a wall-mounted blood pressure cuff were the only furnishings. She was on a narrow stretcher with a thin sheet covering her to the waist. Thankfully, she still had all her clothes on. "Where's my briefcase? My computer's in it. The galleys—"

Alice pointed to the floor. "I have your things right here."

Jenna sighed. "I backed up my latest chapter on a jump drive but I didn't send it off-site yet. If I lost that—"

"Don't worry about any of that." Alice gripped Jenna's hand. "Lie back down. Seriously, Jenna. You went down hard and you need to rest."

"What time is it? We need to get through security." Jenna impatiently threw off the sheet and swung her legs over the side of stretcher. Immediately, her head swirled, her stomach somersaulted, and she scrunched her eyes closed to stop the merry-go-round. "God, I must have a migraine. I've never had one before. I will never badmouth people who say they get migraines ever, ever again."

Alice circled Jenna's shoulders. "We don't know what's going on right now. But you need to lie back down. I've canceled our flight."

"You what?" Jenna gaped. "Alice! I've got a signing scheduled this afternoon and a two-hour event tonight. We'll never make it if we don't take this flight."

Alice braced both hands on her hips, her expression one Jenna couldn't decipher, and she'd seen Alice in every situation imaginable. "I've canceled the rest of the tour."

Jenna gripped the edge of the metal stretcher, panic making her limbs weak. "What are you talking about?"

"You haven't had a vacation in two years. You've been pushing—" Alice looked away, her voice tight. "*I've* been pushing you at an inhuman pace for the last six months. You need to slow down. You need to take a break."

"I can't take a break! I've got deadlines. I need to tour. I've got a new book to promote—"

"Your new book is going to do fine without you schlepping around the country touting it at bookstores. That's what happens when you're a bestseller. Your name sells your books."

"I'm not there yet," Jenna said, alarm flooding her chest. She couldn't go back. She'd never go back. Her writing was her ticket to the life she wanted, the life she needed. "Alice—"

"It's done, Jenna," Alice said. "The tour is off."

Jenna's stomach lurched, letting her know in no uncertain terms if she didn't lie back down, there would be nasty repercussions. Reluctantly, she settled back and covered herself with the sheet. "What did you tell them?"

"That you had an unexpected change in an upcoming deadline and that you're terribly sorry to disappoint any of your readers, but you thought they'd be happier if you were writing your next book so they could get it on time."

"Thanks."

"Don't thank me." Alice stroked Jenna's hair. "Let's just take care of you. You need a thorough physical and a vacation."

"One step at a time. I'll get checked out, if that will make you happy." They could argue over what came after that later, but Jenna was certain of one thing. She wasn't taking a break. "Then we can decide what I'm going to do next."

Alice looked like she was about to protest, but then a ringing cell phone interrupted her. She glanced down at her waist and then at Jenna's briefcase. "It's yours. You want me to get it?"

"No," Jenna said, holding out her hand. "I can take it."

The call had to be business, and business was exactly what she needed.

❖

"Hello?" Jenna said.

"Ms. Hardy, this is Dr. Davis. I'm—"

"That was certainly fast," Jenna said, unable to squelch her irritation. She did not want to deal with any more of this until she could deal on her own terms, not lying flat on her back with a pounding head and a queasy stomach. "I don't have my calendar right at hand, but—"

"I'm sorry?" The woman on the other end of the line had a resonant, alto voice. She also sounded confused and slightly annoyed.

"Really, I'm sure my agent told you we're still at the airport. I'll make an appointment—"

"I'm afraid you might be confused about the reason for my call, Ms. Hardy."

Jenna could see Alice frowning and she held the phone away from her mouth and whispered, "Did you call a doctor's office to set up an appointment for me? Give them my number?"

"No," Alice said. "I'm fast, but I'm not that fast. Besides, you're going to see my doctor. I'll take care of making the arrangements. Who is that?"

"I have no idea." Jenna stared at the phone. "Who is this?"

"As I said a moment ago," the smoky-smooth voice responded, the slight edge having blossomed into unmistakable irritation, "my name is Gardner Davis—"

"You said you were a doctor?"

"Yes, I'm—" She sighed, paused, and finally said, "I'm sorry. I'm sure this call has come out of nowhere and I'm not explaining the situation very well. I'm calling from Little Falls, Vermont. I'm the county coroner. I'm very sorry to have to tell you this, but we believe that a distant relative of yours has died and you're the next of kin."

"Well, you've made a mistake," Jenna snapped. "I don't know anyone in Vermont. In fact, I don't think I've ever even *been* to Vermont."

A dry chuckle came down the line. "From what we've been able to trace through a records search, Elizabeth Hardy would have been a very distant relative. She was in her nineties. We're not a hundred percent certain, which is why I have a few questions, bu—"

"What did you say your name was?"

"Gardner Davis."

"As I said, Dr. Davis, you're mistaken." Jenna hadn't talked to Darlene since she'd left home eleven years ago, a few months before her eighteenth birthday. She thought there might be a half brother or sister somewhere from the father she'd never known, but she'd never met them and didn't care to. That life was far behind her, a different existence—before Cassandra. Before everything that mattered. She didn't have any family, she didn't want any family, and she didn't have time for this now. "I'm afraid I have to go."

"If you could just give me a moment," Davis said.

"This is pointless. I know I don't have any relatives in Vermont."

"Is your father's name Frank?"

Jenna shivered violently, her skin instantly clammy and her heart racing.

"Jenna?" Alice said. "You just went white as a sheet. What is it? Let me take this call."

Alice held out her hand for the phone, but Jenna shook her head. She swallowed but her throat was so dry it hurt. "Yes, but that's an awfully common name. I told you, I don't know anyone in Vermont."

"What about Lancaster, PA?" Davis asked quietly.

Jenna closed her eyes. "Not anymore."

"We believe that Elizabeth Hardy is related to the Frank Hardy who lived in the Lancaster, Pennsylvania area, with a daughter named Jenna. Is that you?"

No. No, it isn't me. Not anymore. I'm not her. Jenna had trouble catching her breath.

"Ms. Hardy?"

Jenna's stomach finally won the battle over her willpower. Dropping the phone onto the bed, she clamped her hand over her mouth and looked desperately at Alice.

"Hold on, sweetheart." Alice yanked open one of the drawers in the metal cabinet. She pulled out a plastic washbasin just in time for Jenna to empty the sparse contents of her stomach into it.

❖

Gard pressed her phone against her ear, straining to make out the distant sounds. The entire call had been disjointed, as if she and the woman on the other end weren't really speaking on the same frequency. She thought she detected someone moaning.

"Hello? Ms. Hardy? Hello?"

She stared at the screen—the readout informed her the connection had been lost. She pushed redial, got voicemail. Damn it, she'd handled that all wrong. She punched in Rina's number, replaying the strange conversation with Jenna Hardy. The woman's strained voice and stubborn denials left her feeling unsettled and uneasy.

"Rina, it's Gard. I didn't have much luck with the Jenna Hardy whose number you gave me. She swears she doesn't have any relatives up here."

"Well," Rina said, "none she knows of maybe. But she's the right woman. I've got a long paper trail to be certain of it. Besides that, I woke Sherm Potter up. Since he's the only attorney in Little Falls, I figured he'd have the will."

"Did he?"

"Yep. And Jenna Hardy is the only heir. The farm and everything else is hers."

Gard sighed. "I'll call her back."

"Problem?"

"Not exactly. She wasn't receptive to the idea of having a relative up here, though."

"A lot of people don't want to get involved, especially with a deceased who's essentially a stranger."

"Yeah, I suppose," Gard said, but what she'd heard in Jenna Hardy's voice hadn't been indifference. It had sounded a lot like fear.

CHAPTER FOUR

"Who was that on the phone earlier?" Alice asked.

"No one," Jenna said without opening her eyes. Her stomach had finally settled, just in time for a short ambulance ride from the airport to Jamaica Plains Hospital. Now, at a little before ten in the morning, they were waiting for an emergency room physician to check her over. "Just a case of mistaken identity."

"That was a pretty long conversation for a wrong number." Alice sounded suspicious.

"It was nothing. Believe me. How long do you think this is going to take?"

"We've only been here fifteen minutes."

"This day feels like it's already been a year long." Jenna risked cracking her lids a fraction, and when the glaring overhead fluorescents didn't ratchet up the awful pounding behind her eyes, she kept them open. "It would be simpler for me just to see a doctor sometime this week. This is a waste of everyone's time."

"Let's not take any chances. Maybe this is just a migraine, but you've never had them before. We don't want to overlook anything serious."

"All right. Fine." Jenna resigned herself to a few more hours of misery. Alice was trying to sound casual, but she was wearing the speckles off the dingy gray tiles with her constant pacing. Jenna had never seen her display anything other than cool control and, occasionally, razor-sharp anger directed at some hapless individual who had dropped whatever ball Alice wanted carried. She must really be worried, and that realization stirred a wave of tenderness that had Jenna grabbing Alice's hand as she passed. "Hey, I'm okay. Sit down. Stop fretting."

"I'm not—" Alice grinned when Jenna raised an eyebrow. With a sigh, she leaned down to kiss Jenna's cheek. "I just can't have anything happen to you, now can I?"

"Nothing will. Sit. We'll be out of here soon."

As it turned out, an hour passed before a pleasant Indian emergency room physician assured Jenna she did indeed have a severe migraine, brought on most likely by stress and malnutrition.

"Malnutrition?" Jenna almost laughed. "That's absurd."

The physician smiled softly. "I'm afraid you're quite anemic and your serum protein level is below normal limits too. Both results indicate serious iron deficiency, an inadequate diet, and in all likelihood, a depressed immune system. The migraine might very well be the first symptom of a more serious problem."

"What do we need to do?" Alice's voice quavered and she looked as if she might faint next.

"I'm prescribing the usual vitamins and iron supplements, regular exercise, plenty of rest, a balanced diet, and"—the doctor looked pointedly at Jenna—"a reduced work schedule for a few months."

"That's ridiculous," Jenna exclaimed. "My work is not taxing. I'm a writer. I spend most of my days at a desk."

"Do you think that exerting mental energy hour after hour is not draining? That the pressure of finding and tapping your creative resources does not produce stress and anxiety?" the physician asked gently.

Jenna felt trapped. By the doctor's logic, by her rebelling body, by the dread in Alice's eyes. She wanted out of the small sterile cubicle. She wanted to escape from the too-critical gaze of the physician and the anxious attention of her oldest friend. She didn't want to be helpless. She was not this woman losing control of her own life—she was Cassandra Hart. Capable, confident, successful. Always one step ahead, always on top.

Jenna sat up. "Thank you for everything you've done, Dr. Singh. May I go now?"

"Of course. The nurses will give you an instruction sheet when you sign out. Please consider the things I've told you, and have a good day."

As Jenna slipped into her pants and buttoned her shirt, she sent Alice, whose worry was like a third person in the room, an exasperated glance. "Stop. I told you, I'm fine."

"It didn't sound that way to me," Alice said. "We're going to need to take a hard look at your schedule and make some adjustments."

"We're going to do no such thing. My schedule is fine. *I'm* fine."

"You heard what the doctor said. Today was a warning," Alice said. "If you want to stay on top of the game, then you're going to need to change a few things. You do want to hold on to your best-selling rank, don't you?"

"That's blackmail and you know it." Jenna grabbed her briefcase. Out, she just needed to get out of the hospital. Away from Alice's too-sharp gaze and well-meaning concern. She wasn't about to change her routine, risk her career—risk her life, for a damn headache. "Let's go."

"I don't want to play hardball," Alice said with surprising gentleness, "but if that's what it takes, then that's what it takes."

"We'll talk about this later." Just as Jenna jerked open the curtain enclosing the cubicle, her phone rang for the fourth time in the last hour. She'd ignored it each time previously. This time, she yanked it out of her briefcase and checked the readout. The same 802 area code number came up again. She pressed the accept icon and said tersely, "This is Cassandra Hart."

After a moment's silence, the husky alto voice she remembered from earlier that morning said, "I'm trying to reach Jenna Hardy. This is Dr. Gardner Davis."

"Yes, Dr. Davis, I know. And my answer is still the same as it was—"

"Ms. Hardy?" Gard asked.

"Yes."

"Our county sheriff—Sheriff Gold—has traced a number of records—birth, marriage, death certificates, that sort of thing—and they pretty clearly indicate that you are indeed Elizabeth Hardy's direct heir. You're named in her will, Ms. Hardy."

"I don't really see how that's possible, but I'll have my attorney contact—who should he contact? You? The sheriff?"

"Sheriff Gold would probably be the best one to help straighten out the legalities," Gard said. "I know this is sudden, but we'll need some instructions on how to take care of Ms. Hardy's remains. There's one funeral home in town that I can recommend."

"This is insane," Jenna muttered. How could she possibly make decisions about someone she didn't even know? "You're satisfied with their services?"

"Yes. Completely."

"Fine. Then that place would be fine. What about in the will? Has she left any final instructions?"

"I don't know. Usually the family has that information—"

"Well, that's obviously not the case this time." Jenna closed her eyes but the shards of glass spearing each eyeball kept right on stabbing. God, she just wanted a dark quiet room and no one asking her for anything. Solitude. Please, God, soon. "I'll let my attorney know he'll need to look into that. Give me the sheriff's number."

"All right," Gard said, her tone stiff. "It's—"

"Wait a minute." Jenna really didn't want to deal with any of this. Not now. Not ever. She half opened her eyes and dug around in her briefcase, finally locating a small pad of paper and a pen. "Go ahead," she said, and wrote down the number. "If that's all, I have other things to attend to."

"I'm sure you do. Good-bye, then."

"Son of a bitch…" Jenna pressed the silent phone to her ear. "I think she hung up on me."

❖

Gard leaned a hip against the side of her truck, berating herself for taking Jenna Hardy's, or Cassandra Hart's, or whatever her name was, cold indifference personally. She should know better than to lose her temper, but the woman's perfunctory, dismissive manner had hit every one of her sore points. She knew this kind of woman—the one for whom simple human niceties didn't even register on her radar. Jenna Hardy was either too busy being successful or too used to the insulation provided by her wealth and power to care about how her actions affected others. All the same, Hardy *was* a bereaved relative and after all this time, Gard should be immune to people lashing out at whoever happened to be handy. Even the people who didn't deserve it.

"Oh for Christ's sake," Gard muttered. She'd let Jenna Hardy get to her because she reminded her of Susannah. And her mother. And her sister-in-law. All the women in her life who had cared more for their social status, their financial security, and public opinion than things like love and trust and forgiveness. She'd thought she was past all that, that she couldn't be hurt any longer by disdain and contempt, but one—no, two conversations with Jenna Hardy had catapulted her a dozen years into the past. How was that possible? She'd moved three hundred miles away, cut all her ties with a family that had made it clear she was no longer a part of it, and rebuilt a life based solely on what she did day in and day out as she made her way from farm to farm. No one up here knew her family, knew her history—or her shame. But in a few brief moments, this stranger had managed to remind her of all of it.

She hoped she never had to talk to Jenna Hardy again.

❖

Jenna awoke from an uneasy sleep in the late afternoon. She'd opened the windows in her high-rise apartment when she'd finally arrived home after convincing Alice she did not need company. Now a thick blanket of hot, humid air weighed on her chest, and for a few seconds, she was back in the tiny airless bedroom in the sweltering trailer. Unable to catch her breath, her mind filling with crushing dread, she gripped the sheets and forced herself to breathe slowly and evenly.

I'm fine. I'm fine. I'm home.

Eventually, the tightness in her chest receded. Panic attack. She'd never forget the last one. She'd been seventeen and had awakened in the eight-by-ten room at the far end of the trailer to the labored grunts of Darlene and her latest boyfriend having sex in the room next to hers. She hadn't wanted to listen, but the walls were thin and Darlene wasn't trying to be quiet.

Jenna wasn't supposed to have been home. She'd told Darlene she was staying over at Betty Sue's house, but she'd come home early, bored with the endless conversation about boys and babies. She'd known since she was fourteen she wasn't going there. Not with the boys, for sure. She'd fallen asleep reading and the groans and dull thud of the platform bed striking the wall woke her. She'd recognized the sounds instantly, she'd heard them all her life. She'd rolled over, tuning them out, and then she'd heard her name.

"You think I don't know the real reason why you been coming around," Darlene said. "I've seen you looking at her. You want something young and fresh, and you think you know just where to find it."

Jenna had shivered, feeling trapped. The only way out was past Darlene's room, and every footstep in the single-wide was audible. They'd know she was home, that she'd been listening.

"I ain't been giving you no cause to accuse me of that sort of thing," Floyd said.

Darlene laughed. "I got eyes. That's all the reason I need."

"You don't sound all that mad, just the same."

Floyd had a playful note in his voice that made Jenna's skin clammy.

"Could be I'm not," Darlene said.

"How's that?" Floyd asked in a cautious tone.

"Could be I'm not opposed to the idea of you and her, if we were to make it a little more interesting."

"Interesting. How would that work?"

"I was thinking we might make it a family affair."

His laughter was as harsh as the hand squeezing Jenna's throat. Her stomach twisted and she could hardly breathe.

"Jesus, Darlene, she's your daughter."

"You know, she's not. Not by blood. She was Frank's, and when he left, I got stuck with her. But at least I get money to keep her." Darlene laughed. "Besides, I'm not into girls that way. It'd just be fun to double up on you. You'd like that, wouldn't you?"

"I don't know. I'll have to think about it."

"That's not what the stiff thing between your legs is saying." Darlene's voice dropped low and Jenna had tried really hard not to imagine what they were doing. "I'd say your thinking is already done."

Jenna hadn't waited to hear Floyd's answer. She'd crept across the room and clicked the flimsy lock on her door. She'd known it wouldn't keep them out if they'd wanted to come in, but she couldn't think of anything else to do right then. By morning, she had known what she had to do. She'd packed her clothes, taken whatever money she could find while Darlene and Floyd snored, and walked the three miles into town. She'd climbed on a bus going north and ridden it until it stopped.

"And here I am," Jenna whispered into the silence. She had nothing to fear. Her past was behind her, except when she slowed down enough to let the memories catch her unawares, and she was careful not to do that. That helpless girl, that empty life, were dead and buried. Dead and buried.

She thought about the phone call and a stranger in Vermont, her distant relative. A woman who had known her name and just because of that, had left her all that remained of her life. Jenna had gone so long without a connection to anyone other than Alice, she resented this person she'd never known reaching out from beyond death to touch her life. Her face heated as she recalled the last conversation she'd had with the coroner. She'd been rude, she realized now. She had the excuse of having felt one step away from death herself, but she wasn't usually so cold and abrupt. But what else could she do?

She had a life of her own, a busy life with many obligations. She couldn't take time out to go… Time out. Time away. Just what the doctor had ordered.

Now that Alice had canceled her upcoming engagements, she'd be stuck in Manhattan for the summer—with Alice worrying and watching her to see that she didn't overwork—whatever that meant. If she wasn't going to tour, she was definitely going to write, and she didn't want the specter of this minor episode hanging over her head. Alice would no doubt want an accounting of her time. If she escaped to Vermont, she could work with no one to bother her. No one could claim she wasn't resting or taking a break if she was sequestered in some off-the-map town in the middle of nowhere, for God's sake.

Jenna threw the sheet aside, her mind racing. She could fly up, take care of whatever paperwork needed to be taken care of, stay on to get a jump on her next book, and make everyone happy. She might die of boredom, but at least she wouldn't be defending her every action to her overprotective agent. By the time she came home, Alice would have forgotten all about this little event and life could get back to normal.

A few weeks in hiding. The perfect solution.

Jumping naked from bed, she needed a second to get her balance. Damn, she was still light-headed. After retrieving her phone, she called Alice.

"Jenna, hi," Alice said when she answered. "How are you feeling? Did you sleep?"

"What? Oh. Yes. I'm good. Listen, can you contact the travel agent? I need you to make plane reservations to Vermont for me. Tonight."

"I'm not following," Alice said.

"I think the doctor's right. I should probably take a little break. That phone call earlier—turns out a distant relative died and I need to take care of—things. I'll need hotel reservations too."

"Can't you go tomorrow or the next day? You need to—"

"I think I should go now," Jenna said. "I should probably see to the funeral arrangements myself."

"I can do that for you," Alice said.

"I know you can, but you shouldn't have to."

"All right, if you're sure."

"I'm very sure."

A few weeks. A month at the outside. She could handle anything for a month.

CHAPTER FIVE

Gard fingered the loose change in the pocket of her khakis while staring out the solitary window at the two Rutland Airport runways. At almost midnight on a weeknight, the small regional airport was nearly deserted. The occasional footstep or distant cough echoed down the empty halls. Behind her in the tiny arrivals waiting area, a prematurely careworn woman in her early twenties juggled a sleeping baby and two fussy toddlers while, despite the din of whining children, an elderly gentleman somehow managed to snooze in the row of black plastic chairs. Replaying the unexpected conversation she'd had with Jenna Hardy a few hours before, Gard tracked the lone set of red lights on the arriving aircraft as it descended through a sea of glittering stars in the inky sky.

"Dr. Davis," Jenna had begun as soon as Gard answered the phone, "I've decided to come to Vermont tonight to take care of the arrangements for my…uh…Elizabeth Hardy."

"Tonight?"

"I want to get things settled. I was hoping you could help with that." Hardy's tone had been brisk and businesslike. And definite. The woman sounded as if she was used to calling the shots, and Gard hadn't wanted another argument with her. Just the same, she bristled at the near command.

"Of course." Gard had still been at the clinic, finishing up her billing and reviewing the financial statements for the last quarter. Her stomach churned with a mixture of fatigue, acid, and aggravation. Her part-time office assistant, Bonnie, had failed to file the last quarterly unemployment taxes and now Gard owed penalties. She was as annoyed with herself as she was with Bonnie since she should have been overseeing the accounts and financial paperwork, but not only didn't she have time, she hated doing it. Growing up, she'd never had to worry about where money came from or where it went. If she needed something, all she had to do was write a check or use the credit card her father had presented her on her thirteenth birthday. Clothes, car, private school tuition. Vacations in the Hamptons. Winter skiing in Vail. She hadn't thought of herself as a spoiled rich kid, she was simply living the life she'd been born into. How could she know her experience was vastly different than that of the majority of people in the world? All her friends were of the same economic and social class. By the time she'd entered Harvard she'd been aware of the great divide between the wealthy and the non, but not until she'd had the blinders ripped away one morning by a stranger did she really understand that privilege came at a price—a price often paid by others.

Annoyed at the plague of memories, Gard stalked toward the gate where Jenna Hardy's flight was disembarking. Pacing behind the TSA guard, she studied the travelers who straggled up the gangway and out into the concourse, trying to pick out Hardy. She pictured Hardy as an icy blonde, haughty and unapproachable, like her mother and Susannah and her brother's wife Daphne. She was typecasting and she knew it, but then, from what she'd experienced of Jenna Hardy so far, she definitely fit the mold of socialite.

A woman appeared out of nowhere, stopping a few feet in front of Gard and perusing her with an amused smile. In low heels, she was almost Gard's height, and expensively dressed in tapered chocolate brown pants and a rust-colored cashmere sweater that hugged her smallish breasts. The reddish-brown top complemented her wavy, chin-length chestnut hair and accentuated her truly remarkable spring green irises. She was slender, with flawless ivory skin that rarely if ever saw the sun. Her pallor, together with the faint smudges beneath her large, luminous eyes, gave her a fragile, vulnerable air.

"Dr. Davis?"

"Yes. Ms. Hardy?" Gard realized she'd been staring and hoped Hardy had not noticed. It wasn't as if she didn't see beautiful women every day. Well, perhaps not every day, but she *had* seen beautiful women in her life before, and still did. But she couldn't remember the last time she'd been captured quite as quickly by the elegant arch of a brow or the seductive slant of a smile. Jenna Hardy's face wasn't perfect, the bridge of her nose had a small bump and her jaw was just a little too square to be classically beautiful, but she was… arresting. And damn it, she was staring again.

Gard held out her hand. "Gard. Gard Davis."

Jenna laughed and took the offered hand—larger than hers, the palm was rough, but the grip surprisingly gentle. Gardner Davis was not at all what she'd expected. On the phone, the doctor had been irascible and gruff, and Jenna had pictured someone sharp-faced, hard-eyed, and humorless. Although Davis's features were boldly hewn, her broad forehead and strong jaw gave her a confident, commanding look, even if at the moment, she appeared slightly flummoxed. Her discomfiture was rather endearing, considering how from across the room her dark good looks had made her seem remote and unapproachable. The appreciative glint in her eyes as she took Jenna in, more than once, was quite nice also. Jenna was no stranger to admiring glances, but she was very aware that the looks were for Cassandra. She hadn't dated a woman who hadn't been dating Cassandra Hart in…forever. Her choice, of course, and one she did not regret.

"Thank you for picking me up, but you needn't have," Jenna said. "I could have taken a cab."

Gard automatically reached for the carry-on Jenna juggled along with a briefcase and suitbag. "Let me take those. You would never find a cab out here this time of night, and even if you did, no one would drive you the forty miles to Little Falls."

Jenna rankled at the suggestion she couldn't manage on her own. "It's been my experience that for enough money and a generous tip, you can find someone to do almost anything."

"Yes, I imagine that's true," Gard said stiffly.

"I can carry my own bags, thank you," Jenna said, annoyed by the criticism apparent in Gard's tone.

"It's quite a hike out to the parking lot. No need for you to struggle."

"Always so gallant, Dr. Davis?"

"Not so you'd notice."

Despite her aggravation, Jenna relinquished her grip on the luggage. She wasn't going to let false pride stand in the way of good sense. Her headache had abated, but her stomach hadn't weathered the flight quite as well. She was still a little shaky, she wasn't going to be able to carry all her luggage, and there were no redcaps in sight. "I have another bag that I checked."

"Planning to stay for a while?"

Jenna wasn't certain why everything Gard Davis said sounded like an accusation, as if she were being judged and found lacking. She'd had a hellacious day, her temper was none too steady under the best of circumstances, and she'd stopped accepting insults in silence the day she'd crawled out of Darlene's trailer. "Is there some reason I shouldn't?"

"Not at all," Gard said. "Baggage claim is this way."

The overly bright, faintly grimy room held three luggage conveyors, two of which sat motionless. A third rattled around with a few stranded bags dotting their black belts in an endless loop. Gard headed in that direction.

Jenna hurried to keep up. "Then what—"

"I doubt you're going to find Little Falls very entertaining," Gard said. "Certainly not what you're used to."

"Oh? What do you suppose I'm used to?"

"The flight you took came up from New York City. Is that where you live?"

"Manhattan," Jenna said. "Does that automatically make me incapable of enjoying a few quiet weeks in the country?"

"Not at all. Plenty of people come up here from the city for a break. But they usually stay at trendy resorts or elegant B and Bs. Little Falls is hardly on the map."

"Believe me, I've had my fill of hustle and bustle for a while. I just spent a month plane-hopping from one glitzy hotel to another." Jenna stopped herself from saying more—she didn't ordinarily reveal details of her personal life, and Davis's thorny disposition hardly inspired confidences.

"Who is Cassandra Hart?" Gard asked just as a loud whine followed by a piercing screech signaled the lurching start of a conveyor belt.

"I'm sorry?" Jenna scrambled to remember if she'd mentioned who she was.

"Earlier, when I called. You answered 'Cassandra Hart.'" Pieces of luggage began to spew from the hidden recesses behind the baggage carousel, and Gard slid closer to make the grab. "What's it look like?"

"That's mine," Jenna said, heading for a large black Pullman. Caught off balance by Gard's reference to Cassandra, she took advantage of the diversion to consider her answer. Before she could tug the large suitcase off the carousel, Gard got to it first and lifted the large bag as if it were no heavier than Jenna's briefcase.

"So?" Gard asked.

"I'm Cassandra Hart," Jenna said.

"You have two names?"

"Cassandra Hart is my pseudonym. The name I write under."

Gard lifted her brow. "You're an author?"

"Yes, actually, I am." Jenna shouldn't have been surprised that Gardner Davis had no idea who she was, but the knowledge was unexpectedly irritating. And the irritation was even more irritating. Why should she care?

"What do you write?" Gard pulled out the retractable handle on the Pullman, grabbed the carry-on, folded the suitbag over the top of the Pullman, and rolled the assembly toward the double glass doors leading outside.

"Novels." Jenna hurried to catch up. "Let me take one of those."

"I've got them."

"Do I look like I'm incapable of carrying my own luggage?"

Gard shot her a grin. "You look like you're used to having an entourage follow you around taking care of your every need."

"Exactly why would you think that?"

"You just do. Should I have heard of you?"

"You do realize that a question like that could be construed as offensive?"

"Really?" Gard laughed. "How so?"

Jenna stopped walking. "Well, in the first place, you don't know who I am, which implies that I'm not important enough to be known. Secondly…" She hesitated, her frown deepening. "Actually, I don't think there is a second place."

"Are you important enough to be known?" Gard asked.

"Cassandra is, at least some people think so."

"And what about you?"

They'd reached the deserted lanes outside the airport, and the mountains rose beyond the sparsely lit parking lot, massive and dark against a moonlit sky. Jenna smelled pine, fresh turned earth, and cut grass—country smells. A visceral memory, both pleasure and pain, of all she'd left behind struck her hard and she jumped. "I'm sorry. What?"

Gard slowed, her expression quizzical and concerned. "Are you famous?"

"Not really, although every one of my last seven new releases has made the *New York Times* top ten list." Jenna wasn't sure why she was trying to impress a stranger, and one who wasn't even all that likable. Maybe being thrown into surroundings so much like those she'd escaped had her off balance, because she certainly didn't care what this woman thought of her. Maybe it was just the damn headache making a reappearance that had her acting out of character.

"What exactly do you write?"

"Romances."

"Ah," Gard said.

"Ah, what?"

"That's why I don't know who you are. I don't read them." Gard pointed with her chin. "I'm parked over here."

"What exactly do you read when you're not reading medical journals?" The parking lot was unpaved, potholed, and muddy. Spotlights hung from telephone poles in no discernible pattern, dotting the lot with thin cones of light that barely reached the uneven ground. Jenna had to step carefully to avoid puddles left by what must have been a recent, heavy downpour. Her shoes were going to be ruined.

"I like mysteries. Puzzles. Things I have to figure out."

"Have you ever actually read a romance?"

Gard passed into one of the swaths of light, and Jenna saw her frown. "*Wuthering Heights* in high school. Maybe. Or that might've been CliffsNotes."

Jenna laughed despite her lingering annoyance. "Then you've missed a few things. The genre has changed quite a bit in the last hundred years or so."

Gard stopped beside a dusty black pickup truck. "How so?"

"Well, there's sex, for one thing." Jenna leaned forward, squinting to read the logo on the side. "This is yours?"

"Yep." Gard unlocked and lifted the cap on the back and began stowing the luggage.

"Little Falls Animal Clinic and Surgery?" Jenna asked.

"That's my place."

"You're a vet?" Jenna exclaimed.

"Yup. I never said I was a medical doctor."

"But you did say you were the coroner when you called," Jenna said.

"I am."

"They let a veterinarian be the coroner?"

"Sometimes it's a funeral director." Gard chuckled. "I've known a couple who were justices of the peace. I think being a vet might actually overqualify me." After securing the back, Gard skirted around to the passenger side door and opened it for Jenna, who trailed behind. "Need a hand getting up in here?"

"I think I can manage," Jenna said icily. She'd no sooner said the words than she stepped into a water-filled rut a good foot deep, lost her balance, and pitched forward. "Oh!"

"Hey!" Gard jumped forward and caught Jenna before she could hit the ground. She swept Jenna up and into her arms. "Are you all right?"

Jenna automatically entwined her arms around Gard's neck, her face almost brushing Gard's cheek. Her knee screamed but the pain was clouded by the scent of sweet clover, something she hadn't smelled in over a decade and hadn't realized she missed. Her breasts pressed against Gard's chest, and when her nipples tightened, she pulled away. "Put me down."

"Sure thing," Gard said, amazed at how light Jenna felt in her arms. Her vet work kept her strong and she could lift as much weight as most men her size, but this woman seemed to be sketched out of the air and as fragile as a wisp of cloud. When she set her down on the ground, Jenna gasped and leaned heavily against her. "What's wrong?"

"Nothing." Jenna straightened, her features tightening as she clenched her jaws.

"Bullshit. Twist your ankle?"

"My knee," Jenna said through her teeth.

"Okay then." Gard bent slightly, slid an arm behind Jenna's shoulders and the other behind her knees, and picked her up again. "Watch your head."

Jenna ducked as Gard eased her into the front seat. "Thank you. I'm fine."

Gard closed the door, circled the front of the truck, and climbed behind the wheel. She started the engine and then shifted in the seat to face her passenger. "There's a hospital between here and Little Falls. We can stop and have you looked at."

"I'm fine," Jenna snapped. "I started the day in the hospital, I'm not going to end in one."

"What happened this morning?"

"Nothing. Please, can we just go?"

"Absolutely. You're the boss." Gard shifted into gear and drove out of the lot.

After a few moments of silence, Jenna said, "I apologize for my bad manners. You've been very helpful all day."

"No need to apologize." Gard gripped the wheel more tightly. Her prejudices were affecting her in ways they hadn't for years. "I should apologize. You've done nothing to warrant my mood. It sounds like it's been a long day for both of us. Why don't we just leave it at that."

"Fair enough." Jenna leaned her head back and closed her eyes. "I don't suppose the hotel has room service?"

Gard laughed. "It's the middle of the night. There probably won't even be anyone at the desk. If you're still hungry when we get to the clinic, there's an all-night diner at the edge of town. Jackie makes the best home fries in two states."

Jenna's eyes snapped open. "What clinic?"

"My clinic."

"What are you talking about?"

Gard shot her a quick glance then focused on the road. "I want to take a look at your knee."

"You're a vet!"

"Knees are all pretty much the same."

"And if I say no?"

"Then I won't take you for an early breakfast." Gard turned on the radio to an oldies station and turned it down low. "Besides, I'm driving, so you don't have much choice."

Jenna swallowed a sharp retort and turned away to stare out the window. What an arrogant, overbearing pain in the ass. She would've argued more, but her knee throbbed and if Gard hadn't caught her she might have fallen. Once in a day was enough for that.

"We've got about a forty-five-minute drive," Gard said. "I don't mind if you snooze on the way."

"I'm not tired," Jenna said, but as the darkness closed in around them, and the old familiar music played in the background, she closed her eyes and drifted on memories of sweet clover, country lanes, and summer nights filled with youthful dreams.

CHAPTER SIX

Gard pulled into the empty gravel lot beside her sprawling clinic on the outskirts of Little Falls, turned off the motor, and studied her passenger. Jenna still slept, her head tilted against the window, her face partially illuminated by silver starlight. The otherworldly glow accentuated the contours of her face and smoothed away the lines of fatigue Gard had seen earlier, giving her the look of a delicately carved ivory statue. She'd been surprised when Jenna had fallen asleep—she seemed too tightly wound to relax so completely with a stranger. But then she'd heard the quiet moans cutting through the low murmur of the radio as she'd driven through the night. Jenna was either having a very bad dream or was in considerable pain. Judging from how she'd looked when she'd arrived at the airport—drawn and exhausted—along with her earlier comment about having started the day in the hospital, Gard suspected she wasn't well. Although Jenna had put on a good show of being totally in command, right now she appeared not only defenseless, but vulnerable.

A surge of protectiveness, coupled with an intense desire to ease Jenna's discomfort, put Gard on instant alert. The reaction was foreign, primitive, and one she was quite sure she'd never experienced toward any other human being. Uneasy with the unwelcome urges, she chalked her mood up to the lateness of the hour and the hypnotic pull of the waxing gibbous moon overhead. Everything seemed slightly unreal awash in the moonlight, including her own feelings.

"Ms. Hardy?" Gard said quietly, carefully pressing her fingertips to the sleeping woman's shoulder.

Jenna jolted upright with a gasp and jerked away from Gard's touch, her expression a mixture of apprehension and combativeness. "What? Where are we?"

"I'm sorry," Gard said quickly, aware that Jenna was not just startled, but threatened. Someone had frightened her in the night, in the dark, before, and the knowledge settled in the pit of her stomach like a hot, hard stone. "You're in my truck. At my clinic. You fell asleep."

Jenna slowly drew air in through her nose, visibly calming herself. She was strong, and admirably self-sufficient. "Sorry. I didn't expect to fall asleep. My apologies."

"None needed. How's your leg?"

Tentatively, Jenna extended her knee and winced. "Stiff, but moving."

"I'll come around and help you out."

"I hardly think that's necessary, Dr. Davis."

"Gard. Call me Gard."

"Then it's Jenna to you."

"All right. Jenna. I'll come around and help you out."

Jenna folded her arms over her middle and glared at Gard. "Are you always this overbearingly authoritative?"

Gard grinned. "Usually just with the horses. You're a special case."

Jenna refused to smile, but she wanted to. God, the woman was infuriating, but on her, even arrogance was attractive. "I can walk."

"Let's find out."

Gard jumped down from the truck, shoved her keys into the front pocket of her khakis, and hurried around to the passenger side of the truck, not trusting Jenna to wait. The woman was independent to a fault, and Gard didn't want her to hurt herself just to prove that she didn't need any help. Besides, she wanted an excuse to lift her out of the truck. And she did *not* want to think very long about why she hungered to hold Jenna in her arms again. After pulling open the cab door, she reached inside and slid one arm under Jenna's knees and the other around her shoulders. "Hold on."

"You really ought to ask permission first." Just the same, Jenna threaded her arms around Gard's neck and let herself be lifted from the cab. She tried to keep some distance between their bodies, but that proved difficult when Gard tightened her hold and pulled her against her chest. The muscles in Gard's arms bunched against the backs of Jenna's thighs and along her shoulders in an unconscious display of strength that was tantalizing and, damn it, arousing. She wasn't usually so quick to respond physically to a casual touch from a woman. Her body was not her own today—her reactions seemed to belong to someone else. She hated being out of control this way, but the pleasure of being cradled in the arms of a woman who looked and smelled as good as Gard did was way beyond her ability to ignore, so she might as well enjoy the tingling in her breasts and other places. Secretly. The last thing she wanted was Gard Davis knowing she was turned on by such innocent contact with her. "Don't hurt your back."

"Hmm?" Gard asked absently, having caught a hint of dahlias and spice, reminding her of hot summer mornings before the dew burned off. But it wasn't morning, and the dahlias hadn't bloomed. "Is that you?"

"What?"

"That…" Gard caught herself trying to catch another hint of the alluring scent and mentally cursed. What the hell was she doing? She never got lost in a woman this way. "Never mind."

"Maybe you should put me down. I think you're shaking."

"I'm not going to drop you." Gard laughed. "Besides, this is nothing compared to a traction delivery or examining a cow's hoof when she's leaning on you."

"I'm so glad I'm easier than the patients you usually have to deal with," Jenna said with a bit of temper. "You know, being compared to a barnyard animal isn't exactly flattering."

"I guess my social patter needs a little work," Gard said dryly. "Hold on to me while I let you down. I want you to put most of your weight on me until you test your knee. Don't try to be a hero."

"Heroine."

"Isn't *hero* a gender-neutral term these days?"

Jenna leaned back and studied Gard appraisingly. "That's an unusual question coming from someone who claims not to read romances."

"What do you mean?"

"That question is hotly debated among some romance authors."

"Why? Isn't there always a hero and heroine? You don't have to read them to know that much."

"Not true in my books."

Gard hesitated in front of the two stone steps leading to the main door of the clinic, holding Jenna easily in her arms. It wasn't that she was super strong, but she enjoyed the weight of the woman against her body. The slight strain in the muscles in her arms was well worth the soft press of Jenna's breasts against her chest. She was probably taking advantage of Jenna's injury, as she doubted Jenna would have wanted to be in this position otherwise, but she welcomed the slow burn in the pit of her stomach. A woman hadn't affected her this way in a long, long time. "I don't follow."

"I guess I didn't mention that I write romances involving two women."

"Lesbian romances?" Gard asked.

"Yes."

"Huh. Is there much call for that kind of book?"

Jenna laughed. "Enough. And getting more popular all the time."

"And are there a hero and heroine or two heroines?" Gard paused. "Or two heroes?"

"Well, I guess part of it depends on your politics or your comfort level or how you view the gender spectrum." As much as Jenna was enjoying the odd and unexpected turn in the conversation, they were standing outside in the dark in the middle of the night. Well, Gard was standing and she was taking shameless advantage of her. She didn't need to be carried, and it was time to relinquish her guilty pleasure. "You should put me down."

"Ready?"

"Yes, go ahead." Jenna carefully shifted her weight onto her injured leg as Gard eased her down. Her knee throbbed even when she wasn't standing, and the more pressure she put on it, the sharper the pain became. She gripped Gard's shoulders harder and tried not to wince.

"On a scale of one to ten," Gard said, "ten being you can't stand on it at all, where are we?"

"About a seven," Jenna said reluctantly.

"Well, let's not test it any further." Gard scooped Jenna up and climbed to the narrow landing. "I want to take a look at this inside."

"I'm sorry," Jenna said. "This can't be what you wanted to be doing in the middle of the night."

"Believe me, there are lots of things I'd rather not be doing right now. Carrying a beautiful woman in my arms isn't one of them."

Jenna's breath caught. "Well that's a clever line."

"That wasn't a line. Could you reach into my right front pants pocket and pull out my keys?"

"Yeah, right. You've got a pretty smooth routine," Jenna said acerbically. "And I am *not* putting my hand in your pants."

"I'm not putting you down again, so just get the damn keys."

"Fine," Jenna muttered, sliding her right hand down until her fingers brushed the fly of Gard's khakis. She tried to ignore the way Gard stiffened at the contact, but she couldn't contain her own response. Heat bloomed in her chest and tendrils of pleasure teased between her legs. She pushed her hand into Gard's pocket, and stone-hard muscles bunched against her palm. Oh now, *that* was nice. She closed her fist around a cluster of keys, careful not to let her hand stray toward the heat she knew was inches away. But she wanted to. Part of her wanted to feel Gard react to her touch again. The power to make a woman respond was an aphrodisiac all its own.

"Here." Jenna jerked her hand free, the keys clenched in her fist.

"Thanks," Gard said, her voice tight. She raised one knee, nestling Jenna in the cradle of her body, and took the keys. After a second of jostling the ring, she inserted a key, opened the door, and stepped inside. "On the wall to the left of the door. Light switch."

Jenna fumbled over the wall until she found the toggle and flipped it up. She blinked against the sudden glare, taking in a square, whitewashed cinderblock room that more resembled the waiting area in an auto repair shop than what she'd imagined she'd find in a veterinary clinic. A waist-high counter ran parallel to the opposite wall and obviously served as a reception desk. Stacks of papers and file folders covered one end. A computer monitor, a phone, and a small adding machine were the only other items visible. The floor was black and gray industrial tile, well-worn, but clean. A soda machine occupied the center of the far wall with a few mismatched metal folding chairs haphazardly clustered directly in front of it. A green plastic trash can stood nearby with a hand-lettered sign on brown cardboard stating "We Recycle."

"My practice is large animals," Gard said as if reading Jenna's perplexed look as criticism. "I don't need a waiting room, although sometimes owners like to wait if we're doing surgery. Most of my calls are actually on-site."

"No dogs and cats or exotic birds?" Jenna said.

Gard grimaced. "Only in emergencies."

Jenna settled back into Gard's arms as Gard carried her across the room toward a single wood-paneled door behind the counter.

"Where do you operate?"

"Through there." Gard tilted her head toward two floor-to-ceiling gunmetal gray swinging doors in the far rear corner. "There's another whole building in the back. We need a lot of space for the hoists, recovery confinement areas, that sort of thing. This used to be a Chevy dealership. I had it retrofitted—" She stopped when Jenna laughed. "What?"

"I thought it looked like you ought to be repairing cars here." Jenna tried to silence her amusement, because each time she laughed her breasts swayed against Gard's chest in an altogether too appealing way. She was in danger of getting seriously turned on.

"Some of the horses can weigh as much as one."

Gard opened the door behind the counter and they repeated the light switch routine, although this time, the room was considerably more hospitable than the stark waiting area outside. Jenna had expected a utilitarian office but this fifteen by twenty foot space was anything but. Dark wood bookcases crammed with a variety of books, some professional and some that appeared to be pleasure reading, filled the left wall from floor to ceiling. An oversized brown leather sofa took up most of the wall across from the bookcases. Directly ahead, a heavy carved-walnut desk sat on a dark chocolate and beige Persian rug in front of a pair of French doors. The walls that weren't covered with framed photos of horses were painted a rich cream. The hardwood cherry floors gleamed. If Jenna hadn't just passed through the barren room posing as a reception area—and doing a crappy job of that—she would have sworn she was in the study of a Park Avenue mansion. "This is a surprise."

Gard glanced around as if seeing the room for the first time. Then she shrugged. "It's comfortable."

Jenna's attention was diverted from her elegant surroundings when Gard gently deposited her on the butter-soft leather sofa, lifted her legs onto the seat, and removed her shoes. Gard's blue cotton shirt was sweat-dampened along the open edges of the collar at her throat, a reminder that she'd had to exert some effort carrying Jenna all that way. While Jenna was well used to looking after herself and liked it that way, Gard's singular attention was…well, exciting.

"So…what next, Doctor?"

Gard frowned down at her and an uncomfortable tension suddenly permeated the air.

"I don't think we're going to be able to roll up your pants leg high enough for me to examine you," Gard said. "You'll need to take them off."

"Oh, wait a—"

"I'll find you something to cover up with." Gard spun on her heel and disappeared.

Jenna experimentally flexed her knee. She really did not want to get half naked in Gard Davis's study in the middle of the night. She hadn't planned on a doctor's visit. She was wearing black silk bikinis. Small bikinis. They'd been handy when she was getting dressed and she hadn't really been planning on an evening out. Had she known she would be disrobing in front of a stranger, she would've worn something nondescript and infinitely forgettable. Maybe she could save them both further trouble.

Unfortunately, when she tried to bend her knee the pain was excruciating. She dropped her head onto the arm of the sofa and glared at the ceiling.

"I cannot believe this is happening to me. Could my life get any worse?"

"Probably," Gard said, coming back through the door they had entered carrying a plaid horse blanket. "This is the best I can do. My patients usually aren't concerned with modesty. It's clean."

"Fine. Let's just get this over with."

After Gard covered her with the blanket, which thankfully wasn't wool, Jenna quickly unzipped her pants underneath it, and immediately realized she couldn't get them off. She could raise her hips, but she couldn't bend her knees. "Would you mind pulling them down."

"Not at all." Gard reached beneath the blanket near Jenna's ankles and carefully tugged on Jenna's pants until they were free. After draping them over the end of the sofa, she sat next to Jenna. "I'm just going to push the blanket up until I can look at the knee area."

"Whatever you need to do."

Gard was gentle, even more than Jenna had expected her to be. As she pressed her fingertips slowly and carefully over Jenna's lower thigh, her knee, and the upper portion of her lower leg, she asked if it hurt.

"No," Jenna said. Pain was not what she was experiencing. Did the woman have to have great hands, too? "Are you done?"

"Just a second."

Gard lightly probed one spot on the outer aspect of Jenna's knee, and Jenna thought a burning poker had been jammed into the joint.

"Ow, God. Ow, damn it."

"Sorry. Might have a little bit of a ligament tear," Gard said.

"They shoot horses for that, don't they?" Jenna gritted her teeth and refused to whimper.

"Not anymore." Gard slid one hand behind Jenna's knee and the other in front. "I'm going to test this now and if I hurt you, I want you tell me immediately and I'll stop."

Jenna wanted something to hold on to, and the thin plaid blanket was the only thing available. She gripped it in both hands. "Go ahead."

Gard bent Jenna's knee in smooth steady increments and Jenna started to relax. Sore. But not terrible. Then, out of the blue, fire blazed across her knee again and she cried out before she could stop herself.

"I'm done," Gard said quickly. She carefully straightened Jenna's leg and rested it back on the sofa.

Jenna didn't realize she'd yanked the blanket above her hips until a gentle tug on the fabric clutched in her grip drew her attention to Gard covering her again. "Thank you."

"I'm sorry I hurt you. You're going to need to stay off that leg for a day or two. Ice, anti-inflammatories, minimal weight-bearing. I think you've just got a bad sprain, but if it doesn't get better with conservative therapy you may need an MRI or arthroscopy."

"I think I'd rather you shoot me."

Gard laughed. "You say that now. Let me find an ice pack and we'll get you over to the hotel and into bed."

"You don't have to do that. You've done enough already."

"I already told you there aren't any other options. You'd be miserable sleeping on this couch and you won't get a cab out here this time of night."

"At least let me pay you for your—"

"Don't insult me." Gard stood quickly, her hands in her pockets, and regarded Jenna tightly. "I've got a knee immobilizer in the back. My part-time office manager left it here when she got tired of wearing it. Softball injury. It ought to allow you to walk if you're careful."

"Thanks."

"Are you going to need help getting your pants on?"

"Oh for God's sake…I can…how much time do we have?"

"I'll take that as a yes." Gard tried to sound casual, but the last thing she wanted was to get any closer to Jenna. She'd been touching her, even if she had been completely professional, for longer than she'd touched a woman in years. Jenna's skin was so soft, and she smelled so damn good. Now she was half naked, and goddamn it, thinking about her naked when she was hurt and vulnerable was wrong. Carefully, she slid Jenna's silk pants over her ankles and guided them up Jenna's thighs. Despite trying not to, Gard caught a glimpse of delicate black panties stretched over the graceful arches of Jenna's hip bones and the inviting hollow just above the mound of her sex. Her mouth went instantly dry and her abdomen tightened with a swift and dangerous hunger that shocked her. She didn't realize she'd stopped moving, the material of Jenna's pants gripped in her fingers, until Jenna spoke.

"I think I can get it from here."

"Of course." Gard released the pants and straightened abruptly, turning her back. "I'll get that immobilizer."

Before Jenna could protest, Gard disappeared. Jenna closed her eyes, the unmistakable image of desire imprinted on her mind.

Chapter Seven

Jenna had been quiet since they'd left the clinic, and ordinarily Gard wouldn't mind silence. She spent so much time alone, or talking to animals who didn't talk back, she'd pretty much lost the art of casual conversation, let alone anything more intimate. Jenna's quiet didn't bother her so much as it concerned her. She couldn't tell if Jenna was in pain, or angry, or sad. She'd sat motionless, looking out the side window, since they got in the truck.

"Are you all right?" Gard asked.

"I'm fine," Jenna said softly.

"Still hungry?"

"It's two in the morning." Jenna turned from where she'd been watching the night pass by in fragmented snapshots of hoary fields back-dropped by the skeletal arms of tree branches stretching into a ghostly sky. She'd cracked the window, and the tang of newly plowed fields, fresh-cut grass, and fecund life transported her back a dozen years and five hundred miles away to a place she'd thought she would never want to go again. How was it that the taste of a summer night could make her feel fifteen again, filled with promise and expectation and restless longing? But she wasn't fifteen anymore, and all that youthful anticipation had been extinguished by the harsh hand of experience. Hopes and dreams were for those who couldn't control their own destinies, but she could. She could. She'd had to learn to shape her own fate, and she'd gotten very good at doing that. "I imagine you'd like to get some sleep tonight."

"I'd say about a third of the month I'm up working all night,"

Gard said. "This is as usual a time for me to have breakfast as it is to have dinner. I guess I don't work by a normal clock."

Jenna shifted around on the seat, trying to get comfortable with the unfamiliar and incredibly aggravating knee immobilizer forcing her to keep her leg out straight. Putting her back against the door, she watched Gard drive. She looked relaxed, her shoulders back against the seat, her hands low on either side of the wheel, her eyes fixed straight ahead. In charge, but comfortable, in tune with her surroundings. Gard didn't look as if she ever had to wrestle with fate to keep her life just where she wanted it. Jenna found that both admirable and annoying.

"Are you married?" Jenna asked.

Gard whipped her head around and hit Jenna with a hard stare, then just as quickly faced front again. "I'm trying to figure out what my discussion of mealtime has to do with that."

"Sorry," Jenna said. "I have a tendency to think in chapter breaks. One of the first rules of novel writing is that every chapter should begin very close to the heart of the scene. I guess I'm not much on leading up to a topic."

Gard laughed. "I'm still not getting the segue."

"Oh. Sorry. I was thinking it must be kind of hard to be in a relationship when your schedule is so erratic. Unless of course, you have a very patient partner."

"Plenty of doctors have stable long-term relationships."

"Absolutely. And plenty don't." Jenna noted Gard very often redirected the conversation to avoid answering a question. She recognized the ploy because she used it herself. Gard, despite her laid-back demeanor, was very guarded. Her name suited her. "Touchy topic, Dr. Davis?"

"Nope." Gard's hands tightened on the wheel. "Not attached. Never have been."

"And is that just because you enjoy working all the time, or you're more of a casual dater?"

"Neither," Gard said, sounding a little as if her answer surprised her. "You're right—I do like my work, and it doesn't leave a lot of time for socializing. But I'm not much for socializing anyhow."

"That's a shame," Jenna murmured.

"Sorry?"

"Nothing." Jenna wondered why she'd asked Gard the question. She rarely gave much thought to the private lives of women she found attractive. The only thing she really cared about was whether they were attached or not. When she'd run away from home and was living hand to mouth in one dead-end job after the other, sex staved off loneliness. She hadn't been above sleeping with a married woman then, but before very long, the excuse that everyone was responsible for their own relationships started to feel a little self-serving. Now she at least tried to determine if the women she bedded were single. Well, usually. Thinking back to Brin—God, had it really only been twenty-four hours since they'd been tearing each other's clothes off?—she realized she hadn't made any effort to find out her marital status. But nothing about Brin screamed married. As to Gard, the answer was moot. The woman was attractive—physically, at least— but she was far too controlling. Jenna liked aggressive women in bed, but just spending time in the same space as Gard was a battle and she didn't need that in the bedroom.

"You never answered my question about being hungry," Gard said.

"Actually, I'm starved." Jenna was wide-awake with nothing to look forward to except an uncomfortable night in a strange hotel. She wouldn't mind spending a little more time sparring with Gard. Verbally at least. "So if you really don't mind—"

"I was the one who offered. You can trust me to tell you what I mean. I don't have time for games."

Jenna heard the word *anymore* hang in the air, and wondered what game Gard had played, and with whom. And if she'd won or lost.

"I'm in then," Jenna said.

❖

Oscar's Road House perched on the side of Route 7 like a wet rooster, bedraggled but feisty. Even at two in the morning, pickup trucks and eighteen-wheelers clogged the dirt and gravel parking lot around the ramshackle barn-red diner. No-frills security lights blazed from under the eaves, as bright as the noontime sun. Jenna blinked when Gard opened her door and helped her down from the truck.

"Popular place," Jenna said.

"Oscar's makes the best homemade sausage in three counties," Gard informed her as they navigated the parking lot. "How's the leg?"

"It'll get me where I need to go, as long as I don't need to be there this week," Jenna muttered.

Gard laughed. "I could always carry you again."

Jenna shot her a look. "Oh, and wouldn't that make a perfect entrance. We're probably going to be the only women in this place as it is."

"That's not true. All the waitresses are female."

"Some things never change." Jenna rolled her eyes, wondering exactly what she was getting into. She knew what these places were like. She hadn't been in one since she was seventeen and slinging hash on nights and weekends to buy clothes for school, but she hadn't forgotten the come-ons disguised as teasing that were always one step away from turning ugly when she refused. As she and Gard stepped through the revolving glass door into the brightly lit long, narrow room, she saw the familiar vinyl-lined booths hugging the front windows and the topsy-turvy counter stools on the other side of the narrow, grease-splattered aisle. Men ranging from twenty to sixty hunched over coffee in all the booths, most of them wearing green work shirts and khaki pants, all with sweat-ringed caps sporting the logos of long-distance trucking companies. And every single one of them turned to watch her and Gard make their way slowly to the counter. She didn't mind being looked at. She was on stage almost every day of her life. But for an instant, she couldn't help remembering the girl she had been—her clothes outdated, her hair home-cut, her eyes haunted by the oppressive neglect of growing up with a woman who saw her as nothing more than a meal ticket. She was expected to accept the offers for a night of fun, no matter how crudely put, because everyone knew she could do no better. The past came rushing back so quickly she abruptly stopped.

"Just a little farther," Gard murmured, resting her hand at the small of Jenna's back. "There're open spaces right over here."

"I'm fine," Jenna said.

"You're ten shades of pale. This was a stupid idea. I'm sorry."

"I'm fine, damn it. Just give me a lift onto the stool. This brace is impossible to move in."

"That's the idea." Despite what Jenna'd said, Gard slid her arm farther around Jenna's waist, worried she might faint. A wolf-whistle cut through the air and Gard swiveled her head, honing in on a scruffy guy with bloodshot eyes leering at them. Leering at Jenna. She wanted to smack the lascivious grin off his face, and then pulled herself up short. Hell, she bumped shoulders with good ole boys like him every day and never gave their off-color remarks and lewd looks a second thought. She blanked her expression and locked on his eyes until he slid his gaze away.

"Here you go." Gard guided Jenna onto a stool and took the one next to her, extending one leg a little into the aisle to protect Jenna's injured knee from careless passersby. Leaning over the counter, she signaled to a heavyset bleached-blonde in a too-short, tight black skirt who poured coffee a few seats away. "Hey, Betty. Could you bring us an orange juice and a couple of those glazed doughnuts right away?"

The blonde glared before spotting Gard, her iceberg expression melting into a hot pink smile. "Of course, darlin'."

"I'm really all right," Jenna murmured, refusing to give in to yet another case of the swirlies.

"You just need a little sugar to counteract all the stress. If you're not feeling better in a few minutes, we'll get something to go."

"All right. Thanks." Jenna hated being so exposed and vulnerable. "I'm not usually such a wimp."

"You mentioned being in the hospital this morning," Gard said. "What happened?"

"Nothing. It was just a...thing."

"Oh. The dreaded thing. They can be a nuisance."

Betty slid two enormous honey-colored glazed doughnuts in front of them along with glasses of orange juice. "Coffee too?"

"Yes," Gard said. "Thanks."

"None for me." Jenna broke off a piece of the doughnut, put it in her mouth, and nearly swooned as an explosion of warm dough and sweet maple assaulted her taste buds. "Oh my God. What is this?"

"Vermont's own maple-glazed doughnuts. They make them here."

"This place is dangerous."

"Wait until you taste breakfast." Gard nodded her thanks to Betty when the coffee arrived and asked for two specials. "So you were telling me about this *thing*."

"No, I wasn't."

"Why don't you anyway."

Jenna sighed. "You are annoyingly stubborn."

"You can add that to overbearingly authoritative."

Jenna laughed. Nothing seemed to faze this woman. "I've been on a really hectic book tour for almost a month. I had a signing that ran late last night, I didn't get much sleep, and I…sort of fainted. That's all. It wasn't a big deal."

"Sort of fainted, or did?"

Jenna swiped a hand through her hair. "Did."

"And then you flew up here, injured your knee, and haven't had dinner or any sleep tonight either. No wonder you're light-headed."

"Who said I'm light-headed."

"Aren't you?"

"Maybe a little." Jenna ate some more of the doughnut, feeling her strength return as the sugar surged through her bloodstream. "I'm going straight to hell for eating this thing. How many does it take before you're addicted?"

Gard glanced at Jenna's plate. "You're about there now."

Jenna moaned. "That's what I was afraid of."

"I'll feel better if you stayed at my place for the rest of the night."

"Really." Jenna pushed away the last half of the doughnut and swiveled on the seat to face Gard. "You work fast for someone who isn't interested in dating."

"If I wanted to date, I'd make it more obvious and I'd suggest somewhere more exciting than my guest room. You've had a hard day and a harder night. I don't know how to say this without insulting you, but you *look* like hell."

"Well, that may be the reason you don't date very much, Dr. Davis. You're somewhat lacking in tact."

"So I've been told," Gard said.

"So far tonight," Jenna said, ticking points off on one hand, "I've forced you to drive for hours in the middle of the night to shuttle me from the airport, then provide emergency medical care, and now you're ferrying me around so I can eat. I'm hardly going to add to all that by having you put me up at your house. I have a perfectly good hotel room waiting. But thank you."

"There's only one place in town and it's perfectly fine, but it's more of a motel. There's one night clerk who, if I'm not mistaken, is barely out of high school. If you have a problem, I don't want you to be there alone. I have to leave at six for my calls. You'll be able to sleep in until I get back around noon. Then I'll take you to the motel."

"No. I'm not inconveniencing you any—"

"If I have to drive you to town it's another half an hour each way. My place is a mile off this road."

Jenna eyed Gard suspiciously. "And you just happened to take me to the diner that was around the corner from your house?"

Gard grinned. "A mile is hardly around the corner."

"Don't give me that. I know what things are like out in the country. This place is practically in your backyard."

"Not always a city girl, hmm?"

Jenna flushed and clasped her hands in her lap before Gard could see them shaking. "You're nefarious."

"Now there is a word I haven't been called in…oh, a century or so."

Jenna couldn't help herself. She laughed. "How about impossible? Does that work a little better for you?"

"I think I prefer nefarious. More sophisticated."

Jenna snorted.

"So are we agreed?"

"You make the motel sound so appealing." Jenna shrugged. "I'm not making you drive around an extra hour to take me to town. If you're sure."

"I'm sure." Gard took in the circles under Jenna's eyes, the pallor that went deeper than the natural hue of her skin, the tightness around her eyes that spoke of pain, both physical and something beyond. For just an instant, she saw Jenna asleep in her bed, secure in the circle of her arms, and knew she'd lied.

When it came to Jenna Hardy, she wasn't sure of anything at all.

CHAPTER EIGHT

J enna went back to watching the night as Gard turned off the serpentine country road onto a gravel lane that wound between regiments of towering oaks and lone spruce sentries. The moon flirted in and out behind smoky clouds while ahead of them an apparition rose, Brigadoon-like from the shadows, to consume the horizon. A stately white clapboard house stretched its wings from either side of the main building into darkness, its tall, narrow windows flanked by black shutters like so many thick lashes. Incandescent lanterns on either side of the double front doors cast pale yellow circles onto a columned porch. Not a mansion built to mimic the elegance and gallantry of centuries gone by, but the real thing. A country manor house preserved in all its glory.

"And to think I passed on the Motel 6." Jenna rapidly revised her earlier assessment of Gard as a simple country vet. Gard hadn't earned enough tending livestock to buy a place like this. Family money, maybe, or inherited. Definitely a mystery, and when the puzzle came wrapped up in a package like Gard Davis, a fascinating one she itched to unwrap.

Gard pulled the truck around the circular drive and stopped. "The walk is tricky. Wait for me."

Peering through the windshield, Jenna got the impression of another sizeable building looming behind the house—the barn, she presumed. When Gard opened the door, the night rushed in, carrying the wild scent of the surrounding farmland and woods. A gust of wind singing with the deep rumble of bullfrogs and the high-pitched rustle of insects whipped her hair around her face, and she reached up to brush the errant strands out of her eyes. She could almost believe she'd stepped through a time warp, and Gard's sudden appearance did nothing to dispel the illusion. Her profile etched in starlight, her dark hair blowing, and one hand held out to Jenna, she might have been the lord of the manor handing a lady down from her carriage.

Jenna was no Cinderella, though, and she knew it only too well. Had she waited to be rescued so long ago, she would still be lugging trays at Benny's. Ignoring Gard's outstretched hand as agilely as she had dodged the unwanted advances of Benny's customers, Jenna gripped Gard's shoulder instead and stepped down onto her uninjured leg.

"How's the knee?" Gard asked.

"Better." Jenna let her hand linger on Gard's shoulder and tested her damaged knee. Sore but serviceable. She relinquished her hold on Gard. "I think the treatment might be worse than the injury."

"Often the case," Gard said, "but this walk is uneven and you won't be able to see the flagstones in the dark."

"This is no little country farm."

When they started toward the house, Gard slipped her arm around Jenna's waist, and Jenna didn't protest the chivalry. She might not need rescuing, but she liked the hard heat of Gard's body. As long as she was the one in charge of the touching.

"Mulberry Ridge was once one of the largest farms in the state. I was lucky to get the house after the family sold off most of the land."

"And there's just you here?"

"Me, Beam, and a couple dozen horses, goats, and chickens."

"Beam?"

A dark form cannonballed out of the shadows and bore down on them so quickly Jenna gasped and pressed close against Gard. "What—"

"Beam," Gard called sharply. "Take it easy. Walking wounded here."

A wriggling Labrador Retriever skidded to a halt in front of them, tongue lolling and eyes glinting in the moonlight.

Jenna laughed. "Your roommate?"

"One and the same."

"Hello you." Jenna released her grip on Gard's arm and leaned down to pet the dog.

"That's enough, Beam. Go on up now," Gard said.

The dog shot up the steps and Gard took Jenna's hand, helping her up to the wide plank porch. After unlocking the front door, Gard led the way inside and flipped on a light switch.

"Beam," Gard said, "go in the kitchen."

Jenna was too absorbed by her surroundings to be more than momentarily impressed that the dog obeyed. A slate-floored foyer led to a large central hall with doors standing open on either side. She noted a library on the left, a sitting room on the right, and straight ahead a huge curving staircase that opened onto a semicircular second-floor balcony that overlooked the central hall. Oh yes, this was definitely the lord of the manor's home. Scattered rugs covered gleaming random-width hardwood floors and a huge chandelier hung in a glass-domed cupola high above their heads.

"This place is exquisite. Have you been here long?"

"A few years." Gard tossed her keys casually onto an oak side table with a beveled mirror. "I'll show you your room, then bring up your luggage."

"All I need is the carry-on," Jenna said, recognizing that Gard was avoiding any discussion of the personal. Gard was a mass of contradictions, and so was Jenna's reaction to her. They'd only just met, but Gard had somehow gotten closer to her than anyone other than Alice had managed in years. Close enough to divert Jenna from her plans to stay at the motel, close enough to convince Jenna to stay at her home, close enough to take care of her, to have touched her more than once. Jenna hadn't *let* her close as much as Gard had crossed the barriers she had carefully constructed as if they didn't even exist, and that made Jenna wary. She felt vulnerable, and not just because Gard held her secrets even closer than Jenna held hers. She was uncomfortably aware of liking Gard's attention. A lot.

"I'll wait here, if you want to grab my bag out of the truck," Jenna said. "I can carry it upstairs."

"No doubt. But I'm not going to watch you struggle with it just so you can prove you can do it."

"Just when I think I'm starting to like you, you piss me off again."

Gard grinned, an appealing, crooked grin that on anyone else would probably have come off as practiced. On her it was completely natural and all the more attractive. "I seem to do that a lot."

"You're right, you do. If you insist on playing the knight to my damsel in distress, just bring in the damn bag. I'm too tired for another power struggle."

"I can't see you in that role—damsel in distress."

"Good. Neither can I." Jenna smiled. She could see Gard as a knight, though. She had that intensity and sense of purpose, and damn it, she liked that about her. Not at all her usual response to women trying to take charge. "I'll get a head start on the stairs while you're gone."

Gard hesitated, then nodded. "All right. Your room is up the stairs, the first on the right. I'll be right up."

"Thanks."

Jenna crossed to the stairs and started the laborious process of ascending. From behind her, she heard a soft "Be careful," and the last of her annoyance melted with the stroke of Gard's deep voice over her skin.

❖

The guest room was country-classic with floral print wallpaper above white beadboard wainscoting, French doors that opened onto a wood-railed balcony, and a canopy bed. An antique writing desk nestled in front of lace-curtained bay windows, the window bench complete with a red velvet seat cushion. The modernized adjoining bath was fitted out with a Jacuzzi and glassed-in shower.

Jenna retrieved her computer from her briefcase and set it on the desk. She hadn't checked her mail since she'd arrived at the airport, and business was a twenty-four-hour-a-day event in the Internet-connected world. She probably couldn't get online way out here, but she could at least respond to her latest messages and send them in the morning. Hopefully the motel had wireless. A rap sounded on the open door and she turned as Gard placed her carry-on next to the mahogany armoire.

"Find everything you need okay?" Gard retreated to the threshold, as if not wanting to invade Jenna's space.

"Yes, it's great. After what you told me about the motel, you may have trouble getting rid of me." Jenna indicated the room with a sweep of her arm. "This is beautiful."

"You're welcome to stay as long as you like. The wireless isn't passworded."

"Wireless?" Jenna sighed. "I may definitely have to move in."

"Can you cook?" Gard stood with an arm braced against either side of the doorway, her hips canted to one side, a ghost of a smile flickering over her wide, sensuous mouth. Jenna had registered her attractiveness earlier—how could she not? Gard's tight body and handsome features were impossible to miss. But she hadn't caught the rush of sexual current until just now. Gard kept that power tamped down very effectively, and Jenna wondered why. And why Gard had dropped her shields now.

Jenna imagined herself naked, spread out on the canopy bed with Gard's strong hips thrusting between her thighs, her palms sliding down Gard's slick back, her will trapped by Gard's hungry eyes. Jenna blinked, and across the room Gard's mouth quirked, as if Gard were reading her thoughts. Jenna quickly averted her gaze. What was she doing? She'd just had an entire night of sex, very good sex at that, so why couldn't she seem to stop thinking of it every time she caught a glimpse of her host?

"Can't cook a thing," Jenna said too quickly. Perfect. Just what she needed. To let Gard see her so off-balance. Getting a grip, she pasted on her practiced smile—the one she brought out for public appearances and casual liaisons.

"Well, you're still welcome to stay. If there's anything you need—"

"I can't imagine wanting for anything here."

"I don't have guests very often." Gard frowned. "Actually, I never have guests. The housekeeper is supposed to make sure the rooms are kept ready, but…" Gard shrugged. "I don't actually check."

Jenna sat on the end of the bed and wrapped her arm around the carved wooden bedpost. Leaning her head against it, she regarded Gard curiously. "This house isn't your usual bachelor pad. And if you're not into entertaining…"

Gard shifted her back against the doorway and crossed her legs at the ankle. Her blue workshirt stretched across her chest, clinging to the contours of her oval breasts, the seductive curves contrasting sharply with her hard-muscled body. A twist of desire struck so sharply Jenna almost gasped. God, her hormones were out of control.

"Never mind, I'm being intrusive." Jenna hoped Gard would just go. Then she'd do a little work, settle herself down, and fall asleep. *Without* thinking of Gard or how good Gard's body would feel covering hers.

"I saw the place and I loved it," Gard said, obviously not interpreting Jenna's message. "It's got character, history, stories in every room." Gard glanced around, her expression distant. "Being here is almost like living with a fascinating woman."

"Really," Jenna said softly. "And you don't get lonely?"

"Always more to learn."

"About the house or the woman?" Jenna wondered just who the woman was—and if she was real or imagined. The twinge of envy for any woman who might have captivated Gard's attention surprised her, but Gard's silence on the subject didn't. After a moment, she said, "Well, that's an amazing analogy. You have the soul of an artist."

Gard snorted. "Hardly. I was raised to be—"

"Raised to be what?" Jenna said, more curious now. Talk about a fascinating woman. Gard was certainly that.

"Nothing. Nothing of consequence."

Jenna recognized the familiar evasion. She spent her life creating stories, many inspired by snippets of conversation overheard in restaurants and airports, and from people passing by in the street.

Her ability to capture those lost fragments and complete the picture was part nature, part cultivated skill. She didn't need any special intuition to know Gard's story was dark and painful, and though she wanted to know why, wanted to know her, she wouldn't satisfy that need at the risk of hurting Gard.

"You've done so much for me today, tonight. Thank you," Jenna said.

"You're welcome." Gard backed into the hall. "My room is across the hall. I'll be heading out early, but the kitchen is stocked with food and coffee. If you wake up before I get back, help yourself."

"I will." Jenna hesitated. "Sweet dreams."

Gard's dark eyes flashed. "Thanks."

❖

Gard undressed in the dark, stripped back the covers, and fell into bed. She'd had no sleep the night before tending to Elizabeth Hardy's remains, had driven a hundred miles from one farm to another during the day, and now had spent almost another entire night up with Jenna. Her body screamed to shut down, but her mind raced with thoughts of the woman in the room across the hall. The first woman she'd invited into her home. A total stranger who had opened doorways into a past she'd long left behind and reawakened memories she'd thought banished. Jenna Hardy. A woman she'd never heard of before eighteen hours ago. How had she let Jenna inside her carefully constructed defenses?

She was usually more careful. She never acted on impulse. She observed, she studied, she analyzed, and then she acted. She wasn't affected by casual encounters, didn't make instantaneous connections, and even when she had been young and willing to get involved with women, she'd made her choices with a clear head. She chose women who shared the same interests, espoused the same values, and populated the same social circles. Jenna was nothing like those women. They were all icy control. Jenna's temper was quicksilver, her wit sharp and insightful. She was heat and passion, not cool intellect. Intelligent, to be sure, but a woman who appealed to the heart, not just the head.

And no one breached Gard's heart. Not any longer. Gard rolled onto her side and punched her pillow, trying to get comfortable. Usually all she needed to do to fall asleep was get horizontal. She smelled dahlias and spice clinging to her skin, or maybe she just remembered the scent, but her thighs tensed. Damn it, even Jenna's perfume was an aphrodisiac.

Sweet dreams.

Jenna's voice lingered along with the flash of sexual interest she hadn't wanted Gard to see. Jenna wasn't the first woman to look at her that way, but she was the first woman Gard had responded to in the years since she'd left her previous life behind. She liked knowing she'd put that hunger in Jenna's eyes. Sometime in the last few hours, Jenna Hardy—or Cassandra Hart, if there was even any difference between the two—had unlocked the chains on her desire, and that was warning enough to stay far away from her.

CHAPTER NINE

Jenna awoke to raucous bird chatter. She rolled over and peered at the bedside table, expecting to discover one of those alarm clocks that lulled you to sleep with the sounds of whale-speak and roused you with nature's songs. She was wrong. A blue jay raced back and forth on the narrow ledge outside the partially open window across from her bed, his feathers ruffled to relay the urgency of his message. She'd opened the windows in the room last night, climbed into the high canopy bed intending to do a little work, and promptly fallen asleep with her computer propped in her lap. The bedside lamp still glowed, overpowered now by brilliant sunlight pouring through the multipaned glass. She'd had the presence of mind to change into an oversized T-shirt and cotton boxers before bed, so at least she'd had a good night's sleep even if she had been half sitting up. Falling asleep over her computer was nothing new, but instead of waking up muzzy-headed and cramped, she was invigorated by the crisp, cool morning air. Taking a deep breath, she caught the pungent odor of fresh manure. She laughed, realizing even *that* fragrance was energizing. The jay kept up his rapid-fire patter, and she wondered if he had a lady bird nesting nearby, and if her own presence in the guest room threatened his fledgling family.

"I'm not going to bother your lady or her eggs," she assured him.

She set the computer aside, stretched her injured knee, and

peeked under the covers. The joint was swollen, a little black and blue, but much less painful than the night before. Carefully, she swung her legs over the side of the bed and stood up. Hallelujah. She could put weight on it. She took a step. Stiff but functional. All systems go. Thank goodness. She did not enjoy the role of patient, even if Gard's care made her feel special. She did not want to win a woman's attentions flat on her back, unless by her own intention. And not under circumstances where she couldn't repay the favors.

After a quick shower, she pulled on loose cotton pants and a ribbed tank top and settled at the antique desk with her computer, curling her good leg under her. She had a strong signal, and when she checked her cell phone, that was good too. Just knowing she could be connected to the outside world, her world, made her feel as if she was once more in charge of her life.

After scanning her mail and downloading several files from her editor, she logged out and called Alice.

"You were supposed to call me last night," Alice said by way of greeting.

"I know, I'm sorry. Things came up and I never got around to it until it was way too late to call you."

"When are you coming back?"

"I have no idea. I haven't even made an appointment to see the attorney yet. I'll know more after I see him."

"What's your number at the hotel?"

"I'm not there yet."

Alice was silent for a moment. "What do you mean, you're not there yet?"

"I haven't checked into the motel yet. And by the way, it's not a hotel, it's a motel. Who made these reservations?"

"Kerry, at the agency. The same person who always does."

"Well, she should know better than to put me up in a motel. I'm not even sure they have room service."

Alice laughed. "Honey, most people don't spend twenty-four hours a day in their room when they stay in a hotel."

"You know how much work I get done when I travel. Hotels

are productive places for me, and I like to have everything I need available in my room."

"I know. I know. I'll double-check next time." Alice was laughing and trying not to.

"Oh, stop. Besides, that's not your job," Jenna said. "I'm sorry. I'm being whiney. It's just been a difficult couple of days."

"I know. And you still haven't told me where you are."

"I'm at Gard's."

Another silence. "Guard? As in palace guard, off guard? What?"

"Gard as in Gardner Davis. She's the vet—I mean the coroner—well, actually, she's both. She's the one who called me about Elizabeth."

"I'm following so far, but what are you doing at her house at… seven thirty in the morning?"

"A better question is what I'm doing up at seven thirty in the morning," Jenna muttered. She didn't usually sleep more than a few hours a night, but after several days with almost none, she hadn't expected to be up so early or feeling so…wonderful.

"You actually sound perky. What's going on?"

"Nothing," Jenna said hastily, wanting to downplay her time with Gard and not even knowing why. She wasn't a kiss-and-tell kind of girl, but she didn't keep her private life a deep dark secret, either. At least not from Alice.

"Not buying it. Are you sure you're all right?"

"Of course. She picked me up at the airport, and then with my leg, she thought it would be better if I stayed here—"

"I think you need to back up a little bit, sweetie. I'm still not on the same page as you."

"I hurt my leg last night—"

"What! Tell me where you are. I'll be there on the next flight."

"I don't need you to come up. I'm all right. Well, I'm a lot better, at least."

"That's not making me feel very good. Besides, I shouldn't have let you go alone to begin with. I don't know what I was thinking."

"Really, Alice. I don't need—"

"Jenna. I know Elizabeth was only a distant relative, but you're dealing with some difficult issues here. I *am* your friend. That's what friends do—lend a hand when things are tough."

Jenna closed her eyes. Alice was her friend and not just her business manager, agent, publicist, cheerleader, and everything else. "I know how busy you are."

"I'm not that busy, and after all, you're my number one client."

Jenna laughed. "Of course you can come up if you want to."

"Give me the details again."

"I'm in Little Falls. I'll be checking into...hold on"—she dug around in her briefcase for a slip of paper—"the Leaf Peeper Inn." She burst out laughing and Alice joined her. "I must really have been tired last night not to notice that."

"You're right," Alice said, "I am going to have to discipline Kerry. What was she thinking? I'll get our reservations switched to a real hotel. Now, how badly are you injured?"

"I only twisted my knee. It was swollen and tender last night, and it was late. Gard thought I should stay here, so I did."

"Tell me about her."

The protectiveness came surging back. More than protectiveness. Possessiveness. She didn't want to tell Alice about Gard. Or the grand old house. Or the beautiful, funny dog. Or any of the things that had made last night almost magical. "There's nothing to tell. She was just being helpful."

"What did you say her name was again?"

"Gard. Gardner."

"And the last name? Davis?"

"Yes. Why?"

"It's ringing a bell, but I can't quite get it clear. And she's a vet, you say?"

"Yes," Jenna said, her antennae quivering. "Alice, honestly, there's no mystery here. Nothing for you to be concerned about."

"I know."

"And I really do intend to work. I'm going to get a jump on my next book while I deal with…whatever details have to be dealt with. There's nothing for you to do up here and you'll be bored."

"When have I ever gotten in the way of you working?" Alice chuckled. "First of all, you never let anyone or anything get between you and a deadline. And besides that, why would I? My job is to keep you on schedule, not derail you."

Jenna laughed. "Is that what you call all the nagging?"

"I didn't hear that. Listen—I'll come up and stay while you sort out your relative's estate. I could use a break myself. I'll…sightsee or go hiking or some such thing. Whatever people do up there this time of year."

"I may have to go along just for the amusement factor."

"What? I didn't catch that." Alice paused. "Is there some reason you don't want company?"

"Of course not." Jenna fought a surge of guilt for holding back the details she ordinarily would have shared. She wasn't even sure where the reluctance came from. Alice was a huge part of her life— but the life she'd made for herself didn't seem to extend into the remote reaches of this sleepy valley. For the first time since she'd left Lancaster County as a teenager, she felt the absence of the protective façade she'd created in New York City, and the realization made her uneasy. "You know what? I'd love it if you came up. We can play tourist together. I could use a little playtime."

"Wonderful." Alice's voice softened. "I look forward to it. See you soon."

"Yes. See you soon."

Jenna tilted her head back and closed her eyes. The house was silent, but a dog barked in the distance, an ecstatic staccato cadence. Beam, probably. She smiled to herself, thinking of the exuberant animal. More birds joined the vociferous jay, and a symphony of song floated through the window. Somewhere a cow lowed in counterpoint to a tractor's rumble. The breeze danced over her skin, bringing memories of sultry nights, rich earth beneath her bare feet, and the promise of a summer of freedom. When was the last time she'd ever believed that kind of freedom existed? Long before that last summer. Jenna sat up, suddenly glad Alice was on her way.

Alice would arrive and life would settle back to normal. Safe and secure and with no surprises.

❖

"Do you think it's a hernia?" Katie Pritchard fidgeted outside the stall, her pretty Irish features twisted in worry. Her blue eyes darted between her stallion and Gard.

"No." Gard carefully palpitated the swollen scrotum while keeping on the lookout for an errant rear hoof. Windstorm was high-strung and irascible under the best of circumstances, and now, in pain, he was completely unpredictable. "This kind of rapid swelling is more often trauma. Did Faerie Queen kick him?"

"Not that I saw, but there's been a lot of teasing going on. She might have."

"He could have an infection, or the testicle could be twisted." Gard didn't feel the stone-hard sign of impending testicular necrosis usually present with a torsion, though. "I'll start him on some antibiotics. Try to keep him quiet and if he's not better by tonight, we'll ultrasound him."

"God, Gard. If I lose his stud fees, I'll be out half my income."

"I know." Gard straightened and squeezed Katie's shoulder sympathetically. The young horsewoman was a regular on Gard's route—hardworking, bright, and a respected breeder. Still, the life of a rancher was hard, physically and emotionally, and Gard hated to see her in trouble. "Try not to worry. I'm being aggressive because I want to be sure he keeps performing for you."

"Thanks," Katie said, relief evident in the softening of her smile.

Gard hefted her kit and stole a peek at her watch. Only eight. Jenna was probably still asleep. Hopefully one of them had gotten some rest. She sure hadn't, not just because she'd had less than four hours before the alarm went off, but because she kept replaying various moments with Jenna. Jenna intrigued her. She was strong and vulnerable, soft and sexy. Her stubborn insistence on doing everything without help, the snap of temper making her green eyes sparkle, the exhaustion she refused to give in to—everything about Jenna stirred her up. She hadn't ever expected a woman to do that to her again.

"Everything okay, Gard?" Katie asked.

"Hmm?"

Katie nodded at Gard's chest. "You all right?"

Gard flushed, realizing she'd been rubbing the spot in the center of her chest where she still felt the heat of Jenna's body cradled in her arms. She quickly dropped her hand. "Fine. Let me set up a couple more doses of antibiotics for Windstorm. Call me later with an update, all right?"

"I will. Absolutely." Katie hesitated, as if she were going to say something else, then blushed and turned away.

Gard stored her equipment and prepared the medication to leave with Katie. She'd read the interest in Katie's eyes and wanted to avoid any awkwardness. She liked Katie and she didn't want to complicate their friendship. Yesterday she would have said her lack of interest was just that—sex or romance or just plain pleasure with a woman hadn't been on her agenda for a very long time. Today she felt differently, and the reason for the change was at home, asleep in her guest room.

❖

Famished and in dire need of caffeine, Jenna grabbed her laptop and went in search of sustenance. The kitchen, a huge room occupying the entire back of the main house, was everything she expected it to be. Although all the appliances were new, they were designed in a traditional country style—a freestanding cast-iron stove with gas burners, a warming drawer, and a big baking oven cozied up to a white enamel refrigerator with chrome handles that could have been transported from the early 1900s. Wood counters topped sage and cream cabinets with inset drawers and glass-paned doors. An oak plank trestle table with benches on either side stood on the natural slate floor in front of an open-hearth brick fireplace that took up the whole wall at one end of the room.

The coffeepot was easy to find. Fortunately, it was a simple electric drip, and the stainless steel canisters lined up in a neat row nearby were precisely labeled *Espresso, French Roast*, and *Decaf*. She couldn't see Gard as a decaf kind of person, not after hearing about how the vet often worked all night, several nights in a row. She'd drunk regular coffee at the diner at two in the morning. No, the decaf was probably for guests. Overnight guests? The thought of someone else coming downstairs, making coffee in the morning after having slept in Gard's bed, bothered her. Then she remembered that Gard said she didn't have guests. Maybe she didn't consider dates in the same category.

"As if who she dates should matter to me," Jenna muttered, watching the French Roast drip into the pot and willing it to hurry. She searched the cabinets and found a heavy white ceramic mug. Comfortable in her hand, no-frills, solid and dependable. She carried it and her laptop to the table in front of a row of double-hung windows. Like those in her bedroom, these were open, and cotton curtains with pale cream stripes the same color as the cabinets fluttered into the room. Outside, rolling pastures lush with green grass stretched to the foothills of the pine forests.

When the coffee was done she dosed it with milk she found in the refrigerator and went back to the view. A spacious back porch complete with Adirondack chairs and a small table looked inviting, but she resisted the urge to explore. She really ought to work. The new publisher wanted three linked romances with release dates six weeks apart. Romance always sold well, but during prolonged periods of economic stress or global strife, they sold even better. Now readers were looking for comfort, as well as passion and excitement, and the small-town setting was enjoying a resurgence. She could understand why.

Contemporaries, though, were not her usual thing. All the same, she could do it. She'd reinvented herself more than once—on and off the page. She just needed a hook—something—*someone*—to make hearts flutter. An image of Gard in dusty jeans and a sweat-dampened shirt astride a big bay, her skin golden in the summer sun, instantly came to mind. God, she could be on the cover of one of her books, she was so gorgeous. And damn it if her heart didn't do a little dance.

"Oh for crying out loud. Time to get a grip." Jenna turned away from the entrancing view and her distracting daydreams and sat down at her computer. Taking a sip of her cooling coffee, she stepped into her past and started to type.

She had no trouble conjuring both the appeal and the stifling familiarity of a tight-knit community, where everyone knew your secrets but pretended they didn't. The people in line at the drugstore knew your name, and if you were buying condoms or pregnancy tests, they noticed. And talked about it. For the past decade, the last thing she'd wanted to think about was small-town living, where corruption existed side by side with friendship and fierce loyalty. Now she thought about the girl she'd been, and the woman she had become, and how things might have been different then if she hadn't been so alone.

The crunch of gravel beneath car tires disrupted the soothing backdrop of birdsong and rustling leaves as effectively as a ringing telephone or doorbell. Gard was back. Jenna automatically clicked Save, anticipatory excitement stirring. Standing, she glanced at the clock above the refrigerator, surprised to find she'd been working for over three hours. 11:15 a.m. Hadn't Gard said she'd be back around noon?

She should probably pack. She'd meant to do that earlier and then gotten sidetracked by sudden inspiration. Gard probably didn't have much time and would want to take her to the motel, glad to dispense with her responsibilities and her unexpected houseguest. For just a minute, Jenna was sorry to be leaving. She understood now why Gard had likened the house to a woman. She felt not just welcomed by the beautiful old house, but embraced amidst the sunshine and the burgeoning earth and the trill of birds. She laughed wistfully—she'd never actually experienced such communion with a lover and wondered if Gard had. She imagined Gard waking up in the arms of a woman on a lazy summer day, sated and peaceful, surrounded by all this splendor, and a twinge of jealousy shot a red flag straight into the heart of her musings.

She snapped her laptop closed, as if that could banish her dangerous thoughts. "Definitely time to go."

Chapter Ten

A knock sounded at the front door and Jenna wondered if she should answer. Obviously whoever had arrived wasn't Gard. Well, why not answer? She had several perfectly good reasons for being in Gard's house—even if the thoughts she'd been entertaining about her host the last few minutes had been anything but businesslike.

"Hi, can I help you?" she asked when she pulled open the door.

A woman in a khaki sheriff's uniform stood on the porch, her legs slightly spread, her hands on her hips. She didn't say anything as she took her time assessing Jenna, her bold dark brows drawn low over wary blue eyes. Jenna was used to being the focus of attention, although this perusal was more intense and unapologetic than the shy glances of her readers. She waited for the woman to speak, and while she did, she made her own survey.

The woman filled out the uniform very, very nicely—the shining Sam Browne belt accentuated the subtle flare of hips and the swell of ample breasts and broad shoulders above a long waist. The sharply creased trousers were not tight, but tailored to fit muscled thighs. She was pretty in an earthy, sensual way. Sultry eyes, full lips, and a wide, generous mouth.

"Is Gard home?" The woman's voice was resonant and warm, as voluptuous as her body.

"No, but I expect she will be soon," Jenna said.

The woman extended her hand. Her grip was strong but not challenging.

"Sheriff Rina Gold."

"Cassandra Hart," Jenna answered automatically, as she usually did in situations where she didn't know the individual. She spent most of her life as Cassandra. Her editors, her publicist, and her public all called her Cassandra. Only Alice called her Jenna. Well, Alice and now Gard.

"Cassandra Hart," the sheriff repeated, sounding surprised. Then she smiled, really smiled, and the heat that had been simmering under the closed gaze flared. "I like your books. In fact, you're one of my favorite authors."

Jenna smiled. "Thank you."

"Might you also be Jenna Hardy?"

"Oh, yes, sorry—I guess I just assumed you'd make the connection. I don't know why." Jenna gestured to the house behind her. "I suppose because I'm here. Why else would I be?"

"Well, hell could have frozen over and Gard might have…" Rina grimaced, swept off her wide-brimmed Smokey-style hat, and brushed her forearm over her damp brow. "Never mind. Out of line there."

She gave Jenna another long look, and the question in her eyes said the sheriff had a bit more than casual interest in Gard. Jenna considered how she must appear to the sheriff—barefoot, her hair a little tangled from her shower, and alone in the house when Gard wasn't home. She probably looked like more than a casual guest, but she wasn't about to discuss her relationship with Gard with the sheriff.

"Sorry about the wasted trip," Jenna said.

"Not at all," Rina said. "I would have wanted to meet you anyhow. My condolences about Elizabeth. Everyone in town knew and liked her."

"I wish I'd had a chance to meet her." Jenna doubted she would have made the effort had she simply discovered the presence of a great-great-aunt under other circumstances, but now she'd been drawn into Elizabeth's world and she was curious about her. "Do you need me to do anything today? I was going to check in at the hotel—motel—and then make an appointment with the attorney. Is there something I should—"

"No, there's nothing pressing. The coroner—that being Gard, which I guess you know—will provide you with a death certificate. Sherman Potter, Elizabeth's attorney, will guide you through the rest of the paperwork. I do need to know what you want to do about securing the house."

Jenna let the screen door close behind her and settled into one of the rockers on the porch. The sheriff leaned against the white railing opposite her, her arms braced on either side of her hips. The posture accentuated her breasts and Jenna appreciated again how attractive she was. She wondered if the sheriff and Gard had ever dated. Were still dating. Just as quickly, she reminded herself *again* that Gard's personal business was none of hers. "I'm sorry. What do you mean, secure the house?"

"I'm sure the crime rate around here isn't what you're used to in the city, but we do have our share of vandals. Elizabeth has some pricey farm equipment in the barns, and an empty house is going to be an invitation for someone to break in. If you're planning on selling, the real estate agent may be able to advise you as to the best way to protect the place. In the meantime, I'll try to have a car sweep by Birch Hill at least once a night."

Jenna rubbed a spot between her eyes that had started to twinge. She hadn't even thought about the house or its contents or what she would do about the property.

"How much property are we talking about?"

Rina shrugged. "The attorney will pull the deeds for you if he doesn't already have them, but I think Elizabeth's place runs about a couple hundred acres or so. Used to be a pretty big dairy farm with a few hundred head of Guernseys, but Elizabeth hasn't done anything on that scale in over twenty years. The house and barns are in pretty good shape. She's still got a few cows, the stray chicken, an old donkey or two."

"Cows and donkeys and chickens." Jenna stared at the sheriff. "What does one do with them besides milk them or eat them?"

The sheriff laughed, a clear, melodic laugh that made Jenna think of water rushing in a crystal brook. Oh, yes, she was very attractive. Funny, though, the sheriff's lush good looks seemed to pale in comparison to Gard's. *And we're not going* there *again, are we?*

"Pretend I'm clueless," Jenna said, "which obviously I am."

"They're probably pets at this point," Rina said, still smiling, "None of them would be much for eating unless you were desperate."

"I can see this is going to be a lot more involved than I thought. I'll have to look at the house after talking to the attorney. I suppose I can get an agent to handle the sale of the estate." Jenna rubbed her eyes. "What about the animals? Will they be all right without someone there?"

Rina's face registered surprise and then what might have been respect. "I asked a couple of the neighbors to look after them, but you'll want to decide what to do about them too."

"Of course. Thanks for doing that." One thing Jenna knew about country folk—even the laziest, most irresponsible among them—would pitch in to help a neighbor in need, because community was more than a concept. People were raised knowing the next person in trouble might be them. "I still can't really believe I'm here. I have no idea why Elizabeth left all of this to me."

"Elizabeth was no fool. She must have had a reason. Maybe intuition."

"Intuition. I guess we'll find out." Jenna grinned wryly just as the roar of an engine cut through the quiet and a truck tore down the lane, spewing gravel and leaving a cloud of dust behind it. Gard slammed to a stop beside the sheriff's cruiser and jumped out, leaving the door ajar as she sprinted toward the house. Beam shot out after her and raced in circles around Gard's long legs.

"Jenna," Gard charged up the four steps to the porch two at a time, "are you all right?"

"Yes." Jenna rose carefully on her sore leg, feeling unaccustomedly shy. Beam skidded to a stop between her and Rina, her butt rotating as her tail cut wild figure eights in the air. Jenna scratched behind the dog's ears and used the diversion to enjoy her first look at Gard in daylight. She'd been gorgeous by moonlight. She was heart-stopping now in dusty jeans cut low on lean hips, scuffed boots, and a blue work shirt unbuttoned to the middle of her flat abdomen. The white T-shirt underneath hugged the shadow of her breasts like the snow capping the distant peaks—alluring and ever so remote. Her thick black hair lay in damp swirls on the tanned skin at the back of her neck. Jenna's throat went suddenly dry. "I'm fine."

"Okay. Good. That's good. I saw the cruiser..." Gard slid her hands into her back pockets and rocked on her heels. "What's going on?"

Rina said, "I've just been talking to Ms. Hardy about making arrangements for Elizabeth's place."

"I realize now there's more to it than signing a few papers," Jenna said. "The house can wait, but I want to make sure the animals—"

"I'll take care of that," Gard said. "I was planning to run out there and check on them after we got you settled at the motel."

"No," Jenna said quickly. "You don't need to. You've been wonderful, but I'm sure you've got plenty to do with your own job."

Rina's gaze swiveled between Gard and Jenna as if she were waiting for the serve on match point in the finals of a Grand Slam tennis tournament. "I'm heading back through town. If you need a ride—"

"I'll take her," Gard said forcefully.

"If the sheriff is going that way—" Jenna protested.

"It's no trouble." Gard paced a few steps and fixed Jenna with an intense stare. "We can run by the Hardy place on the way. See what might need to be done before you talk to Sherm."

Jenna couldn't argue the logic, but she still wanted to. She didn't let anyone take charge of her life, not even Alice. Alice was her detail woman, true, and she did more than organize her schedule. Alice was the wall between Jenna and the rest of the world, the buffer between her and the outside forces that disrupted her concentration and made it hard for her to work. Alice wielded more power than Jenna had ever granted anyone, even her occasional serious lovers, but not even Alice crossed beyond the barriers Jenna had erected around her body and her soul.

Gard Davis didn't even seem to recognize those barriers, or if she did, she didn't care. She shouldered past them, steamrolled over them, while insisting on being part of Jenna's life as if Jenna had no say whatsoever. The intrusion irritated her, but she resisted the urge to argue, and not just because she didn't want to expose herself in front of Rina Gold. Part of her, maybe a bigger part than she wanted to face right now, liked Gard's arrogant chivalry. She would never have asked for Gard's help, but Gard didn't seem to need an invitation.

Until this moment, Alice had been the only one in her life who put her first, who cared about her welfare more than about what she could get from *pretending* to care for her. For all of that, Alice had never looked at her with the consuming intensity Gard did. Alice loved her as a friend, and sometimes, possibly—more. But even Alice didn't care for the fragile places in her heart because Jenna didn't let her. If she had, she knew Alice would be there for her. She wasn't offering those vulnerable places to Gard, either, but Gard didn't seem to need permission to cross boundaries. She just did it. Jenna had never really met anyone like her before.

"You're sure you have time?" Jenna asked. Spending a little more time with Gard wasn't exactly a hardship, especially when the alternative was sitting in the motel.

"Positive." Gard jiggled her truck keys in her pants pockets while watching the war wage across Jenna's face. She thought she knew why. Jenna was independent, even more independent than the farmers and ranchers she bumped shoulders with every day in the quiet countryside. She hadn't thought there could be anyone more independent than these people who prided themselves on doing for themselves and living by their own rules. But Jenna was. She didn't want help from anyone, as if help were a sign of weakness. As if letting anyone ease her way would somehow lessen her. She had shadows under her eyes this morning, and although she probably wasn't even aware of it, she was favoring her injured leg. Strain lines marred the smooth skin around her eyes and at the corners of her mouth. She was exhausted and in pain but ignoring both. Knowing that made Gard's insides twist and her chest hurt. She wanted to take away that pain. She'd never had the desire, the need, to do that with another woman. The strangeness of it jangled her nerves. "Look, we should get going."

"All right. Fine." Jenna knew she sounded ungracious, but God, the woman taxed her patience.

"I'll get your things when you're ready," Gard said, needing to move. Needing to do something to burn off the restless energy that was always with her but magnified a thousand times in Jenna's presence. She wanted to touch her. She wanted to catch the scent of flowers and sweet spice again. "Then we'll head into town so you can get settled in at the motel."

"I want to see the Hardy property first," Jenna said.

"Your call."

"I'll go pack." Jenna held out her hand to the sheriff. "It was nice to meet you. Thank you for the help at Elizabeth's."

"Anything you need while you're here, just let me know," Rina said. "I take it, then, you'll be staying a few days?"

"It sounds like I'll need more than just a few days," Jenna said. "Maybe a few weeks."

"Really," the sheriff said dryly, her gaze shifting to Gard.

Curiosity flickered in the sheriff's eyes, and Jenna wondered what misconception the sheriff had about her and Gard. If she thought the two of them were anything other than acquaintances, she was way off base. She and Gard had nothing in common and practically everything at odds. If anything, the sheriff should have noticed that they could barely have a conversation without irritating each other. Besides, she should hardly pose a threat to a beautiful woman like Rina Gold, who obviously had more than just a friendly interest in the local vet. Jenna had no trouble at all imagining Gard and Rina together, and the instant she did, the flare of possessiveness hit her so hard she almost gasped out loud. This wasn't like her. She just wasn't the possessive type. She rarely indulged in a relationship long enough to have any feelings for her dates other than fondness. Jealousy? Never. Possessiveness? Irrelevant. She hadn't even kissed Gard Davis, and the thought of another woman touching her made her blood run hot.

"I'll just need a few minutes. Good-bye, Sheriff." Jenna quickly ducked inside, needing to put distance between herself and Gard. And Rina Gold. Whatever was between Gard and the beautiful sheriff did not concern her.

As she climbed the stairs as quickly as her aching knee allowed, leaving Gard alone with Rina, she refused to consider why every step she took was more difficult than plodding through quicksand.

Chapter Eleven

H ow's the knee?" Gard asked when they were settled in the front seat of her truck.

"Much better." Jenna rolled down the window as Gard pulled out onto the road. The thick, sultry air felt more like July than June, the kind of hot, hazy day she associated with skinny-dipping in placid ponds, hiding away in the shade of a huge maple with a book, and relaxing in twilights resonant with the sound of distant thunder. She'd lost touch with those pleasures all these years living in the city, where the summer brought only the pungent stench of automobile fumes, trash left out too long, and throngs of humanity coursing over the steaming sidewalks like schools of fish fleeing for their lives.

"Sorry there's no air-conditioning," Gard said.

"Don't be. I hate it."

"Me too." Gard slowed as a string of geese with goslings scampering behind waddled haphazardly across the road. "You might feel differently in August, though."

"I can remember putting ice cubes on my chest to fall asleep some summer nights," Jenna said, laughing.

"Inventive." Gard imagined Jenna as she would appear now, nude in the moonlight with trails of cool clear water streaming between her breasts and over the curve of her abdomen to pool on the soft white sheets tangled around her hips. Her skin gleamed with reflections of starlight and Gard saw herself leaning down to brush her mouth over the glimmering diamond ice chips. Lust kicked in her belly and she jerked her thoughts away from the fantasy. "I notice you *forgot* the immobilizer today."

"You do realize it's hateful?"

"I've had the pleasure." Gard smiled.

"Then you know why I'm not wearing it." Jenna liked Gard's smile, the way her lips canted up at one corner, softening the angular planes of her face and hinting at a dark sensuality she found hard to ignore. Gard had changed while in the house, and now she wore a pressed button-down tucked into charcoal work pants. Her boots were still the same low-heeled scuffed farm boots, and a tooled brown belt encircled her waist. Her wrists and hands below the rolled-up sleeves of the crisp white shirt were faintly corded and darkly tanned. If she hadn't seen Gard's elegant, stately house, she might have been surprised at the pressed and starched shirt. Gard had to be sending her shirts out to be done. Not exactly what she would have expected from the usual country vet, but nothing thus far was ordinary about Gard. She remembered Alice's comment that Gard's name had rung a bell.

"Where are you from?"

The smile disappeared and Gard's jaw tightened. Another sensitive spot for the enigmatic doctor—so attentive one second, and so distant the next. Someone else might not have noticed, but Jenna made it her business to notice the small details that revealed feelings and moods. She'd learned to watch people for the subtle signs of tempers about to snap after the first time a hand she hadn't seen coming had struck out and landed on her face. Darlene hadn't resorted to physical violence very often, but once had been enough to teach Jenna to be vigilant. She'd been lucky. She'd taken those lessons and turned them around, just like she'd turned her life around, and made them into something she could trust. She'd become an expert people watcher. Being a writer, much of what she conveyed about her characters was through the nuances of expression, and she'd learned to trust the signals others gave off unconsciously. She had to if she wanted to be safe.

"Touchy subject?" Jenna was suddenly sorry she'd brought up

something that stirred a painful memory. "Never mind. I shouldn't pry."

Gard took a deep breath, obviously trying to force herself to relax. "You're not prying. It's a simple question."

"Not always, and I should know better." Jenna suspected Gard never truly relaxed and wondered what haunted her. She seemed to be the kind of person who needed to be moving, maybe because there was something she was trying to outrun. Impulsively, Jenna rested her hand on Gard's forearm and squeezed, finding the muscles beneath her fingers more like steel than flesh. She rubbed her palm up and down over the soft cotton, knowing some pain couldn't be soothed with a simple touch, but needing to try all the same. She didn't want Gard to hurt. "It's not important. The past is the past."

Gard turned her head, her smoky eyes as impenetrable as a dead fire. "Is it? Is yours?"

"Long dead and buried," Jenna said.

"Is it hard for you, then, having a relative like Elizabeth suddenly appear in your life?"

"You are astute, Dr. Davis," Jenna murmured, surprised at Gard's perceptiveness. "I didn't say everyone in my past was dead and buried, did I?"

"You ask questions but you don't say much about yourself." Gard lifted her shoulder, her gaze moving between Jenna and the road she could probably drive with her eyes closed. "The quintessential observer who keeps her secrets to herself."

"I'm not alone in that." Jenna delighted that Gard could read her, even as yet another warning pealed. Gard could read her, and that wasn't a good thing. "You do realize you've completely diverted the conversation from my original question?"

"Have I?" Gard slowed and turned onto yet another hard-packed dirt road. This one was lined on either side with fences, pastureland, and copses of thick birches. As they rounded a curve, a homestead came into view.

"Oh! Is that it?" Jenna's heart raced.

"That would be Birch Hill."

"It's beautiful."

A rambling pale yellow farmhouse that had been added on to many times over the centuries, if the varying roof heights and façade details were any indication, sat on a slight knoll shaded by huge maples and slender white birches. Several weathered gray barns were visible behind the house and a fat round silo jutted into the skyline between them. A broad porch with plain square-capped columns and no railing circled the front of the house and ran along both sides as far as she could see. Where Gard's home was a grand manor house, this was every inch a traditional New England farmstead.

"They don't come any finer than this place." Gard slowed even more as they approached the house, waiting for the golden-feathered chickens to peck their way out of the path of the truck.

"Rina said there were cows. Are those going to wander out next?"

Gard laughed, a deep resonant laugh that stirred an echoing rumble in Jenna's depths. God, she was sexy.

"They ought to be in the back pasture."

"What about the donkeys?"

"Fred and Myrtle have their own shelter on the other side of the back barn. As long as they've got food and water, they should be fine. I'll check on them before we go."

Gard turned off the truck and Jenna sat, her hands loosely clasped in her lap, surveying what was now, apparently, hers. The place couldn't be more different from where she had grown up. The trailer park had been situated in a hollow, shaded by the rise of surrounding mountains, damp in the spring, hot and humid and bug-ridden in the summer, barren in the fall, and bitterly cold in the winter. She doubted that everything here was as beautiful as it appeared on this crystal June morning, but she knew she would always remember it this way. Tranquil and still and lovely, steeped in the indolent passage of time. She itched to write.

"This is a house meant for romance," she murmured.

"You think?" Gard said softly.

Jenna flushed. "Sorry. Some places just beg for a story."

"What about people? Do they do the same thing?"

Jenna shifted to put her back against the door. "Not always. Sometimes the story's better left untold."

"What about yours?"

Jenna shook her head. "No. Mine isn't interesting."

"More so than you think, I imagine." Gard leaned over the space between them, her body slanting above Jenna's, and braced her arm on the door beside Jenna's shoulder. Her face was so close their mouths nearly met. Her arm caged Jenna in.

Gard was going to kiss her and she was going to let her.

Jenna blinked and caught herself before she could gasp aloud. Gard hadn't moved. She slouched behind the wheel, one arm casually tossed over it, her expression curious.

"Are you okay?" Gard asked.

"Yes, perfect," Jenna said, too fast she knew. Her imagination was on hyperdrive and had been since she got off the plane. Her usual boundaries were distorted, as if her trip from the city to the country had somehow reset her inner compass. She needed to be more careful. She needed to reroute the conversation to safer ground. "I guess I should take a look around. I need to have some idea what to tell the realtor. And I want to be certain the animals are being properly cared for."

"Let's go."

"Do you have keys? I never thought—"

"I took Elizabeth's, but the door isn't locked."

Jenna arched her brows. "Isn't that a little reckless?"

Gard shoved open her door. "Not really. Wait for me, I'll come around."

Jenna didn't plan to wait, but when she opened her door and considered the drop from the truck to the ground, she hesitated. She couldn't risk re-injuring her knee. In another day she would be completely mobile again. When Gard appeared, Jenna rested a hand on Gard's shoulder and let Gard slip an arm around her waist and lift her to the ground. She might get used to the lady-of-the-manor routine. The whimsical idea made her laugh.

Gard relaxed her hold but didn't move away. Their shoulders and thighs touched. "What?"

"Nothing," Jenna said, barely resisting the urge to bury her face in the curve of Gard's neck. Gard smelled of soap and sunshine. Simple, strong. The sun glinted in her hair, gilding the ebony curls on her neck, and a fine mist of sweat sheened her skin, tempting Jenna to taste the salt and heat of her. Jenna took a step back. She'd need a lot more than a few feet to ensure immunity to Gard's appeal, but she would damn well find a way to resist. She wasn't against a healthy roll in the proverbial hay—she almost laughed again when she considered the barns nearby, no doubt full of the stuff—but Gard already made her mind cloudy and they hadn't even kissed. She wasn't risking full-out sex with a woman who wouldn't keep her distance.

"If you don't lock the door, aren't you inviting vandals?" Jenna stepped carefully around the chickens on her way to the house.

"If someone wants to get in, they'll break a window. Why create false barriers that don't keep anyone out and prevent the ones who should have access from getting in?"

Jenna wondered for a moment if they were still talking about the house, but they must be. What else would they be talking about?

❖

"Doing okay?" Gard turned on lights as they slowly traversed the first floor, checking that windows were closed and the gas turned off in the big six-burner cast-iron stove in the kitchen, where their journey ended. The kitchen resembled Gard's in the same way a vintage Rolls resembled a sleek new Mercedes. All the classic elements with an added touch of grace. The solid oak cabinets were fronted with beveled-glass doors and cut-glass knobs. The pie safe and hutch had carved lion's-feet legs. The oak plank floors were worn down in front of the sink and counters from generations of cooks shuttling back and forth. Bright rag rugs were strategically placed in front of the back door that led in from a wide porch overlooking the back forty and barns. The spacious heart of the house was neat and tidy and had clearly been lived in, and lived in well.

"I feel a little like an intruder," Jenna said. "Did you know her very well?"

"Not personally, not really." Gard rested her hand on Jenna's shoulder. "I saw her in town and stopped out here occasionally when her stock were ailing. If it helps, she seemed happy and content."

Jenna leaned into Gard's steady presence, folding her arms beneath her breasts. "She…died peacefully, you think?"

"I do."

"Good." Jenna squeezed Gard's hand. "I guess we should check upstairs before we go. Make sure all the windows are closed and things like that."

"All right. Then we'll take a look at the stock."

The stair treads dipped in the center from years of passage. A wide hall with a faded oriental runner bisected the house, with rooms opening on either side. Jenna peeked into a room with a double sleigh bed, dressers covered with personal effects, and a cane rocker with a wicker basket of knitting beside it. Elizabeth's bedroom. A colorful handmade quilt covered the bed, smooth and neatly tucked at the corners. She wondered who had straightened it and glanced at Gard, who shook her head.

"Probably one of the neighbors came in," Gard said. "I'm afraid I wasn't thinking of it when I was here."

"Of course you weren't." Jenna smiled at Gard. "You were seeing to Elizabeth. I'm glad it was you."

Gard's chest tightened at the sadness in Jenna's voice. She'd grown pale again, and her limp was more pronounced. When Jenna turned her head, Gard caught the shimmer of tears glistening on her lashes and reacted instinctively. She clasped Jenna's shoulders and drew her into her arms. Cupping the back of Jenna's neck, she guided Jenna's head against her shoulder and held her. "You've had a pretty rough few days. Why don't we leave the rest of this for another time."

"Sorry, just give me a second," Jenna whispered.

"Long as you need." Gard held her breath and would have stopped her heart if she could—anything not to break the spell of having Jenna in her arms. Jenna's heart beat against her chest and warm breath fluttered over her throat. She felt as if she were holding a fragile work of art that might shatter at any second, even though she knew Jenna was neither fragile nor a priceless object. She was a flesh-and-blood woman, strong and stubborn and self-sufficient. Still, she wanted to shelter Jenna in a way that was completely new to her. The urge was so intense she shuddered with the force of it.

Jenna ran her hands up and down Gard's back, drawing her fingers along the edges of the muscles bracketing her spine. "I'm all right."

"I know," Gard murmured. Blood pumped like oil from an uncapped well into her belly and pounded between her thighs. She was hard and swollen, her nipples rigid. She tightened her thighs to keep from rocking her pelvis into Jenna's. She was just a little bit taller than Jenna, and they fit together perfectly. She gritted her teeth when moist warm lips skated over her neck.

"You taste like a summer afternoon," Jenna whispered. "I knew you would."

"Jenna," Gard groaned. She didn't want to let her go, but if she didn't, she was going to kiss her, and that would be a mistake for more reasons than she could count. Jenna made a small sound in the back of her throat, half whimper, half want, and Gard's control slipped. She skimmed her hand from Jenna's hair over her neck, along the curve of her shoulder, to the swell of her breast.

"Mmm, yes." Jenna sighed, her breath a hot wind blowing through Gard's blood.

When Jenna trembled, Gard snapped back to reality as if she'd been doused in cold water. She had no business touching this woman. Certainly not here, not now. She clasped Jenna's shoulders again and eased away until their bodies no longer touched. "Jenna, I'm sorry."

Jenna's eyes went from hazy to crystal clear in a heartbeat. "No need to apologize. I'm here too, remember?"

"I just wanted to—"

"It doesn't matter. Shall we finish up?"

"Sure," Gard said, a muscle jumping along her jaw.

Jenna strode off before the flush creeping up her chest above her low-cut tank top gave her away. God, she'd lasted all of two seconds up close and personal with Gard before totally losing her sanity. She loved the way Gard's tight body molded to hers, and the way she tasted. Rich and tangy and oh God, she was so wet now just thinking about it. She needed to get out of the house. She needed to remember her Number One Rule. Never go to bed with a woman she couldn't control. This meltdown was proof enough that woman wasn't Gard Davis.

"This ought to be the last." Jenna pushed open the door to a room at the back of the house and stopped so fast Gard's front brushed her back and warm breath stirred the fine hairs on her neck. Just what she so didn't need—more stimulation from Gard, accidental or otherwise. She almost leapt into the twenty- by forty-foot room to put distance between them. Light washed through three skylights and a bank of windows that hadn't been visible from the front of the house. An easel stood in the center of the room, and at least two dozen canvases rested in stacks along one wall. This was an artist's studio, and an active one, judging by the number of canvases. "I didn't realize Elizabeth was a painter."

"Neither did I." Gard frowned, walking around Jenna to look at the painting on the easel. "I've never heard anyone mention it."

Jenna followed and studied a nearly completed painting. A bold sunset rendered impressionistic with thick slashes of bright primary colors highlighted a craggy mountain range. The perspective was that of someone looking down from a great height, and Jenna had the instant sensation of flying. "I'm no expert, but this seems very good."

Gard removed a canvas from one of the stacks and held it out at arm's length. Another impressionistic view of mountains and this time, a starlit sky. "I feel like I'm lying on my back in a field and the sky is rotating over my head. Jesus. I can't believe I left the house unlocked with these in here." She carefully set the painting back. "You're going to need an expert to appraise these, but I have a feeling they're going to be worth something."

"Well, if they are, they're going in a museum."

"You might want to find out what they're worth before you decide not to sell them."

Jenna shook her head vigorously. "No. This is her legacy. This is her life. Look around you."

Gard looked at Jenna, her eyes contemplative. "Maybe she knew you'd understand."

"You don't think this is why she left all of this to me?" Jenna said. "Could she have known I'm a writer?"

"Why not? You don't keep your given name a secret, do you?"

"Not exactly, but I don't use it professionally." Jenna didn't want to explain that everything she owned was held by Cassandra Hart Enterprises. In the unlikely event Darlene ever wanted to find her, it would be damn difficult. Not impossible, but difficult. Fortunately, her phone sounded with Alice's ring tone, and she gratefully turned away to answer. "Hi."

"Hi, sweetie," Alice said. "I have plane reservations for tomorrow morning. I've rented a car and I've got GPS and God willing, I won't end up in Canada. Will you be okay until then?"

"I'll be great." Jenna laughed, incredibly relieved to hear from Alice. Now maybe life would get back to normal. "Call me when you get in, and I'll let you know where we can meet."

"I will. What are you doing?"

"We're at Elizabeth's, checking the house."

"We?"

"Yes."

"That would be you and Gard Davis?"

"Yes," Jenna said, lowering her voice even though she knew Gard couldn't hear Alice's side of the conversation.

"She's more than just a country vet, Jenna. Be careful."

"I can't talk right now," Jenna said, suddenly protective. She didn't want Alice prying into her relationship with Gard. Even though there wasn't any relationship, and wasn't going to be one. "I have to go. I'll see you when you get here."

"Jenna, I'm not trying to—"

"I know. See you tomorrow." Jenna disconnected and slipped

the phone into her pocket. She avoided Gard's searching gaze and indicated the room with a sweep of her arm. "Perhaps the attorney can shed some light on all of this."

"Maybe so," Gard said. "Ready to go?"

"Yes."

"Company coming?"

"My agent. A good friend." Jenna strode out of Elizabeth's studio, confident that soon this strange pull she felt to Gard would disappear. Their worlds were about to spin out of orbit as quickly and as unexpectedly as they had collided.

CHAPTER TWELVE

Jenna didn't need to see Alice's face to know she was the one driving the sleek Audi roaring toward the corner of Main and Maple where Jenna waited. The red convertible was the newest, cleanest vehicle within sight, and the only one without a trailer hitch. Most of the vehicles parked diagonally at the curb, front-end-in, were Ford pickup trucks like Gard's, or SUVs and Subarus. Practical, hearty, and snow-worthy. Main Street, a ubiquitous name for the central thoroughfare in every small American town, formed the heart of Little Falls. Three- and four-story brick and clapboard buildings stood shoulder to shoulder on each side of the street for three blocks and housed the bank, post office, city hall/sheriff's annex, drugstore, diner, beauty shop, pizza parlor, a law office, a real estate firm, and three taverns. The residential streets where the doctors, lawyers, bankers, and businessmen used to live ran perpendicular to Main and were named for trees. Maple, Willow, Elm, and Oak were the prominent ones she'd noticed as she'd walked through town after finishing up with the attorney. Many of the once-grand houses with spacious grassy lots and detached garages larger than the trailer she'd grown up in had been divided into apartments when the mills had closed, the jobs had disappeared, and the wealthy had left for the cities.

The elms had long been lost to blight, but the sweeping maples still cast cool shadows over the uneven slate sidewalks, and when the breeze wafted over her skin, making her shiver in the steamy heat, she might have been back in Lansingville, PA, population 673, on her way to a bone-wearying, soul-sapping night of hefting trays and dodging passes from truckers and locals at the diner. She'd outrun the memory on her brisk walk back to Main, and now she smiled with an unanticipated rush of pleasure as Alice screeched to a halt at the curb, one hand holding her streaming blond hair back from her face.

"Nice entrance." Jenna tossed her briefcase on the floor and slid into the passenger seat. "How was the trip?"

"What is it with the drivers around here?" Alice frowned, an inverted V marring the smooth contour between her brows. "If they're not passing you in pickup trucks going ninety miles an hour on roads that look like they ought to be traversing the Alps, they're poking along at thirty. And don't even get me started on the tractors—"

"You're in the land of rugged individuality now"—Jenna leaned over to kiss Alice on the cheek—"where rules were made to be broken and laws are merely suggestions, usually for the other guy."

"Were they serious about the population? Eighteen fifty-seven?" When Jenna nodded, Alice shook her head and laughed. "Where to?"

"We can get you checked in at the hotel—it's another forty minutes from here according to MapQuest—or if you want to start your adventures today, you can stay at the motel with me."

"Kerry hasn't changed your reservations yet?"

"If she did, she didn't let me know about it. But no matter. I've got a marvelous room with an absolutely striking view of the parking lot. As near as I can tell only three other lifeforms currently inhabit the bathroom, and whatever sticky substance is on top of the dresser—"

"Stop. Please. I haven't had lunch yet."

Jenna glanced at her watch. Almost two p.m. Somehow the day had slipped away. More than twenty-four hours since Gard had dropped her off at the Leaf Peeper Inn. They'd filled the silence on the ride into town from Birch Hill with small talk. The polite talk of strangers who hadn't nearly shared an unplanned intimate moment. She'd come very close to kissing Gard in the hallway of Elizabeth's house, or inviting a kiss from her. She hadn't intended either thing, and that spontaneous lapse was frightening. She always planned her liaisons, made the decision to share her body with a cool head, even when the rest of her had already moved to the next stage. Being around Gard sent her well-rehearsed and reliable patterns topsy-turvy, and she didn't like the feeling. She didn't like that she was still thinking about the almost-kiss either.

"Jenna?" Alice grasped Jenna's hand and drew it into her lap, squeezing gently. "Are you okay? How are you feeling?"

"What? Oh, I'm fine. Really."

"How's the headache?"

"Gone."

"Really? You're sleeping all right?"

"Well enough. Stop worrying." She'd learned to half-sleep while listening for Darlene's late night party guests and she was still a restless sleeper. At Gard's she'd slept soundly despite her injury, feeling safe with Gard across the hall, but last night her dreams—fractured bits of a long-ago life and frustrating fragments of a kiss that almost was—had left her uneasy and tired in the morning.

"And your knee?" Alice tilted her head and peered at the object in question as if she might see through Jenna's pants. "How bad is it?"

"Seventy-five percent better already. I think getting off it right away made all the difference. Gard was right about that."

"I take it you're completely moved out of her house?"

"Let's have lunch." Jenna didn't want to talk about Gard, and Alice's warning tone was hard to miss. "Then we can draw up a game plan if you really want to stay a while. You really don't need to, you know."

"I told you," Alice said, "I'm looking forward to a mini-vacation. I saw all sorts of bumper stickers on the way here with delightful places to visit. Caves and caverns and other exotic places. Pottery barns. I assume those come without livestock."

Jenna couldn't help but laugh. Alice was the epitome of a

city girl. An elegant and sophisticated woman who always knew the right wine to choose, the best restaurant, the finest hotel. She had guided Jenna into a world that had been completely foreign to her, and had never once pushed Jenna to be anyone other than who she was. Jenna had taken what she needed from Alice's repertoire, and kept, she hoped, the core of herself—even if she had hidden it away.

"Lunch first," Jenna said. "Head straight through town and I'll take you to Oscar's."

"Italian food?" Alice asked hopefully.

"Ah, well, just about any kind of food you might want."

Once out of town, Alice unleashed the Audi and took the curving roads at breakneck speed. Surrounding fields blurred into ribbons of green, lush streamers cast on the currents of ocean sky. Alice laughed joyfully and Jenna joined her, feeling seventeen again. Freedom was suddenly as simple as the wind on her face. They'd gone five miles over empty roads when a white cruiser pulled out behind them, followed an instant later by the sound of a siren. Jenna looked behind them and saw the revolving red light on top of the sheriff's car.

"Crap," Jenna shouted.

"Well hell," Alice called back, flipping her turn signal and pulling onto the gravel shoulder of the narrow two-lane road. The cruiser pulled in behind them. Alice leaned over the seat for her purse. By the time the officer approached the side of the car, she had her license and car rental papers already out.

"License and registration please." Rina Gold removed her sunglasses and hooked them onto the flap of her shirt pocket as her gaze slid from Alice to Jenna, one dark brow lifting. "Good afternoon, Ms. Hardy."

"Sheriff Gold." Jenna knew her face was flaming.

Alice turned in her seat, putting her back partially to Jenna and tilting her face up to Rina. The sun caught the silver highlights in her hair and she seemed to glow. "I'm sorry, Sheriff. I'm afraid I was too busy admiring this gorgeous countryside to pay attention to my speed."

For half a heartbeat, a smile threatened to break Rina's tight-lipped grimace. "Yes. I hear that a lot. One moment, please."

As soon as she was out of earshot, Alice rounded on Jenna, her eyes sparkling. "Who is that? She is drop-dead gorgeous."

"The county sheriff. I met her out at Gard's."

"Is she—" Alice waggled her eyebrows suggestively.

"I don't know. It's not the first thing I usually ask a stranger." Jenna sounded testy and she knew it. Did everyone think that Rina Gold was gorgeous? Just because she was. Damn her.

"You don't know, or you don't think so?"

"I don't know," Jenna said, keeping her voice low because the sheriff was on her way back.

Rina handed back Alice's papers. Then she braced both hands on the edge of the car door. "I'm going to give you a warning this time, Ms. Smith, because I see that you've just arrived in Vermont. Those little signs that you see along the side of the road with numbers on them? They denote the speed limit. On this road that's fifty-five."

"I'm sorry. I really was having a wonderful time driving through your county, Sheriff. It's like nothing I've ever seen before."

Jenna could hear Alice's eyelashes flutter and choked back a groan.

The sheriff studied Alice a long moment and said, "It would be nice if you lived long enough to see more of it. These roads are treacherous. Be careful."

"I will," Alice said seriously. "Thank you."

Rina touched the brim of her hat with one finger, glanced over at Jenna, then turned away. "You ladies have a nice day."

When the crunch of the sheriff's boots on the gravel faded, Alice said under her breath, "I want her. Is it too soon to ask for her number?"

"Just try to behave for a few more minutes. She's going to wait until you drive away. For God's sake, don't peel out."

"What's going on between you two?" Alice eased the convertible onto the road and kept well below the speed limit until the cruiser sped past in the left hand lane a few minutes later and disappeared over a rise in the road.

"Nothing. I hardly know her."

"I could feel the tension between you. Oh no. Wait. Don't tell me. She asked you out?"

Jenna snorted. "Not likely."

"Then wha—the vet? You're both chasing her?"

"No. I already told you there's nothing going on—"

"Oh, please. So is she worried about you and the good doctor?"

"You know, I forgot why I wanted you to come up here. But I think I want you to go home now."

Alice shook her head, her usual playful smile having gone suddenly grim. "You and I need to have a talk about Gardner Davis."

❖

Gard squeezed her truck between Rina's cruiser and a rusted-out Chevy pickup with two mud-splattered ATVs strapped into the open rear bed. Oscar's was jammed, and once inside she stopped next to the register to scan for Rina. She spotted her perched on a stool at the end of the counter, her hat claiming the adjacent stool, and at the same instant, she saw Jenna. Jenna, looking gorgeous with her hair windblown and her color high, sat in a booth halfway down with another woman whose back was to her. When her gaze met Jenna's for a second, Jenna quickly looked away. The brief connect followed by the obvious dismissal jarred her. She'd made a big mistake putting her hands on Jenna, but damn it, Jenna had been upset. And she'd needed to comfort her. That need had caught her by surprise, and now she was paying for giving in to it. She could still feel the press of Jenna's breasts against her chest and the whisper of warm lips against her neck. Fortunately, she had only to remind herself that Jenna would soon be returning to a world she wanted no part of to squelch the temptation to repeat the folly.

Gard headed for Rina but was forced to stop next to Jenna's booth to let Trish, one of the day waitresses, sidle by her with a full tray of burgers and fries.

"Hi, Gard," Trish said in passing.

"How's it going, Trish."

"It's going."

"Afternoon, Jenna," Gard said. Only an inch of space separated her hip from Jenna's shoulder but the chill in Jenna's eyes made it feel like a long, cold mile.

"Hello," Jenna said, her smile fleeting and forced.

"Sherm called. All the arrangements have been made."

"Thank you." Jenna hesitated, then added, "Gard, this is my friend Alice Smith."

Gard held out her hand to a woman she pegged instantly as another big-city sophisticate. Poised, polished, and perfectly turned out in faux-casual clothes that probably cost more than half the trucks parked out front. "Nice to meet you. Gard Davis."

"A pleasure," Alice replied. "Jenna's been telling me how helpful you've been."

"Not at all. Just being neighborly."

Gard watched Jenna as she spoke, searching for some sign that what had almost happened hadn't been all in her imagination. Jenna looked up at her then, and the heat in her eyes was a kick in her gut. Jenna might act like they were strangers, but her eyes said otherwise. Some of the knots in Gard's insides unraveled a little and she barely resisted the urge to brush a loose strand of hair off Jenna's cheek.

"More than neighborly," Jenna murmured. "Busy day?"

"About average. I've still got a few calls to make."

"Well, I know you're busy. Don't let us keep you."

"Enjoy your lunch." Gard continued on and settled onto the stool next to Rina. "Did you order already?"

"Uh-huh. I hope you're in the mood for your usual." Rina cocked her head, giving Gard a quizzical look. "Rough day?"

"Not particularly," Gard said, trying to shrug off the taste of lingering desire.

"I see you've met our newest visitor," Rina said.

"Who?"

"The lovely blonde with Jenna."

"I just had the pleasure."

"They brighten up the place, don't they?"

Gard tried to decipher what was behind the tension in Rina's voice. "What happened?"

Rina slid her fork back and forth on the counter. "Nothing, really. I pulled them over for speeding."

"Wait. Let me guess. The red Audi in the lot out front?"

Rina smiled. "That would be the one. Alice likes speed, it seems."

"Does she?" Gard wondered what the relationship was between Jenna and Alice. Jenna had said Alice was her agent and good friend. Maybe that meant good friend with benefits. That seemed to be popular among busy professionals these days. Why complicate matters having a relationship when you could just have sex with one of your friends. Maybe she should consider it with Rina. She pegged that idea as bullshit as soon as she thought it. Rina deserved better.

"They've been turning quite a few heads in here," Rina noted.

Before she could stop herself, Gard swiveled on her seat in Jenna's direction to check out who was nearby. Wanting to know which men—or women—might've taken an interest in her. Wanting to warn them off. As if it was any of her business. Which it wasn't. She turned back. "It's not like we don't have plenty of beautiful women in town."

"Oh, I agree with you." Rina laughed. "I can think of any number of hot women, but they all seem to be clueless."

"Present company excepted, of course." Gard grinned.

Rina laid her hand on Gard's forearm. "Of course."

❖

"It seems your friend and the sheriff are a little more than friends," Alice murmured.

"What are you talking about?"

"The sheriff looks like she wants to take a bite out of the good Dr. Davis's neck. And she can't keep her hands off her."

"You sound envious." Jenna was glad she couldn't see Gard and Rina together. Imagining Rina leaning into Gard, touching her… She shook the picture out of her mind before Alice picked up on her irritation.

"I confess," Alice leaned on her hand, her expression pensive, "I wouldn't mind being in the vet's place right now."

Jenna fell silent as a waitress slid enormous platters of French fries, coleslaw, and triple-decker turkey sandwiches in front of them. Somewhere between now and the time Gard had walked away to join Rina, her appetite had waned. She picked at a French fry halfheartedly. She hadn't expected to run into Gard again so soon, and she definitely hadn't expected her heart to do a cartwheel the instant she laid eyes on her. Women didn't affect her this way. They just didn't.

"You're muttering to yourself," Alice whispered.

"I am not."

"You don't know who she is, do you?" Alice said, all levity gone from her voice.

Jenna looked up from her plate, surprised by the solemn note in Alice's voice. "No, should I?"

Alice lifted her shoulder infinitesimally. "Probably not. You don't pay attention to society news, and this was quite a while ago. Not that long after you arrived in New York City."

"I don't really want to hear gossip about—"

"It's not gossip, it's fact. If you don't believe me, we can have someone in the office pull the newspaper archives. It's all documented."

Jenna schooled her expression to reveal nothing, but what was left of her appetite fled and her headache made a reappearance. "We all have pasts."

"We do. That's absolutely true," Alice said. "But most of us haven't been—"

"I don't want to hear this," Jenna said sharply.

"Damn it, Jenna. Your friend over there has a criminal past. Along with all the rest of her family."

"I don't believe it."

Alice's eyes widened. "Why not? You don't know anything about her."

"Yes, I do." Jenna knew Gard had cared for her when she'd been hurt. She'd tended to Elizabeth even in death. She'd been nothing but sensitive. Jenna knew people and what they tried to hide, and she couldn't believe Gard was dangerous or evil.

Alice shook her head. "Sweetie, just because she's kind to animals and too good-looking to live doesn't mean she can't also be trouble. Especially for you."

"We just met," Jenna protested.

"Tell me you aren't contemplating a little up close and personal."

"I'm *not*." She wasn't lying—her runaway libido where Gard was concerned was not voluntary. Splitting hairs, maybe, but she didn't need to give Alice any further ammunition.

"Listen," Alice went on as if Jenna hadn't said a word, "I'm all for you having a break. I know how hard you've been working. I heard what the doctor said. And if spending a few weeks in the mountains and having a fling is going to help you feel better, go for it. But not with her. The last thing your career needs is word getting around that you're consorting with someone like her. Your image is too important and you've worked too hard to—"

"You can't be serious," Jenna said. "My personal life has nothing to do—"

"You don't think so? Don't be naïve. The economy has been in the toilet for two years, and publishers are suffering. Bad publicity will hurt you. The last thing publishers want is to invest money in a risky author. Believe me, at the first sign of negative press Edith Reynolds will dump the deal we have in progress and find someone else to make into a best seller. Is your career worth a couple of nights with a hot body and a gorgeous face?"

"No," Jenna whispered, unable to lie about something so essential. Her career wasn't just a job. Her career was her life. She couldn't risk losing it. If she lost all she'd built as Cassandra Hart, she would lose herself.

CHAPTER THIRTEEN

Gard turned down the long lane to Birch Hill, planning to make a quick stop to check that Elizabeth's—now *Jenna's*—stock were doing okay before she went home. She hadn't gotten by the previous night what with one call after another, and today had been just as bad. An emergency case of postpartum hypocalcemia had taken longer than she'd expected, and she'd just gotten the milk fever treated when two more calls had come in. The afternoon had slipped into evening and finally night while she'd finished up. Now it was close to ten p.m. As she rounded the last bend and emerged from beneath the dark canopy of maples into a night nearly bright as day under a full moon, she saw lights blazing from the Hardy homestead. The red Audi sat in front of the house. Of course Jenna and Alice would be together. Alice had flown up to support Jenna and was probably inside doing that right now. The thought of Jenna leaning on Alice shouldn't bother her, but it did.

Disgusted with herself for begrudging Jenna the comfort, Gard pulled the truck in behind the Audi, turned off the lights, and cut the engine. What the hell was she doing here? And why should she care who comforted Jenna? She ought to turn around and leave. Get back to her life. She was reaching for the keys when a rap on the window stopped her. Jenna peered in at her through the driver's window. She rolled it down. "Hi. Didn't mean to bother you."

"You're not," Jenna said. "I…I didn't expect to see you."

Beam tried to climb over the seat from the extended cargo space behind Gard to get to Jenna. A wet nose raked across her neck.

"Beam," Gard complained. "Stay in the back."

The lab settled down with a mournful expression. Gard grabbed the hand towel she kept in the front seat to dry her hands after cleaning them with antibacterial gel, which she did frequently during the day, and swabbed her neck. "I thought I'd be sure the stock were secure for the night."

"I checked them after dinner and they had food and water."

Jenna's face was luminous in the starlight, and when she smiled, something shifted in Gard's chest. The shields cracked just a little and heat seeped into the cold core of her.

"You don't need me, then." Gard reached for the ignition key. She should have known her excuse to stop by was pathetic. She just couldn't get rid of the tight ache in her chest that had been there since she'd almost kissed Jenna, since she'd had her hands on her. She thought maybe if she saw her, she might be able to break the crazy hold Jenna had on her. That sure wasn't working—she was more twisted up than ever. Her insides seethed like a nest of hornets. "I'll get out of here—"

Jenna grasped her arm through the open window. "It's awfully nice of you to check."

"I wasn't sure if the neighbors were still coming by. After all, if any of the animals wander away in the dark and get hurt, I'll just have to take care of them. Plus the chickens are a temptation to the coyotes. I want to make sure they're in the coop."

"Coyotes?" Jenna sucked in a breath. "As in…coyotes?"

Jenna tugged on her arm and Gard half leaned out the window. Hell, she felt like Beam, just wanting to breathe the same air as Jenna. Could she be any more pitiful? "We've got a lot of them."

"Okay. Out of the truck."

"What? Why?"

"We're going down to the barn, and I'm not going by myself."

Gard laughed. "There's nothing to be afraid of."

"I didn't say I was afraid. I'm just…cautious."

"All right."

"And I still say it's very thoughtful of you." Jenna stepped back and before Gard could climb down, Beam shot out, ran twice around Jenna, then threw herself down in front of her, panting to be petted. Laughing, Jenna scratched behind her ears while Gard got her flashlight from a box behind the seat.

Gard held out her hand. "The track to the barn is pretty rutted. Watch your footing."

Jenna hesitated for a second, then took Gard's hand. Their fingers fit easily together. "Thanks."

"What are you doing here so late?" Gard played the light over the worn dirt path that ran around the side of the house, past the back porch, and down toward the barns. The grass in the front yard needed cutting and her pants legs were quickly soaked with night dew.

"I wanted to get another look at the paintings before contacting an appraiser. Alice suggested I take some photographs to send along by e-mail." Jenna hugged Gard's arm to her side, leaning into her as they walked.

"Your leg okay?" Gard asked. Jenna wasn't limping, but she wouldn't—even if the knee was killing her. Jenna didn't court sympathy or help. Thinking of her in pain made Gard's stomach knot, and she wanted to slide her arm around her. Another excuse to touch her, and if she did, she'd just want more. Hell, she was like a horse in a grain bucket, unable to stop even though it was going to hurt later. She needed a dose of reality. "Where is Alice?"

"She's on her computer back at the Peeper, taking care of some urgent business. I'm not her only client and she pretty much dropped everything to come up here." Jenna laughed. "That motel is growing on me, which definitely means it's time to get out of there."

"She's staying with you?" Gard tried to sound casual, but the picture of Jenna and Alice sharing intimate quarters sent the hornets buzzing out of her belly and into her blood. Christ, she needed some sleep or a drink. Something to calm the hell down.

"She cancelled her reservation at the inn." Jenna laughed. "Said it was too far to drive, but I think she just wanted to share my pain."

"That was nice of her."

"Yes, it was."

An eerie howl rose, followed by another, then another, finally culminating in a chorus of song. The piercing notes rang sharply on the still night air and Jenna pressed closer.

"Is that them?"

"Mmm-hmm. Pretty, isn't it." Gard slid her arm around Jenna's shoulder and the embrace felt...right. "They're harmless, you know. They won't approach people."

"What about the animals? The cows? Fred and Myrtle?"

Gard squeezed her gently. "Coyotes won't fool with the large stock. The chickens are a different story, but they'll usually head into their coop at night."

"I certainly hope so."

"Stay here." Gard quickly checked the barn and attached shelters. The cows and donkeys were settled for the night. When she shined her light into the row of coops off to one side, she was rewarded for her concern by disgruntled cackles. Rejoining Jenna she said, "Everybody's tucked in."

"I really appreciate this," Jenna said as they turned back up the path. "I'll have to add finding some part-time help to my to-do list."

"I know some of the teenagers in the local 4-H. Any of them would be glad to pitch in for a few bucks. I'll get you their numbers tomorrow."

"You're a lifesaver."

Gard grimaced. "Not so you'd notice."

"Are you just finishing work?"

"Yes."

"That's an awfully long day for you."

"Longer than I expected."

"Have you had dinner?"

"No."

"I've been getting things organized over here today." Jenna grasped Gard's hand. "The refrigerator and freezer are stocked with food. Let me make you something to eat. It's the least I can do after you came all the way out here."

"You don't have to do that."

"I know I don't, but I want to. Let me repay your kindness."

"I thought you said you didn't cook?"

Jenna shrugged. "I'm no match for Oscar's but I can do simple. Come in. Please."

Gard knew she should say no. Leave. The more time she spent with Jenna, the more things she found to enjoy. She liked the way Jenna's hand fit in hers. The softness of her skin, the firm certainty of her grip. She liked the way her stomach tightened as their shoulders brushed with each step. Even when she'd thought she'd been in love, she hadn't felt the same combination of excitement, contentment, and desire. She ought to back away but heard herself say, "That would be great. Thanks."

"Good." Jenna squeezed Gard's hand, pleased to finally be able to take care of Gard in a small way. She'd hardly believed it when she'd heard the truck pull in and had looked up to see Gard parked in the drive. She'd just been walking through the house, recalling her sadness during the first visit, thinking how comforting Gard had been. She hadn't expected to grieve for a woman she didn't know, and she certainly hadn't expected to be consoled by a stranger. Gard didn't feel like a stranger now, even though she knew very little about her, really.

"You never did tell me where you're from," Jenna said as they climbed the back porch steps.

"Does it matter?" Gard said, and the wariness was back in her voice.

"No." Jenna had told Alice the past was the past, even though she knew the past never completely disappeared. Hers was like a living presence in the back of her mind, whispering reminders of what she'd escaped and warnings of how tenuous the present might be. She wondered if Gard's past haunted her as hers did. "Are you happy here?"

Gard reached the screen door and held it open for Jenna to pass into the kitchen. "Yes. I like my job."

"Grab a chair and relax." Jenna flicked on a wall switch and the round globe in the kitchen ceiling bathed the room in a pale yellow light. If anyone had asked her if she was happy, she would have instantly said yes. She loved her work, thrived on the demands of her busy schedule and the pleasure and security she got from making her own way in the world. Evidently Gard was the same way. Neither of them was attached, apparently by choice. Gard could surely have any number of women if the admiring glances of the ones in the diner—and Rina Gold—were any indication. Neither of them wanted anything serious, neither wanted complications. What could be better? If she was going to be here for a few weeks, she could do much worse than Gard for company. Once she returned to New York, this would just be another piece of the past that had nothing to do with Cassandra Hart's life.

Humming lightly, Jenna opened the refrigerator and took out all the vegetables, then removed a package of chicken from the freezer. "Stir-fry okay?"

"Sounds pretty perfect. Want help?"

"No. There's not much to do."

"Probably safer."

Jenna laughed. "I take it you don't cook?"

"Not much reason to, really. Beam is happy with whatever I give her, and I'm not home enough to spend time fixing a meal."

When Gard turned her chair around from the table to face her, Jenna paused, a half-peeled carrot in one hand. Gard's long legs stretched out in front of her and she'd draped one arm over the back of her chair. With her dark hair tousled and her rangy body so utterly untamed, she was about the sexiest woman Jenna had ever seen. A knot formed in her throat and she had to swallow before she could speak without a tremor in her voice.

"I forgot, you're not big on entertaining, so you probably don't have any reason to do much cooking." She went back to peeling the carrot and hoped Gard couldn't read her thoughts. She was usually much better at this game.

"I'm afraid culinary arts are not in my skill set," Gard murmured.

"I'm sure you have others." Jenna gave her a slow smile, aware she was flirting. Enjoying herself. She was usually the one being pursued, and even then the seductions often bordered on transactions. This reversal was unexpectedly exciting, and her slowly building arousal even more acute. Gard's expression seemed to have sharpened, her gaze darker and heavier by the moment. Hoping for casual, Jenna rinsed the package of chicken neatly labeled and frozen in a clear plastic bag under lukewarm water until it began to defrost. "I've been thinking I might stay here while I make arrangements for the estate."

"Here?" Gard straightened. "By yourself?"

"Yes." Jenna looked over her shoulder. "Is there some reason I shouldn't? Isn't it safe?"

"Oh, it's perfectly safe," Gard said quickly. "It's kind of out in the middle of nowhere. I guess I didn't picture you wanting to be that far from civilization."

Jenna laughed. "Do you really think I'm some kind of spoiled city girl?"

"Ah, I didn't say that." Gard shrugged. "Rina tells me you're a celebrity, though. You didn't mention you were an award-winning author."

"Why would I? Those awards don't mean anything to anyone outside the industry. The only thing that really matters is how popular your books are with your readers." Jenna turned and pointed her wooden spoon at Gard. "And you don't read romances, remember? So I have no chance at impressing you."

"I wouldn't say that." Grad stood quickly and strode toward her, so graceful and powerful Jenna's pulse tripled. "I would imagine being a *New York Times* best-selling writer is pretty damn amazing for anyone."

"I'm always happy about having my work recognized, of course," Jenna drizzled olive oil in the pan and set the burner on medium, "but it's not something I chase after."

"No?" Gard stepped close to Jenna to peer into the skillet, so close Jenna caught a whiff of hay and clover. "What do you chase after?"

A night without dreams. A life without fear. Maybe, for a few weeks, you. "The next great story," Jenna said lightly.

"I imagine you spend a lot of time in the limelight."

"I suppose." Jenna grimaced. "Occupational hazard. I'm selling a product, and I'm only as popular as my last book. If I'm not out there reminding people of who I am and what I write, there are plenty of other authors who will step up to fill the gap."

"You make yourself sound ordinary, and I know that can't be true." Gard rested her hand on Jenna's back and leaned closer to the stove. "That smells great."

"You're very good for my ego." Jenna scooped a mushroom from the pan and held it out to Gard. "Here. Try."

Gard cradled Jenna's wrist and held her gaze while she softly blew on the morsel and then slowly closed her mouth around it. Jenna couldn't look away from her mouth. Oh God, she had a beautiful mouth. Her insides went liquid. If she didn't step away, she was going to embarrass herself and chase after that mushroom.

"So you think it's all right if I just move in?" Jenna scooted out from under Gard's hand and searched the cabinets for plates. "I feel a little presumptuous even cooking in here."

"Elizabeth left this place to you—I'd think she'd like knowing you were here." Gard took the plates from Jenna and set them on the table. "In fact, it will be a lot easier to inventory the house. And it's got to be better than the motor court."

Jenna rolled her eyes. "Oh, you have no idea. At least here I won't be tempted to carry a gun to shoot the cockroaches."

"What about Alice?" Gard asked, her voice carefully neutral.

"She'll stay here too while she's visiting." Jenna laughed as she filled the plates. "I give her three days before the quiet gets to her."

"What about you? How long do you think you might stay?"

Jenna turned from the table. Gard was inches away. "I haven't decided. I have a really hectic schedule starting in a few months and I need to get a lot of writing done before I take to the road again. This looks like it will be a great place to work."

"You don't think you'll miss all that big-city excitement?"

Jenna couldn't miss the bitterness in Gard's tone and wanted to put the smile back on her sinfully sexy mouth. "I think I'll be able to find something around here to keep me entertained."

A second passed, and Gard grinned wryly. "At least for a few weeks."

"At the very least," Jenna said.

CHAPTER FOURTEEN

Gard was pretty certain she was reading the signals right. Jenna was flirting with her. All through dinner, while they talked about Gard's job and Jenna's next book and Elizabeth's paintings, the conversation drifted easily, like so many leaves on a slow-moving stream. Every now and then, she had to force herself to focus, having gotten sidetracked by the way Jenna tilted her head when she was concentrating, the way her lips parted when she was amused, the way she leaned forward intently when she was excited by an idea, her breasts peaking the cotton fabric of her short-sleeved shirt. Jenna's eyes flashed and glowed with emotion. Her body, her voice, her movements were a beautiful symphony playing along Gard's nerve endings, exciting her, intriguing her, enticing her. By the time they finished the meal and Gard stood up to help clear the table, she was vibrating with the urge to run, or to touch her. She backed up, out of arm's reach.

Jenna turned, a question in her eyes. "What?"

Gard shook her head, mesmerized as Jenna carefully set the plate she'd just rinsed down on the counter and dried her hands. Behind Jenna, through the window above the sink, the moon rode on silver clouds, dark lakes swirling indolently across its surface. She'd seen a similar moon a thousand times, seen the trees shimmer and the pastures radiant with starlight, but she'd never been pierced by the beauty until all that splendor framed Jenna's face. She should thank Jenna for the dinner, turn around, and walk out the door.

Jenna took a step closer, then another.

"Jenna," Gard warned.

"I'm listening." Jenna was inches away, her mouth so close their lips would meet if Gard bent her head an inch. Carefully, ever so carefully, Gard rested both hands on Jenna's bare arms, lightly clasping her soft, warm flesh.

"Why?" Gard asked.

The corner of Jenna's mouth tilted upward. Her pupils, black lakes rimmed by forest green, expanded and contracted. Jenna rested both hands on Gard's chest and rubbed her palms back and forth, her fingertips tracing the arch of Gard's collarbones through her T-shirt. "Beyond the obvious?"

Gard's breath kicked up and she stood absolutely still, letting Jenna explore her. She shivered and thought of the way the horses shied away, knowing they were prey, fearing their defenselessness but still wanting to be close, wanting to be touched. She wasn't nearly as brave—she'd stopped inviting touch, stopped desiring connection, knowing the deadly vulnerability that followed. Knowing the soul-crushing pain of betrayal. Against her will, she leaned into Jenna's caresses, inviting, seeking, needing more as Jenna's fingers traced the outer contours of her breasts, coming close to but never touching her nipples. She shuddered as her nipples tightened into hard, tingling knots.

"The obvious escapes me right now," Gard said hoarsely.

"Number one," Jenna murmured, bowing forward until her pelvis snugged neatly into the curve of Gard's crotch, "you're gorgeous."

Gard clenched her teeth as their thighs and bellies cleaved. From Jenna's pleased smile, it seemed she hadn't been very successful in hiding her response. Jenna played her fingertips up and down the center of Gard's torso, as if painting her with sensation.

"But I don't just love the way you look. I love the way you feel."

Gard sucked in a breath, her stomach tensing as Jenna's light strokes became firmer and their hips started a slow thrust and retreat all on their own. Jenna looked up, her gaze hot on Gard's. "I love turning you on. Am I turning you on?"

"Mission more than accomplished."

"Oh good."

Laughing softly, Gard wrapped her arms around Jenna's waist and tugged her sharply forward until their gentle melding transformed into a hard fusion.

Jenna pressed the flats of her fingers against Gard's mouth. "I like to see you laugh."

Gard teased the tip of her tongue between Jenna's fingertips. Jenna tasted a little bit sweet, a little bit tangy. Gard wanted more, and the wanting was what worried her. "Maybe I shouldn't have asked. Maybe the whys don't matter."

"Maybe only this moment matters," Jenna said, her breath coming fast, the green of her irises darkening almost to black. "I want you to make love to me."

Gard cupped Jenna's hips, her hands closing possessively over firm muscles. Need flared as swiftly as a summer storm. She wanted hot, bare flesh beneath her fingers and the heady musk of desire in her mouth. The wild pulse in her belly made it impossible to think. "Jenna, God..."

"Don't think," Jenna whispered, her mouth an inferno on Gard's neck. "Just feel me, right now."

Jenna's teeth closed on her skin and Gard threw her head back, her vision tunneling into darkness. What were they doing? What was *she* doing? Her hunger, so sharp after being so long denied, was a beast she feared would turn and ravage them both. "I don't...I can't."

"All right," Jenna said quickly, curling her fingers inside the waistband of Gard's jeans. Her light grasp might as well have been iron, for all Gard's ability to deny her. "Something safe then."

Gard snorted, her skin so hot she feared it would melt from her bones. "I don't think there is such a thing with you."

"Just kiss me. Just a kiss." Jenna traced her fingertips over Gard's mouth. "Safe enough, for now."

"I doubt it," Gard muttered, but the need rode her hard and she took a chance. Gripping Jenna's hips, she lifted her onto the counter. Jenna's arms automatically came around her neck, and Gard caged her with her hands pressed flat beside Jenna's hips, stifling Jenna's cry of surprise with her mouth. She wanted to devour her. She wanted to plunge into the heat and promise of Jenna's body. She wanted to lose herself in the sanctity of flesh and blissful oblivion of passion. For an instant she remembered how it had been with Susannah, the blind race to annihilation, the desperate quest for ultimate escape. Making love with Susannah had been a battle, a struggle to find union when they'd never quite been able to connect in any other way. For those few brief seconds when the world exploded with sensation, when thought was obliterated by white fire, she'd believed herself to be satisfied. She'd believed she'd been connected. She'd believed she'd not been alone.

She'd believed a lie. So many, many lies.

Gard pulled her mouth away, panting. "I don't want to do this. Not with you."

Jenna laughed shakily, her fingers closing convulsively on Gard's shirt. "You have a way of insulting me more often than any woman I've ever met."

Gard closed her eyes and rested her forehead against Jenna's. "Sorry. That came out wrong."

"I'll cut you some slack this time." Still in control—but barely—Jenna forced her fingers to relax and stroked Gard's back. She was horribly aroused, more than she had ever expected to be from an almost-kiss. For a few seconds, she'd felt the power of Gard's passion on the verge of exploding, and she'd wanted to be caught in the blast. She'd wanted the detonation to carry her over the edge into the maelstrom, tumbling her into a whirlwind of pleasure. They'd barely begun, and Gard had jerked away from her. If she hadn't registered fear in that single jolt, she might have been angry, or at the very least insulted. Instead, she was anything but. She was captivated. And she was furious at the woman who had wounded Gard so deeply.

"It's all right." Jenna stroked Gard's cheek and skimmed her fingers through her hair. "Really, it's all right."

"No, it really isn't." Gard straightened, her eyes stormy now, cloud-filled and impenetrable. "You're a beautiful woman. Anyone in their right mind would be lucky to be standing where I am right now."

"You don't really know that, but thank you." Jenna continued tracing light patterns down Gard's neck and over her tense shoulders. The muscles beneath her fingertips tightened until she feared something might snap. "But this doesn't have to be hard. It doesn't even have to be complicated. And it doesn't have to be tonight."

Gard stepped away. "Dinner was great. I...Just in case you're wondering, I didn't stop because—"

"Oh no," Jenna said abruptly, holding up one hand. "We're not going down that road."

Gard frowned. "What do you mean?"

"We're not doing the 'it's not you, it's me' routine. There is no fault here, no blame." Jenna jumped down from the counter. "Maybe another time."

"Sure. Maybe."

Gard quickly strode to the door and pulled it open. She paused, her eyes bleak. "What I was going to say is that I stopped because I *wouldn't* have stopped with just a kiss."

❖

Jenna pulled into the Leaf Peeper parking lot just after midnight. The only light came from the unit she now shared with Alice. The single-pane glass windows in the adjoining units looked like the flat dead eyes of mourners at a funeral.

"Hi," she said when she let herself into the room. Alice, in sweats and a New York Yankees T-shirt, sat on one of the two double beds, pillows propped up behind her back, her computer balanced on her knees. Jenna didn't think she'd ever seen her look so casual. When they traveled, they had separate rooms and she'd never seen Alice in anything less formal than pants and polo shirts. Usually she was in full business uniform. Tonight, with her hair loose, dressed in baggy sportswear, she looked a decade younger. Softer. Even more desirable than usual.

"Oh for God's sake," Jenna muttered, stalking across the room to the dresser where she'd left her electronics. What was wrong with her? Hormone storm?

"Have a good night?" Alice asked.

"Marvelous. Are you really sure you want to stay here?" Jenna grabbed her laptop and carried it over to the other double bed. The space between her bed and Alice's was just wide enough to accommodate a nightstand with an alarm clock and a lamp. "It's pretty cramped."

"You worry me." Alice clicked a few keys, then set her laptop on the mattress by her side. "You really can't be serious about staying up here, so what does another day or two matter?"

Jenna opened her mail program and scanned it as she answered. "Actually, I'm going to move into Elizabeth's house. The farmhouse. It's silly to pay to stay somewhere when the house is mine. You're welcome to come."

Alice's brows drew down. "You're really going to stay long enough to make the move worthwhile?"

"Since you canceled my tour, I'm free—travel-wise at least—for the rest of the summer. I've got to get a jump on the new books, and I feel like it's going to come easily here." She played the work card without the slightest twinge of guilt. Alice would never argue with anything that helped her work, and in this case, it was true. "It's perfect, really. What better way to stay motivated than to be immersed in the environment? I'll be killing two birds with one stone. Handling Elizabeth's estate, which is going to be a little more complicated than I anticipated, and cranking out the first book."

"Three birds. You'll be resting too." Alice stretched and wiggled her bare toes, flashing the bright red polish on her pedicured nails. "Because God knows, you're not going to be busy with much of a social life around here."

"Uh-huh." She wasn't about to tell Alice the social life around here was a lot more exciting than anything she'd experienced in the big city, or that she didn't have any trouble at all thinking of just who she'd chose for company. She hadn't stopped thinking about Gard since the moment Gard had walked out on her. She didn't make a habit of casual encounters, but intimate company wasn't all that difficult to come by when she needed it. And damn it, she really needed it now.

No sexual foray in memory, not even the great marathon sex with Brin, came close to the intensity of the interrupted kiss with Gard. The woman turned her on like no one she'd ever been with. She bet she could come right now with barely a stroke, a theory she would have loved to test if Alice hadn't been three feet away. She couldn't remember the last time a woman had gotten her so excited she'd had to take matters into her own hands. She usually had far better control than that.

Of course, maybe Gard affected her so strongly because Gard pulled back first, catching her when she'd already let down her defenses. When she'd ached to have Gard take her. Gard had wanted her, she'd seen the desire in her eyes. But something held her back, and that something nagged at Jenna like a splinter just under the surface of her skin. She could see it, could feel the constant little stabs of pain, could hear the constant taunts of do it, do it, *do it*. She wanted to dig beneath the surface and find out what caused a woman like Gard—handsome, smart, accomplished—to resist something as simple as a kiss. What was that all about?

"Where did you just go?" Alice sat up, her expression moving from curious to suspicious. "What's going on?"

Jenna considered making something up. She wasn't in the mood for an argument with Alice. She was still too unsettled after the near miss with Gard. But lying wasn't her style. And this was Alice, after all. "The social opportunities around here are just fine."

"You're stalling."

Jenna laughed. "I am. I, uh, kind of made a move on Gard tonight."

"Jenna!" Alice looked like she was going to take flight. "I told you not her. Why, why, *why* can't you ever do anything I say?"

"You're kidding, right? You've *got* to be kidding. I always listen to you." Jenna was laughing so hard at the absurdity of Alice's statement she could hardly catch her breath. "I'm like a good little soldier. You give me my schedule, I follow it to a T. You tell you want a manuscript yesterday, I deliver the day *before* yesterday.

I'm sorry my love life isn't quite as easy to arrange as my writing schedule."

"What did you do? Please God, tell me you didn't sleep with her."

Suddenly serious, Jenna said, "And if I had?"

"Just tell me. Did you?"

"No, but I wanted to."

"Okay. Clearly, compromise is needed."

Jenna shook her head, but before she could say that her personal life was not something she was going to let Alice manage, Alice interrupted.

"Here's the deal. Go ahead and sleep with her, because I have a feeling you're going to no matter what I say. But it stays here. Kind of like Vegas. What happens in" —she frowned— "Bumfuck, Vermont, stays in Bumfuck, Vermont."

"Agreed," Jenna said, because that was her plan as well. "If we sleep together, it ends when I leave."

"You mean it?"

"Absolutely," Jenna said with certainty. After all, what other alternative was there?

❖

"A beer—Dogfish Head if you've got it," Gard said to the bartender in the roadhouse one county over. She didn't drink where she worked, unless she was meeting Rina for a quick beer and burger in the evening. If she showed up at one of the taverns in Little Falls at one in the morning, everyone would know about it by breakfast. One of the simple realities of small-town living. So she'd driven close to an hour for a little anonymity. She needed to burn off some energy or she'd be up pacing around half the night again. All she could see was the hazy want in Jenna's eyes. Her clit still pounded with frustrated arousal. Maybe a beer would dull the desire.

"Here you go." The bartender slid a sweating bottle across the counter to her. Two wet trails like fat snail tracks followed the bottle's path. She pushed a five back. "Thanks."

The bar was one big room divided into a small seating section with tables and chairs at one end, a couple of booths across from the bar where she sat, and a pool table tucked into an alcove just to the left of the door. She and three men in long-sleeved green work shirts and canvas pants occupied the bar, each with an empty stool between them, defining their territory and their isolation. She drained her beer and asked for another. This one she sipped, knowing it had to be her last.

Lust curled inside her, gnawing at her flesh while the memory of Jenna's mouth seared the surface of her brain. She had sworn off women because of Susannah, but she hadn't wallowed with a broken heart. She hadn't been interested in getting to know anyone beyond the casual conversation that would lead to a night or two of sex, and she hadn't even had that in a couple of years. She knew more about Jenna Hardy than she'd known about the women she'd slept with, and the disruption of the pattern she'd grown comfortable with disturbed her. Jenna disturbed her. She was beautiful and sexy and smart. Who wouldn't want to sleep with her? Hell, she *did* want to sleep with her, was practically sick with wanting her. But Jenna pulled up her shields and retreated from intimacy just as she did, and that was damn scary. She knew a little bit about why people put up barriers, and if Jenna had unhealed wounds, she didn't want to expose them. She didn't want to know about them or care about them or risk making them worse. She didn't want the responsibility, and she sure as hell didn't want the pain.

She looked down and saw that her bottle was empty and now she had no excuse to stay. She reached for her keys on the bartop and stopped when a feminine hand settled on her wrist. A young blonde, maybe twenty-five, slid onto the stool next to her and leaned against Gard's shoulder.

"Get you another one?"

"No, thanks. I've hit my limit," Gard said.

"Not a big drinker."

"No. Can I get you something?"

"Coke?"

"Two Cokes," Gard called to the bartender. She didn't know

the young woman, and she didn't look or sound like a local. She was wearing tapered blood-red pants that ended mid-calf, a skimpy white spandex top, and low-heeled sandals. The men at the bar paid them no attention. "Are you staying around here?"

"I'm organizing summer conferences at Bennington College. I was just on my way back from a weekend in Boston. That's where I live."

"How did you end up in here?"

"I was starting to get a little sleepy so I thought I better stop." She lowered her voice. "You were the safest-looking one in here. I hope you don't mind."

Gard laughed. "I think they're all pretty safe, but I definitely don't mind. I'm Gard Davis."

"Madison Elliott. My friends call me Madison."

Gard laughed again. "Nice to meet you, Madison."

Madison looked pointedly at Gard's left hand when Gard handed some bills to the bartender. Madison's thigh pressed a little more firmly against hers.

"If you're too tired to drive," Gard said, "I can take you to Bennington. You can have someone drive you back here tomorrow to pick up your car. It should be safe enough in the parking lot, and I know the county sheriff. She can have someone check on it. If you like."

"You'd do that? Drive me to Bennington tonight?"

"Sure. I'm used to being up at all hours. And we wouldn't want you to get in an accident."

"You could stay with me—I've got my own room—and drive me back here tomorrow." Madison drank some Coke and pushed the glass away. She caught Gard's gaze, held it unblinking. "If you like."

Gard collected her change. "Let me drive you home."

CHAPTER FIFTEEN

Oh my God," Alice moaned, staring at her breakfast plate as if it might leap off the table and bite her in the neck. "If I keep eating like this, I'm going to have to hire a moving van to get me back to Manhattan."

"I told you not to order the Trucker's Special." Jenna started in on her own more modest plate of eggs and ham.

The diner was full at shortly after seven a.m. She and Alice weren't the only women, but they were the only ones among the long-distance truckers, contractors, and farmers who didn't look like they were about to put in a very hard day of physical labor. She tried not to search for Gard each time the door opened, but she couldn't help herself. She'd gone to sleep with the memory of Gard's mouth on hers and the sensation of the hard muscles in Gard's shoulders flexing under her fingers. Gard's strength was exciting, but it was the look on her face—barely restrained hunger—that had her tossing and turning half the night. Now every time the door whooshed open and someone who *wasn't* Gard walked in, a wave of disappointment rippled through her. Foolish, probably, but the anticipation itself, a kind of sweet agony, was new and different. She'd never longed for a woman, not like this.

Alice leaned across the table conspiratorially. "It's not safe for you to stay up here alone. You're supposed to be taking a sabbatical for your health. This place is going to kill you."

"Dramatic much?" Jenna smiled.

"You say that now. Give it a couple of weeks." Alice narrowed her eyes in warning, but didn't seem deterred from attacking the mountain of food on her plate.

Eating absently, Jenna checked e-mail on her iPhone. Just as she was about to fire off a response to a query from one of her readers asking when her next book was due out, she heard a female voice whisper, "So did you hear the latest about Gard Davis?"

Jenna almost turned her head toward the two waitresses leaning on the breakfast counter directly across from her booth, but managed to keep her eyes on her phone while she eavesdropped shamelessly.

"No, what?" the other waitress said.

"I heard from Shirley that Jerry Benson said that Gard was out to Ramiro's way over in West Dover last night."

"Well hell, a body ought to be able to drink wherever they want. What of it?"

"Seems odd she'd go almost an hour away when we have a perfectly good tavern right down the street, don't you think?" the first cigarette-roughened voice shot back.

"I guess maybe she wanted a little privacy, which sure is hard to get around here."

"Well, I'd say you're right, considering she left the place with some young girl."

The second woman scoffed. "What do you mean left?"

Jenna's stomach took a wild dive.

"I mean left, as in drove off with her in her truck. Left the girl's car right there in the parking lot."

"Left the car, huh?" The second woman sounded curious now. "Who was the girl?"

"Jerry didn't know her. Said she looked like a city girl." The waitress made *city girl* seem unsavory. "Maybe Gard's got a girlfriend she keeps someplace else. You know you never see her with anyone."

"Maybe unlike some people, she doesn't care to parade her private life all over the streets."

"Oh, are you ever gonna let me forget that time Jimmy Williams and I got a little frisky in the back of his pickup truck?"

"Frisky?" the second woman exclaimed. "You two were buck naked and half the town saw you."

"Ain't that the truth." The cigarette smoker laughed, her tone suddenly years lighter. "And I'd do it again too. He had the biggest damn—"

"Shh," the other woman chided. "Not in front of the customers."

Chuckling, the two women disappeared into the kitchen, reemerging a few seconds later with trays laden with enough food per plate for a family of four. Jenna wasn't hungry any longer and pushed her plate aside. She reached for her coffee, pleased her hand was steady because the rest of her wasn't.

"I gather you heard that," Alice said with unusual nonchalance.

"Rather hard not to." Jenna hated the annoyance in her voice, and of course Alice would pick up on it and know she was bothered. Damn it. So what if Gard blew her off because she had a date waiting somewhere else? They hadn't planned anything. Dinner had been a spur-of-the-moment thing. The kiss had been completely unexpected, and *she* had been the one to start it, after all. Even if Gard had been interested, she wasn't the type to stand someone up. Oh, hell, none of that mattered. Gard was a completely free agent. Just like she was.

Jenna carefully lined her fork and knife up on either side of the plate, drank her coffee, and wiped her mouth with a paper napkin. She met Alice's appraising stare with what she hoped was unconcerned cool. "You should be pleased."

"Not if it hurts your feelings."

Jenna sighed. "I told you if anything should happen between us, it won't go anywhere. And I'm fine."

"All right then." Alice took another bite of pancakes and pushed her plate away with a groan. "At least it didn't sound like it was the sheriff."

"Huh. So you do have designs on the local constable."

"If the circumstances were different, I certainly might. I don't know how one goes about getting a date around here, though."

"I imagine it's the same as any other place," Jenna said dryly. "People still eat, so why not ask her out to dinner?"

Alice snorted. "Out where? Oscar's? With the whole town watching?"

"There are lots of upscale bed-and-breakfast places around here. Some of them have got to have nice restaurants. You ought to be able to find a swanky place to take her."

"You're pushing the sheriff pretty hard, aren't you? Trying to eliminate the competition for the vet?"

Jenna thought back to the conversation she'd just heard about Gard and her date. "If I were out to squash the competition, I'd have quite a big job."

❖

Gard spotted the red Audi parked in front of Oscar's and told herself to drive on by. Jenna might not even be inside. Alice could be in there alone, having breakfast by herself. Even if Jenna was there, she'd be with Alice and Gard would be interrupting. Besides, she couldn't think of a single plausible excuse to stop, other than she just wanted to see her. And hell, that crazy impulse was reason enough to keep on going. She had a dozen calls to make.

None of them were urgent, though.

Just the same, her schedule might be light but she had mountains of paperwork to plow through after rounds. While she catalogued reasons to keep driving, her truck seemed to be navigating all by itself. Her Ford bumped off the road into Oscar's and parked, completely on its own. She sat with the engine idling, her hands on the wheel, wondering what she would say when she saw Jenna again. *The kiss was amazing, but not nearly enough? I want to sit and watch the sun go down with you beside me. I want to see the sunrise with you in my arms and make love to you before the world wakes up. I'm sorry I left—I wanted to stay.*

Jesus Christ—she'd sound like a lunatic.

The dilemma was solved for her when Alice and Jenna came through the revolving door and headed for her. She'd parked next to the Audi. Not wanting to appear like some kind of stalker, just sitting in the lot, she shut off the engine and jumped out of the truck. Jenna made her way between the two vehicles toward the passenger door of the Audi. Gard had to jam her ass against her truck to make enough room for Jenna to get by because Jenna acted as if she weren't even standing there.

"Morning." Gard sucked in a breath as Jenna pulled open the car door. Jenna looked great in tight faded jeans and a navy top that was just clingy enough to show the curve of her breasts. Gard's mouth went dry.

"Good morning," Jenna said with a decided chill. She slid into the convertible and closed the door. Loudly.

Gard frowned. Where had the woman with the hot eyes gone? The freeze in Jenna's gaze this morning was so icy she felt cold to the bone. Maybe Jenna regretted the kiss. Or more likely she was insulted by Gard putting her hands all over her and then walking out. She couldn't blame her. She'd been sending mixed signals, and wasn't proud of it.

Placing both hands on the open window ledge of the convertible, Gard leaned over as Jenna jerked her seat belt across her body and shoved it into the clasp. Alice, behind the wheel, started the engine, stared straight ahead, and did a pretty good job of pretending that she didn't see Gard.

"I don't blame you for being mad," Gard murmured. "But—"

"You don't owe me an explanation," Jenna said tightly. "And I'm *not* mad. I don't do mad where women are concerned."

"Okay, but—"

"I'm sorry I put you in an awkward position last night. My mistake."

"You didn't—I—"

"Let's just forget it happened. We got our signals crossed, no harm done." Jenna gave her an empty smile that was worse than a slap. "I've got a lot to do this morning, and I need to be going."

"Of course." Gard took her hands from the door and glanced at Alice, who had swiveled in her seat and was regarding Gard with what might have been pity. "I'll let you go."

She backed up another inch as the Audi shot backwards, rocketed across the gravel lot, and bounced out onto the road. She watched for a few seconds until it disappeared. She was about to get back into her truck when the sheriff's cruiser came from the opposite direction, angled off the highway, and pulled into the spot Alice had just vacated. Rina climbed out, glanced once back up the highway in the direction Alice had disappeared, and shook her head. "You'd think if she was gonna drive like that, she'd get a car that wasn't quite so obvious."

"Do they ever?"

"Nope." Rina laughed. "Red convertibles are always a gimme when I need to fill my ticket quota. Not that I have a quota, mind you. Buy you a cup of coffee or are you just leaving?"

Gard wasn't sure if she was coming or going. She was still trying to figure out the disjointed conversation with Jenna.

"Coffee sounds good."

They walked in together and scored a booth. After the waitress poured coffee and disappeared, Gard said, "Thanks again for having your deputy check on Madison's car."

"Not a problem." Rina turned the heavy white ceramic mug in a slow circle on the scarred wooden tabletop. "Did you take her back out to Dover this morning?"

"No. She was going to get someone in the dorm where she's staying to give her a lift. I have calls and none of them are in that direction." Gard paused, wondering about Rina's cautious tone. "Are you trying to ask me if I spent the night with her?"

Rina raised her eyes. "None of my business."

Gard waited.

"But, yes. I guess I am." Rina glanced around the diner and lowered her voice. "Quite a few people are curious about that."

"What do you mean?"

"You know how it is around here. Not much to talk about except your neighbor's business. Jerry Bensen was coming in to Ramiro's when you were leaving last night. Saw you pull out with her in the truck and was naturally curious. Then he told someone else, who told someone else, who told Shirley Palmer when she served early breakfast this morning."

Gard groaned. "I guess I didn't drive far enough for that beer after all."

Rina laughed. "You're a good-looking single woman and you don't make any secret of the kind of company you like. You don't think everyone around here is curious about who you're seeing and what you're doing with her? You'd have to go to another state, and I'm not even sure that would be enough."

"I'm not running," Gard bit out. She'd run enough.

Rina's eyes widened. "Whoa, I'm just giving you a hard time. All the gossip was good-natured and most of it was pretty vague. You've got every right to see whoever you want and nobody ever said otherwise."

"Sorry." She was being way too sensitive. She knew the score, had known it when she'd moved here. She had opted to trade the false anonymity of elite society for the open scrutiny of a small, close-knit community. Despite the generally good-natured gossip, most people around here really did live and let live. "For what it's worth, I dropped her off about two and went home to bed. Alone."

"Well, that certainly isn't what I'd call juicy gossip."

Gard laughed. "Sorry to disappoint."

"I didn't say I was disappointed."

Gard thought back to the encounter with Jenna in the parking lot. If Jenna'd heard the same rumors that Rina had, her cold shoulder made sense. Jenna probably thought she had gone directly from groping her to sleeping with someone else. Jenna was almost right too. She'd still been so wound up from being with Jenna,that when Madison had slid across the front seat while she was driving and started playing with the hair at the back of her neck, she'd gotten hot again even though she hadn't wanted to. She'd tried to hide it but Madison must have noticed, because when she pulled into the parking lot where Madison directed her to stop, Madison had kissed her and she'd kissed her back. She was horny and Madison promised to douse the flames that simmered deep down inside her. She'd let the kiss go on for almost a minute before she'd picked up on the change in Madison's breathing. When she registered the urgent way Madison moved against her, she called a halt before things really went too far. She wasn't about to say no twice in one night to a woman she'd led on.

"Nothing happened," Gard said.

"You don't sound all that happy about it."

"No. I'm perfectly happy with it. I'm not looking for any kind of entanglement. Even casual."

"That's nice—that you're not looking for anything, I mean." Rina sipped her coffee. "But you know, sometimes life comes calling all the same."

CHAPTER SIXTEEN

Jenna didn't want to think about Gard, and she knew exactly how to put the irritating vet out of her mind. The same way she had always handled disappointment, anger, or fear. She'd settle into her Cassandra-mindset and work. When she was writing, she disengaged her conscious mind from all the stress and obligations of her daily life, and she lost herself—no, that wasn't quite right—she *immersed* herself in the lives of her characters. She couldn't write her best while straddling two worlds. She needed to be in one or the other, and for most of her life, the world she preferred was the one she created. The joy, the heartache, the passion were just as real as any emotion she had ever experienced. Growing up, when her life had been drab and bleak and dangerous, she'd always found refuge in other worlds, other lives. Becoming Cassandra had taken hard work and a lot of luck, but she could count on the life she'd made not to let her down. Once she got lost in the new book, Gard would cease to haunt her thoughts.

After breakfast, she checked out of the motel, and she and Alice drove to Birch Hill. They started upstairs and spent the morning carefully packing away Elizabeth's keepsakes. Jenna wasn't certain what she was going to do with them, but at least in the short term she would store them. They put fresh linens, pillowcases, and covers on the beds in two of the bedrooms, emptied drawers, folded away clothes—working in silence, reverently, careful with what Elizabeth had left to Jenna. When they stopped for lunch, Alice wanted to look through the studio while Jenna put sandwiches together. When Alice came down to the kitchen, she pulled out a chair at the table, her expression pensive.

"I know a gallery owner in Manhattan," Alice said. "I think we should have her come up here and look at those paintings." She drummed her fingers on the table, the clear polish flashing in the sunlight. "What do you think about some kind of event playing off the family art connection? An Elizabeth Hardy and Cassandra Hart joint show—we could display her art in combination with you doing a reading. There are dozens of independent bookstores in this state alone, and I bet we could get a lot of them interested in this."

Jenna picked up the paring knife she'd used to peel cucumbers and wiped the blade with a wet cloth. "You want me to do a book event up here? Why? You've always wanted me to stick to the big cities before."

"I know, because that's where the sales are concentrated. But," Alice held up a finger and waved it back and forth in the air, "with the new direction you're taking for this series, and this new development in your life, it's a perfect opportunity to pull in a different kind of reader. The grassroots, lifelong romance reader. You know we have them—being gay doesn't change the profile. And it's good promotion to show we're interested in the small bookstores too."

"Since when? You're always harping at me to conserve my energy for the big—"

"You won't have to travel—that's my whole point. I'm not talking about the gay bookstores. Just about every town has an indie bookstore." Alice made a face. "Well, any town that's bigger than a blink, which lets out Little Falls."

"I'm more than happy to do any book event, you know that," Jenna said. "If you want to set something up, go ahead. And as far as the gallery owner goes—if you trust her judgment, that's enough for me. It's one less thing I have to worry about."

"Perfect. I'll make some calls." Alice stood up and rubbed her hands together, never happier than when she was planning and promoting.

"I'm going to spend the rest of the day in my office." Jenna really liked the sound of that, even though at the moment her office was actually a sitting room off the parlor. She thought the room that jutted out from the house, giving it three walls of windows, was meant to be a sewing room, but it was perfect for her to write in. Situated at the back of the house, the view was of the barns and the fields and the mountains beyond. Whenever she looked up, she'd be surrounded by nothing but nature. She knew some of her colleagues liked to work in rooms without windows because they were never distracted, but she found changing her focus actually helped her sometimes, especially when she wasn't quite sure where the next scene was going. "Will you be able to entertain yourself?"

"I've got plenty to do," Alice said. "And I really *am* planning to do some sightseeing. I haven't had a vacation in…since before you became a star."

"Good," Jenna said absently, her mind already on the next scene she intended to write. "I'll see you at dinner."

"Does that mean Oscar's again?" Alice put on a brave face.

"Why don't we live a little and explore the countryside. Maybe find an inn with a restaurant."

"It's a date."

A date. Could it be? Jenna watched Alice as she gathered her keys and briefcase from the sideboard in the kitchen. She'd changed into khaki shorts and a sleeveless white blouse, and she looked fresh and toned and quite beautiful. Jenna had always found Alice attractive in an objective kind of way. They'd been friends for a long time. She trusted Alice in a way that she didn't trust anyone else. And spending time with her up here, relaxed and companionable, was easy. Comfortable. Maybe that was enough to build a relationship on.

Alice turned as if to say something and stopped with a quizzical expression on her face. "What?"

Jenna shook her head, feeling the color rise to her cheeks. "Nothing. I was…nothing."

Alice raised her brows, a playful expression in her eyes. "You were cruising me."

"Oh God," Jenna said. "I'm sorry."

"Why?"

"Because we're friends?" Jenna wrapped her arms around her middle. The sudden awkwardness turned Alice into a stranger, and the space between them seemed to shrink even though neither one of them had moved.

"And friends can't be attracted to each other?" Alice's voice had gotten husky and warm. "I've always been attracted to you, but I felt it would be inappropriate. Not because of the business, but because…"

"Because why?" Jenna asked gently and Alice swallowed, the movement causing her throat to shimmer. She was so very lovely. Why had she never noticed, and why now? "How could anything that happened between us be wrong?"

"Not wrong, no. Just…" Alice sighed. "I know you can take care of yourself. God, you proved that by surviving on your own when you were only a teenager. But I guess I've always felt a little responsible for you."

"I'd be lost without you," Jenna said honestly, "but not because I need you to take care of me. You're the only constant in my life. You're the one I trust."

They stared at one another and the air thickened with summer heat and possibility.

"I think I should go for a drive," Alice said quietly, "and let you work. And maybe we should both think about what we're saying. Because I don't think it would be casual, Jenna."

"I know," Jenna said softly. "I'll see you tonight."

Alice smiled a little wistfully, and then she was gone. Jenna listened to the sound of the Audi roaring down the drive, imagining herself kissing Alice, holding her. Every time she tried, she remembered the demanding press of Gard's mouth and her lean, hard body and the picture dissolved.

❖

Gard knelt in the dirt next to the anesthetized pig. She inserted the oral speculum and checked the boar's canines. All four were extruded, but one was close to four inches long and about to pierce his lip.

"We'll have to take that one down," she told Mike Burns, pointing to the longest of the four teeth. "The others don't really look like they're a problem, but I can saw them off if you want."

"I think just the one for now."

"No problem." She grabbed the Gigli saw from her kit and hooked the eighteen-inch-long strand of woven wire, fitted out with a rod-like handle at each end, around the left mandibular canine. "You want to stabilize his head? This will just take a minute."

Mike held the pig's snout as she positioned the wire blade a few millimeters above the gum line. She thought she saw the pig twitch, but when she waited a few seconds, watching, he didn't move again. She'd given him a hefty dose of ketamine and Telazol, so he should be out for a few more minutes. He was a big animal and she didn't want him waking up while she was working. Just as she began to cut, a sharp crack reverberated through the air. This time she was certain the pig twitched.

"Gunshot," Mike muttered. "Somebody jumping the gun on hunting season."

"Great," Gard muttered, sawing through the tooth with as much speed as she dared. She didn't want to violate the pulp space. The pig would bleed and be in pain, and the open tooth root would be a setup for infection. Two more sharp cracks, followed by a volley, thundered overhead just as she completed the cut through the tooth. The pig jerked, reared his head up, and slashed her forearm with the canine of his upper jaw.

"God damn it!" Gard jerked back and fell on her ass. Mike let go of the snout rope, and the boar staggered to his feet. He took a few steps and went down again, still heavily anesthetized. Gard rolled to her knees, made sure he was breathing, and got to her feet. Blood ran down her forearm and trickled between her fingers.

"Shit! Did he get you bad?" Mike asked.

"I don't think so." Gard grabbed a handful of gauze pads from her kit and wiped the blood from her arm. A five-inch gash gaped across her forearm midway between her elbow and the top of her hand. She could extend her fingers, so none of the tendons were damaged. She'd be sore, but once it was sutured, it ought to be okay. "Nothing too serious."

"You want to come up to the house and get cleaned up?"

"I'd better wash it out," Gard said. "Then if you wouldn't mind giving me a hand bandaging it up, that ought to do it."

Mike looked at the pig, then at Gard. His face clouded. "I'm really sorry, Gard. If you want to send me a bill for the doctor—"

"Don't worry about it, Mike. It was an accident. Not your fault. We'll send you a bill for the tooth trim. The rest is on me." Gard tilted her chin at her med box. "Can you get that?"

"If you're sure," Mike said, hurrying to gather up her kit.

"Hey. He'll need those other teeth done sooner or later, right? I'll be back for those and charge you double."

Mike laughed.

After she got the wound irrigated out and a clean bandage wrapped around it, she stowed her gear with Mike's help and drove slowly down the narrow lane that wound between his cornfields. Once she reached the dirt road that fronted his property, out of sight of the house, she stopped and called Rina.

"Sheriff Gold," Rina said.

"Hey, it's Gard. Are you working?"

"Got the night shift. Lucky me. What can I do for you?"

"I'm out at the Burns place, off Route Seven. I could use a ride to Bennington."

"Got another date?" Rina asked.

"Not so you'd notice. I just got gored by Mike's stud boar. My arm's bleeding pretty good and I—"

"Jesus, Gard! Why didn't you just say so. I'll be there in ten minutes. Can you hold on that long?"

"I'll be fine. I'm just a little bit worried about driving all that way. Once I get stitched up—"

"Just sit still. I'll be there."

Rina's ten minutes was more like seven. She must have torn up the highway to get there. The cruiser pulled in sharply behind

Gard's truck, and Rina jumped out, leaving the motor running. Gard pushed her door open and climbed down.

"I'm okay," Gard said. "I just didn't want to take any chances driving."

"Let me see."

Gard held out her left arm. "It's into the muscle but not as bad as it looks."

"Uh-huh." Rina gently cradled Gard's hand, assessing the blood-soaked bandage. "Come on, let's get you in the cruiser."

Gard didn't argue. Now that she was standing, she felt a little dizzy. She doubted it was from blood loss, more likely just from the aftereffects of adrenaline surge, but she was just as glad she wasn't going to drive the thirty miles to the hospital. She patted her leg. "Come on, Beam." The dog jumped down and trotted along beside her. When Rina looped an arm around her waist, she didn't resist. "I appreciate this."

"You thank me for something like this and I'm going to kick your ass."

Gard slid into the front seat of the cruiser after Rina opened the door for her. Beam crowded in at her feet. She let her head fall back on the seat and laughed. "Love you too."

❖

Four hours later, Rina pulled in behind Gard's truck and stopped with the engine idling.

"I can take you all the way home," Rina said.

"I should be fine now," Gard said. "I don't want to leave my truck out here any longer. It'll be dark in another hour or so, and I've got equipment and medications onboard. Besides, don't you need to get to work?"

"I'm the sheriff, remember? I can be late if I want."

"It's not that far, and I didn't let them give me any narcotics. The arm feels good now. I've got probably an hour before the local wears off. I'll be home and tucked up by then."

"I'll follow you all the same."

Gard opened the truck and motioned for Beam to hop in, got behind the wheel, and opened her window. "You don't have to follow me, but I suppose I can't talk you out of it."

"Humor me," Rina said.

"Don't I always?"

Rina grinned wryly. "Not so's you'd notice."

Gard waited for Rina to get back to the cruiser and then she headed for home, driving carefully with Rina behind her. She was about a mile from her own driveway when a red convertible came zooming around a curve and passed her going a healthy eighty or ninety miles per hour. She glanced in her rearview mirror, caught the flash of Rina's headlights signaling to her, and then the sheriff's car made a fast, tight U-turn and screeched off after the convertible. Gard smiled as she pictured Rina locking horns with Alice Smith.

❖

"What do you mean, she chased you down?" Jenna took one last look at the paragraph she had just finished, decided it was adequate, and closed the document. Turning in her chair, she gave Alice her full attention. She'd only been half listening the last few minutes until she registered the words *sheriff*, *speeding*, and *fine*. "How fast were you going?"

"I don't know. Maybe a little over the speed limit—whatever that is—certainly not too fast for the roads around here. There's never any traffic!" Alice threw up her hands, the picture of innocence. Jenna narrowed her eyes. She didn't look contrite, she looked exhilarated.

"You enjoyed it, didn't you?"

"Which part? The part where she kept me sitting on the side of the road for thirty minutes while she did a crossword puzzle in the front seat of her cruiser? Or the part where every single car, truck, hay wagon, and tractor that went by slowed to approximately a quarter of a mile an hour so everyone could peer into my car? I thought some of them were going to fish out cameras and take my picture."

Jenna smothered a smile. Not just exhilarated, completely thrilled. "I bet you were hoping she'd get out her handcuffs."

"You don't know me well enough to suggest that."

"The hell I don't."

"Believe me, the only thing she wanted to slap on me was a great big juicy fine. Which she did." Alice folded her arms beneath her breasts and looked thoroughly put out.

"How much?"

"Two-fifty."

"Wow. You must've really been going fast."

Alice shrugged and looked sheepish before she managed to don her outraged expression again. But that little break had been enough to tell the story.

"What else did you do?" Jenna rose. "Come on. Let's make some iced tea and sit outside and you can tell me all about it. The sunsets are gorgeous here."

A few minutes later, they occupied matching rocking chairs on the broad back porch. Below them in the fields, the cows clustered in a patchwork quilt of brown and white. Broken shards of sunlight cascaded over the mountaintops, the golden light fracturing into reds and oranges, bleeding down the mountains. A breeze cooled the perspiration on her neck, and Jenna felt very close to peaceful.

"So. You were going to tell me exactly what you did to get such a whopping fine."

"Nothing," Alice said far too quickly.

"Come clean." Jenna sipped her tea.

"I suppose I irritated her a little bit when I accused her of lying in wait behind Gard's truck. And I might have suggested that speed traps were illegal or something. Maybe the word *attorney* slipped out."

"Wait, back up. Gard was there too?"

"Well, sort of. They were coming back from the hospital, apparently, because the sheriff got very snarky when she said that she was actually doing something important when she had to stop to deal with an irresponsible, arrogant city girl who didn't—"

Jenna's breath caught. "Hospital. What does that mean, hospital?"

"I don't know. She didn't exactly give me the details."

"Think," Jenna said sternly.

"I was a little bit preoccupied at the time," Alice protested. "It's not like the world stopped for me when she mentioned Gard's name, you know." Alice must have figured out from Jenna's glare that Jenna was serious, because she sighed and looked thoughtful. "All right, she said…she shouldn't have to leave a responsible citizen like Gard, who'd just been released from the hospital, to deal with—" Alice waved her hand in the air. "And then that was the part about the irresponsible, arrogant city girl."

"Gard was hurt?" Jenna said quietly.

"Well, she couldn't have been hurt very badly, she was driving her truck."

"But the sheriff was following her. And she said that Gard had just come from the hospital." Jenna stood. "Why didn't you tell me that right away?"

Alice looked confused. "Which part? The part where I was humiliated, or the part where I got the fine, or the part where I was insulted by—"

"Never mind."

"Where are you going?" Alice called as Jenna hurried into the house.

"To be a good neighbor," she called back.

CHAPTER SEVENTEEN

Gard closed the refrigerator door with her knee, juggled the jar of mayonnaise and packet of lunch meat in the crook of her right arm, and fumbled them onto the table just as the doorbell rang for the second time.

"Coming," she shouted as she made her way down the hall. Clicking on the porch light, she peered through the vertical windows beside the heavy oak door, jolting in surprise when she saw Jenna peering back. Hastily, she pulled open the door. "Hey."

"Hi," Jenna said quietly, her attention shifting to Gard's forearm. "How are you doing?"

Frowning, Gard followed her gaze, then shrugged. "It's nothing. How did you know?"

"Alice said the sheriff said something about you being at the hospital—" Jenna's eyes widened and even in the waning daylight, her blush was vivid. "Oh my God! I'm starting to sound like the people in the diner. I am so sorry. You must think I'm completely invading your privacy—I *am* completely invading your privacy. I'm leaving right no—"

"No, don't." Gard pulled the door open wide. "Come on in. I was just making dinner." She grimaced. "Except it's baloney and cheese sandwiches and somehow I don't think that's quite what I ought to be offering you for your first meal here. Not after what you made for me."

"I didn't come over to be entertained." Jenna walked in and Gard closed the door. "I was worried. How bad is it?"

"It's really nothing." Gard led Jenna back to the kitchen. "A few stitches."

Jenna regarded her suspiciously. "How many stitches?"

Gard put her good hand into the pocket of her pants, but she didn't have any coins to jiggle and pulled her hand back out. Glancing sideways at Jenna, she said, "Twenty, if you count the ones inside, but—"

"Sit down," Jenna said, pointing to a chair. "I'll fix you something to eat. Only it's not going to be baloney and cheese. If you don't mind me knocking around your kitchen, I'll cook."

"No way." Gard got between Jenna and the refrigerator. "*You* sit. You're my guest tonight."

"You're hurt." Jenna's eyes flashed with a little bit of anger, a little bit of worry.

Gard had never noticed the tiny flecks of black diamond swirling through the green, but now, so close to her, she was mesmerized. "You've got beautiful eyes."

"Shut up." Jenna caught her lower lip between her teeth, the flush creeping down her neck. "Don't say anything else, and whatever you do, don't touch me."

"Why is that?" Gard stepped closer until they were only a few inches apart. Jenna was breathing noticeably faster, the tip of her tongue peeking out to moisten her lower lip when she released it from between her teeth. "You look so damn kissable right now."

"I don't know why it is," Jenna said, her voice breathy and low, "but you make me want to be kissed like no one I've ever known."

Gard traced a finger along the edge of Jenna's jaw. "I don't think I want to know how many women that's been."

"Jealous?" Jenna knew she was teasing, wanted to tease her. She'd rushed over to Gard's to be sure she wasn't hurt badly, but just one look at her had rekindled the wanting. The wanting had quickly caught flame and by the time they'd reached the kitchen, she was fully involved. All she could think about now was Gard touching her, kissing her, holding her. She snapped herself back to the present. Gard was hurt. "We are not doing this tonight."

Gard brushed her thumb over Jenna's lower lip, then pushed in just a little farther until the pad grazed over the moist inner surface of Jenna's lip. "What are we doing? Huh?"

Jenna licked the tip of Gard's thumb, aching to suck it. Aching to taste her. And where in Hell had her brains gone. She jerked her head back but Gard's hand on her jaw blocked her escape.

"What are we doing?" Gard stroked Jenna's lip, sending sparks showering straight to Jenna's core. "Jen?"

Jenna planted her hands on Gard's chest and pushed her backwards, one slow step at a time. "What we're *not* doing is fooling around."

The muscles in Gard's chest and shoulders tightened beneath Jenna's hands. God, she had a gorgeous body. Jenna couldn't help but imagine what all that strength would feel like moving on top of her, moving inside her, and she felt herself go liquid. Go ready. Gard's eyes flared, and Jenna knew she knew.

"I never heard how you got hurt," Jenna said hoarsely, maneuvering Gard back the last inch until her legs hit the kitchen chair and she sat. "Tell me while I make your sandwich. But I'm not eating one of those things."

"There's some leftover pizza in the refrigerator."

"I'm not really hungry." Jenna set about assembling the sandwich, aware of Gard watching her. She concentrated on the mindless activity to keep her mind off the way Gard always made her feel like the absolute center of her attention. She'd been ignored as a child, and as Cassandra was used to being on stage, but rarely had anyone looked at her with such intensity. Having Gard's gaze on her was as exciting as being touched. "Do you want something to drink?"

"Want to join me for a beer? There're a couple of Long Trails in the refrigerator."

"I will, thanks." Jenna pushed the plate with the sandwich on it over to Gard, got out two bottles of ale, found the bottle opener where Gard directed her, popped the tops, and set a bottle in front of Gard. She sat down next to Gard and sipped from hers.

Gard took a big bite of the sandwich, then another. "Good."

"It's baloney. How could it be?"

Grinning, Gard finished chewing, tilted the beer bottle, and took three long swallows, her eyes never leaving Jenna. "How's your writing coming along?"

"My new book?" Jenna was surprised that Gard would care.

"Can you tell me what it's about so far, or is that a trade secret?"

"You really can't be interested."

"Wrong," Gard said softly. "I am."

"I've really just started." Jenna laughed, hoped she wasn't blushing. "Something a little bit different for me. I'm writing a love story, of course, that's what I write, but this one is set in a little town a lot like this one."

Gard's brows rose. "Really? And who's the hero?"

Looking at her, Jenna realized immediately who she'd written that day. "You. I mean, a character a lot like you. I'm going to make her a vet—I just decided that right this minute."

"Not biographical, I hope."

"Only insofar as she's devastatingly handsome, effortlessly charming, and drop-dead sexy."

"Is that what you think?"

"Oh, that's exactly what I think." Jenna recognized she was flirting again, and the feeling was a little bit intoxicating. "Of course, I don't really know what it is that you do, but that's what the Internet is for."

"Why get it secondhand, when you could experience it yourself?"

Jenna wondered if they were talking about her book anymore. "What did you have in mind?"

"Why don't you come out with me on some of my calls? That would be better, right? Give you more of the details that you need?"

"That would be amazing." Jenna sat forward, excited. "You wouldn't mind? Believe me, the character wouldn't be recognizable, even if anyone in Little Falls did read my books."

"You think they don't? Rina knows who you are."

"She might be the only one in Vermont, then."

"I doubt it. Cassandra Hart sounds a lot more famous than you like to let on."

Jenna waved that away with a flick of her hand. "Never mind that. You're sure I can come out with you?"

"I'll pick you up tomorrow at five."

"Wait a minute, you can't be working tomorrow." Jenna brushed the bandage on Gard's arm. "You need to recover."

Gard laughed. "Sweetheart, I can't stop working because I've got a little scratch."

"I can't believe that's a little scratch. And you've very neatly distracted me so that you didn't have to tell me what happened." She stood up and pointed a finger at Gard. "I'm going to clean up and you are going to tell me what happened."

"Oh yeah?" Gard grabbed Jenna's hand with her uninjured arm and pulled Jenna onto her lap. She looped an arm around Jenna's waist, holding her. "You sure?"

"Talk," Jenna said. Being this close to Gard was dangerous, but she didn't care. She laced both arms around Gard's neck and leaned back so she could watch her face. "No touching."

"It was a boar." Gard stroked the outside of Jenna's thigh below her shorts. Each gentle caress was a streak of fire. "I was doing some dental work and—"

"Wait a minute. A pig?"

"A very *big* pig," Gard said with some heat.

Jenna almost smiled. "All right. A very big, mean pig, I gather."

"All pigs are mean," Gard said. "This one is especially nasty when he's awake."

"Wasn't he?"

"He was supposed to be anesthetized," Gard said. "He was getting a little light and some idiots were firing rounds in the woods out behind the farm. The unusual stimulation was enough to wake him up. I was almost done when he got me."

Jenna cradled Gard's injured arm in her lap, carefully stroking the white gauze wrapped around Gard's forearm. "I'm sorry. Will it be all right?"

"Yes. It'll be sore for a few days, and I'll need to take it easy with the heavy work for another week or so. But it'll be fine."

Gard's voice had dropped and the slow strokes on Jenna's leg had become firmer, trailing over the top of her thigh and lightly down the inside, just above her knee.

"I need to get off your lap," Jenna whispered.

"Why?" Gard nuzzled the side of Jenna's neck.

"I'm going to forget you're injured in another few seconds."

"You don't need to worry about me." Gard slowly, deliberately, kissed her way up Jenna's neck and tugged gently on the gold stud in her pierced earlobe.

Jenna arched, unable to stifle a faint whimper. The little pinpoint of pleasure streaked down the center of her body and struck her clitoris. She realized she was grinding her butt into Gard's lap, an invitation she hadn't meant to make and was afraid she couldn't stop. With more strength than she thought she had, she pushed herself up and away from Gard.

"Sorry," Jenna muttered. "Sorry."

"My fault." Gard didn't want to let her go and barely restrained herself from yanking Jenna back into her arms. Her stomach was rigid, a hard hot plank of desire. She hadn't meant to touch her in the first place, but watching her move around the kitchen, bantering with her a little, just *being* with her had been so damn easy. So damn good. "Sorry."

"No, you didn't do anything." Jenna shook her head and backed up another step. "I can't seem to think straight around you."

"I don't believe what we were doing had anything to do with thinking."

"My point exactly."

"The other night you wanted me to kiss you. You wanted me to do more than that," Gard said.

"The other night you didn't want me."

Gard's jaw clenched. "That's where you're wrong. I wanted you. I haven't stopped thinking about wanting you."

"Even when you were with your girlfriend?"

"Girlfriend." Gard blew out a breath. "So you did hear the rumor. Look—"

"Never mind. God damn it. It's none of my business and I know it." Jenna turned to leave. "We're not having this conversation. It's completely unnecessary. I just wanted to make sure you're all right."

Gard stood up. "That's bullshit. You came over here for something else."

"You don't know me well enough to read my mind."

"Can anyone?"

Jenna shook her head. "No."

"What about Alice?"

"What about Alice?" Jenna asked.

"She knows you, doesn't she? I got the feeling Alice didn't think too much of me."

"Alice is a good friend. She cares about me. That's all."

"You're not lovers?"

Jenna paused. "No."

"Do you want to be?"

"It would make sense." Jenna glanced at Gard. "We're compatible. We have the same passion—we work too much and we both get more satisfaction from work than anything else. It would be easy and comfortable."

"Convenient."

"Yes. Would that be so bad?"

"Probably not." Gard lifted her shoulder. "If more relationships were like that, they might last."

"What about you and the girl last night?"

"I just met her."

"That doesn't tell me anything."

"Her name is Madison. We bumped into each other at a bar. She'd been driving all night and was pretty played out. I took her home. That's all."

"Rescuing the damsel in distress." Jenna nodded. "That seems to be your thing—taking care of people."

"You're reading that all wrong." Gard wanted her to know the truth—that she wasn't anyone to look up to. "One thing I'm not is a hero."

"I didn't say it was a bad thing."

"I don't want you laboring under any misconceptions about me." Gard saw a shadow flicker in Jenna's eyes, saw Jenna swallow a question, and she knew. She couldn't escape her past, even here. "What have you heard?"

"Nothing," Jenna said.

"Jenna," Gard said, shaking her head.

Jenna knelt in front of Gard's chair and put both hands on her thighs. Her eyes were fiery. "Listen to me. Alice recognized your name and said there'd been some kind of trouble. She didn't know the details."

Gard snorted. "I find that very hard to believe. Alice doesn't look like anything gets by her. She told you I'd been in trouble with the law, didn't she?"

"Yes."

"Then why are you here?"

"Because I don't care."

"You would, sooner or later."

"You don't know that."

"And you don't know me."

"I know you took care of me when I was hurt. You consoled me when I was sad. You make me laugh. You turn me on."

"How long are you going to be here?"

"A few weeks," Jenna said, but even as she did, she wondered if that was true. She had no obligations for the rest of the summer. She liked being at Birch Hill, and she liked being around Gard.

"Then we don't really need to know anything more about each other, do we," Gard said.

"Not really."

"So why don't we leave things at that."

"That's fine with me." Jenna pushed upright. "I should go. Let you rest if you aren't going to take time off."

"One more thing." Gard stood, caught Jenna by the shoulder, and kissed her. She slipped her tongue into Jenna's mouth and Jenna's arms came hard around her neck. Jenna was electric in her arms, pressing into her, molding to every curve and hollow of her body, hips circling demandingly. When she caressed the rise of Jenna's hip and squeezed her small tight butt, Jenna moaned and sucked on her tongue. The sound of her pleasure, the bite of her teeth, was a shot to the gut. Gard gasped and murmured against her mouth, "You came here because you wanted to kiss me."

"Cocky, aren't you." Jenna nipped at Gard's lip, hard enough to make her wince. She tugged Gard's shirt out of her pants and ran her nails over Gard's stomach, just above the waistband of her pants.

Gard flinched, her breath coming fast. "And you like to tease, don't you?"

Jenna's mouth curved, luscious and ripe. "You have no idea." She circled Gard's navel with her fingertips, then pressed her palm hard against the tight muscles. "I want to make you work for your reward."

Gard jerked Jenna closer and pushed her thigh between Jenna's legs. Jenna's small gasp of surprise made her clit twitch. "I want to make you beg for yours."

"Never happen."

"Oh yeah?" Gard scraped her teeth along the underside of Jenna's jaw, then sucked lightly at the delicate skin in the hollow at the base of her throat.

"You're slick but hardly irresistible." Jenna shivered and knew from Gard's satisfied chuckle her body had betrayed her. She couldn't resist, didn't even want to try. She threaded her fingers through Gard's thick dark hair and forced Gard's mouth harder against her throat. Gard sucked until her skin burned and she wanted Gard inside her right then, right there. She wanted it so much, she was about to fly apart into a thousand pieces. If she did, she'd never be able to glue the bits of herself back together again. She'd never be able to find the safe solid place where she controlled all her feelings.

"Oh God, wait," Jenna whispered.

Gard stilled instantly, her open mouth pressed to the soft skin high between Jenna's breasts. She trembled and Jenna stroked her hair.

"I'm sorry," Jenna said. "You get me so excited. Just…just let me settle a minute."

"Why?" Gard skated her good hand up Jenna's side and cradled her breast. Jenna's head fell back.

"Because I think you could make me come just from kissing me."

"Maybe I want to."

Jenna laughed shakily. "God, you're arrogant."

"If I had two good arms I'd pick you up right now, take you to bed, and shut you up."

"Would you?" Jenna pushed her hand up under Gard's shirt, found the small, firm mound of her breast, and squeezed the tight nipple. Gard jerked, groaning deep in her chest, and the sound vibrated against Jenna's palm. "Would you really?"

"We need to take this out of the kitchen."

"Not tonight." Jenna brushed Gard's nipple lightly and trailed her fingertips down the center of Gard's belly and out from beneath her shirt. "When we make love, I don't want to think about anything except how hard you're making me come. I'm not going to be able to do that until your arm is better."

"I'm not going to wait that long." Gard eased away but kept her hand on Jenna's hip. "I know you don't want me to."

"You have no idea what I want you to do." Jenna took a breath. Steadied herself. Got control. "Are we still on for five?"

"Do women always do what you want?"

"I never ask for anything they're not willing to give."

"Is that the deal?"

Jenna nodded. "Clean and simple."

"No strings."

"No strings."

Gard's gaze bored into Jenna's, the gray shimmering to midnight. "Five it is."

CHAPTER EIGHTEEN

When Jenna got home, she wasn't in the mood to recap the evening, but Alice was sitting on the front porch in the semidark, barefoot in striped boxers and a short-sleeved white T-shirt. Even though the table lamp in the parlor behind her threw a crescent of pale yellow light onto the porch, Alice was mostly in shadow. Each time she rocked forward into the moonlight her face appeared, ghostly and beautiful.

Jenna dropped into a rocker next to her and plucked at the bottom of the boxers. "Going native?"

"Ha ha." Alice rocked slowly and rattled the ice cubes in the rock glass she cradled in her right hand. "It's so quiet here. Sometimes I think it's wonderful, and the rest of the time terrifying. I'm not used to being so alone with myself."

"I know what you mean. It's easy to feel lost, isn't it?"

"I don't think I could be happy here for very long."

"Not enough happening?" Jenna had spent the first seventeen years of her life desperate to escape a place very much like this, on the surface at least. She'd been convinced if she could make her way to the city, opportunity would abound and anonymity would be her protection. Now she knew that safety wasn't a place, or even a person, but a state of mind. She'd carved her safety out of nothing, and guarded it with all her will.

"I don't miss the action," Alice said, "at least not the way you think. Oh sure, I miss the easy access to the theater and good restaurants and first-run shopping. But it's more personal than that. I'd slow down too much if I didn't have all the competition around, pushing me just a little harder, just a little faster." She laughed. "Maybe I'm not as much of a self-starter as I thought."

"Afraid you might lose your edge?"

"Exactly. I guess my energy tends to synchronize with my environment." She rocked a little faster. "Isn't there a name for that?"

"Yes, a very big one, and I don't think you'd really like the analogy." Jenna laughed. "You know—the cold-blooded creatures that stop moving below a certain temperature?"

"Are you calling me a snake?"

"Absolutely not. And I do know what you mean."

"But it's not that way for you, is it?"

Jenna hesitated, thinking over her day. "I can write anywhere. As for the rest of it—I haven't made up my mind. I feel like I've lost a layer of skin up here, as if I'm closer to the air and the earth and—well, everything. And I'm not really sure I want to be."

"You mean you feel vulnerable."

Just the word made Jenna anxious. "Maybe."

"I take it you went over to Gard's tonight." Alice drained her glass and set it on the floor next to the rocker. "How is she?"

"I think her injury is a little worse than she wants to let on, but she'll be all right."

"I was wondering if you'd be back tonight."

"I almost wasn't. If she hadn't been hurt, I might've stayed."

"Moving a little fast, aren't you?"

"Hardly." Jenna didn't share every detail of her private life with Alice, but Alice knew her pattern. She most often slept with women she'd met at an industry meeting or business event. After an evening of conversation, enough to establish the unspoken agreement that one night was all she was available for, she'd have an enjoyable few hours of physical satisfaction. She hadn't been with a woman she'd spent more than a superficial hour or two getting to know in months. Now that she thought about it, in years. Without consciously deciding, she'd limited her personal interactions to the wholly impersonal.

"She's not your usual type," Alice said.

"I don't know about that. She's intelligent, good-looking, sexy as sin."

"Uh-huh. No argument there." Alice propped her bare feet up on the railing. Her legs were smooth and sleek, a fine ridge of muscle etched along the length of her thigh. "But that's not what does it for you with her, is it? She's under your skin. I don't think I've ever seen anyone able to do that before."

Alice was right. Gard was under her skin. Suddenly restless, Jenna strode to the edge of the porch and wrapped her arm around a column, trying to see through the dense night beyond the faint circle of light. Everything she'd said to Alice was true. Gard was interesting, bright, good-looking, sexy. But that wasn't it. That wasn't what made Gard so hard to get out of her mind. What was it that made Gard so different? Not just one thing—big things and little things. The way Gard had caught her when she'd fallen that very first night—so steady and sure, her insistence on taking her home and caring for her when she had no reason to care at all, asking—really asking—about her work. Gard made her feel special. And the way she touched her—God, the way she touched her. Jenna closed her eyes. Her lips tingled with the memory of Gard's mouth traveling over her throat, pressed between her breasts. Her nipples tightened and her clitoris ached. And underneath the arousal, she yearned for the connection she had been so certain she didn't need.

"Oh my God," she whispered.

"Serious, isn't it," Alice murmured.

"No. No, no it isn't." Jenna felt panicked in a way she hadn't since she'd run away from home. Her life wasn't out of control, she wouldn't let it be. She wasn't falling in love with Gard Davis. She wouldn't let herself. They'd already discussed it, they'd already agreed. A few weeks. Neat and simple and no strings.

❖

Gard couldn't sleep. Her arm throbbed, but the pain wasn't keeping her awake. After Jenna left, she'd rattled around the house for a while, walked down to the barn and checked on her animals, and ended up sitting astride a pasture fence listening to the night. The cool air helped dampen some of the fire from kissing Jenna, but nothing could douse the simmering coals deep inside. Back at the house, she lay naked on top of the sheets, staring at the ceiling or out the window at the waning moon, trying to figure out what was happening to her. When she'd been young, she'd desperately longed for a woman and thought her craving was love. Looking back, she recognized it as loneliness. The wealth and privilege she'd grown up with had been poor substitutes for intimacy, and she'd never quite fit in with her father and her brothers, and never known why.

Then Susannah had blown into her life with the force of a hurricane, whipping through the empty rooms of her heart and blinding her to what really lay between them. Had she known the devastation that was coming, she doubted she could have walked away. The elation of having Susannah, of believing they shared desire, passion, need—the exhilaration was too addicting. The union she'd thought they'd had was everything she'd ever wanted. But what she'd thought was love proved to be only her own need, and she'd been left battered and bitterly alone. Abandoned at heart, renounced by her family and peers, she'd turned her back on wealth and status and empty dreams. She'd rebuilt a life where the storms of passion would not seduce her. And she'd been, if not happy, satisfied. Until Jenna came along and woke the sleeping dragon. Now she wanted again. God damn it. God *damn* it.

Close to four she gave up trying to sleep. After a quick shower, she dressed methodically in jeans, a blue cotton shirt, and her work boots. She fed Beam, double-checked her appointment list to be sure she had the necessary equipment in the truck, and drove to the Hardy place. The house was dark when she pulled in front and cut her lights and engine. She sat listening to the engine tick and watched the front door, wondering if Jenna had changed her mind. Wondering if that might not be a good thing.

She wasn't sure why she'd invited Jenna to come with her, to spend time with her. To be part of her daily life. None of that would really matter when Jenna finally heard the whole story, from Alice or someone else. As much as Jenna said her past didn't matter, she didn't believe it. Right now, Jenna was on sabbatical from her life, but she was Cassandra Hart every bit as much as she was Jenna Hardy, and Cassandra Hart did not belong in Little Falls, Vermont. Cassandra Hart did not belong with her.

Gard draped her arms over the steering wheel and watched the sun rise.

"Sorry. Did I keep you waiting?" Jenna said through the open passenger side window.

"No problem. I'm early. I didn't see you come out."

"I was down at the barn. I couldn't sleep."

"Must be contagious."

"Do you still want me to come with you?"

Just at that moment the first ray of sunshine struck the yard, painting Jenna in a swath of gold. The red highlights in her hair shimmered like flame and the sky reflected in her eyes. Framed in the truck window, she might have been an image painted by an Old Master. Gard stretched across the seat, popped the handle on the door, and pushed it open with her fingertips. "Climb in. We're going to have a busy morning."

Jenna smiled and eclipsed the sun.

"You look great," Gard said. "Gorgeous."

"You'll need to refrain from any compliments if you expect me to pay attention to work this morning," Jenna said quietly as she got in and closed the door. "I'm serious about this research, you know."

Gard turned the ignition key. "I know."

Jenna slid over to the edge of the seat, wrapped her hand around Gard's arm, and kissed the corner of her mouth. "But I had to do that first. You look pretty good yourself."

"You ready to go to work now that we've taken care of the important business?" Gard said it teasingly but her heart was racing like a rabbit with a fox hard on its trail.

"Taken care of it?" Jenna laughed and settled back into her seat. "Oh, I don't think so. Not by a long shot."

❖

Five hours later, Jenna climbed into the truck and moaned. "Oh my God. How far did we just walk? Ten miles?"

Grinning, Gard backed down the narrow path between the pasture fences on Warren Jones's back ninety. "I told you to sit this one out. You didn't need to go all the way up the hill with me."

"I wanted to see the baby lambs." Jenna peered down at her sneakers. What was left of her sneakers. "I need new shoes."

"If you're going to do any more of this kind of activity, you do." Gard waved to Warren's wife and kids, who were clustered on the porch, all waving vigorously.

"I'd forgotten how everyone waves," Jenna murmured.

Gard pulled out onto the road and headed away from Little Falls toward Route 7 West into New York. "You grew up a country girl, didn't you? It doesn't show any longer."

Jenna stiffened. "No, I don't imagine it would."

"Cassandra Hart didn't grow up in the country, though, did she?"

"Cassandra Hart is me."

Gard nodded. "What about Jenna Hardy? Is she you too?"

Jenna smiled wryly. "You do realize that anyone listening to this conversation would think we were crazy."

"Probably."

"Where are we going?"

"I thought I'd take you someplace other than Oscar's for lunch."

"Oh no, I can't go to lunch. Look at me."

"Not while I'm driving."

"You know what I'm talking about. I've got dirt and...other things, all over me. I can't—"

"You look beautiful." Gard reached between the seats and

grasped Jenna's hand. "We aren't going anywhere that you need to be dressed up. You look fine."

"What about your work?"

"What about yours?" Gard shrugged. "We need to eat, right? I'm not due in the clinic until late this afternoon. And you're trying to change the subject."

Jenna cradled Gard's hand in both of hers, tracing the nicks and scrapes on the back of her knuckles. She wanted to kiss each tiny cut. She wanted to kiss her, had wanted to for hours. "Your work is harder than I imagined. How is your arm?"

"Stiff. No problem, though."

"Good." When Gard moved her hand to the stick shift, Jenna held onto Gard's wrist, liking the way the tendons tightened and the muscles flexed and relaxed when Gard shifted. She'd never taken such pleasure in another woman's body before. They weren't doing anything remotely sexual and she was becoming so aroused she was having trouble concentrating on the conversation. That was dangerous. Gard had a way of getting her to talk about things, admit things, she didn't want to reveal. She released Gard's arm as if that would break some deeper hold, and Gard somehow plucked her hand out of the air without ever looking away from the road. She let Gard lace their fingers together. Her stomach trembled at Gard's silent refusal to let her go, at the way they effortlessly connected. Oh God. She was in terrible trouble.

"What are you trying to forget?" Gard asked softly.

"I thought we agreed neat and simple. Let's not go there, all right?"

A muscle jumped at the edge of Gard's jaw. She finally looked away from the road, her dark eyes searching Jenna's face. "Did someone hurt you?"

The force of Gard's question, the anger that leapt into her eyes, made Jenna's heart stutter. For one insane instant, she wanted to tell her everything. As if somehow Gard could change it all. Take away the hurt and the fear and the disappointment. But that was foolish. No one could do that for her. She knew that. What was it she wanted, then? Just for another person to know? No. Not any person. This person. Gard.

"It doesn't matter now," Jenna said, nearly breathless. "It was a long time ago. You know what I mean."

"I do." Gard drew Jenna's hand onto her thigh, anchoring Jenna to her. "Didn't mean to push you."

"I know. It's okay." Jenna pressed her fingertips into Gard's leg. She was so solid. So strong. The knot that had formed in her stomach when she'd thought of Lancaster and Darlene melted away. "I had a great time this morning. Thank you."

"Even when you stepped in the cow shit?"

"Maybe not then so much. But I loved watching you work."

Gard laughed.

"No, really. I mean it. It's obvious you're good at what you do, and the farmers trust you. That must mean a lot to you."

Gard's shoulders tightened. "What do you mean?"

"I just meant it's got to feel good when people appreciate what you're doing."

"Is that what you meant." Gard let go of Jenna's hand and gripped the wheel, the skin over her knuckles tightening until the scratches stood out like angry red welts.

"I don't know what you think I was getting at, but you're wrong," Jenna said softly. Something had hurt Gard, and she hated not knowing what it was. She'd just told Gard they should leave the past out of their relationship, but she'd only meant they should leave her *own* past in the dark. She wanted to know everything about Gard. About where she grew up. About what she dreamed. About who had hurt her and why. She wanted to erase the angry pain that poured from her in waves, filling the truck's cab with past sorrows. Cautiously, the way she'd seen Gard gentle a frightened horse just that morning, she rested her fingertips on Gard's shoulder. "I'm sorry."

"Nothing to be sorry for." Gard's voice was so tight it sounded like a branch cracking under the weight of winter ice.

"I'm sorry for whatever hurt you. And for reminding you of it."

Gard exhaled in a rush. "My history is not your problem."

"Fair enough." Jenna rubbed Gard's shoulder, then leaned closer so she could massage the back of her neck. The muscles quivered beneath her fingers. "Do you think we could stop—"

"You want to cancel lunch?"

Jenna spread her fingers through Gard's hair, then tugged a little. "No. I want to buy a new pair of shoes. I'm not eating when my feet are this muddy."

Gard glanced at her, her lips pressed down on a smile that finally erupted as she laughed. "Shoes. Where are we going to get you shoes out here?"

"I'm sure there must be somewhere people buy shoes."

"There is. Hold on." Gard put her blinker on and swerved into a gravel parking lot in front of a long metal-sided building that looked like a gas station on steroids. A big white sign with green letters announced *Agway*.

"Oh no," Jenna said. "I'm not buying farmer boots."

"They'll be better for you the next time you're out on a call with me."

The next time. Would there be a next time? She hoped so. She looked at Gard and, foolish as it was, hoped for a lot more than that.

CHAPTER NINETEEN

Don't look," Jenna said, crouching with her back to the truck in the rear corner of the Agway parking lot, the passenger side door open to block her from view of anyone driving in. "Am I clear?"

Gard swiveled behind the wheel and checked out the back to make sure no one was watching them. "You're good to go."

Jenna unzipped her pants. "I can feel you looking."

"I have my eyes closed, but the cows up on the hill probably have a terrific view."

"Liar. Get my new jeans out of that bag and hand them to me, would you?"

Gard rustled through the shopping bags on the floor, pulled out the new Levi's, and quickly removed the labels. "Here you go."

Jenna half turned and her eyes met Gard's. "I knew you were looking."

"You've got a really cute ass." Gard's throat went dry as Jenna's smile flickered between amused and inviting. She did have a great ass, round and tight and just the right shape to fit into her hands. She remembered cradling Jenna's butt while they were kissing in the kitchen and imagined Jenna naked on top of her, smooth muscles flexing under her fingers, hot slick skin sliding over hers. "Put your pants on."

"That's not what you were thinking."

Jenna's eyes had gotten hazy and her lips seemed to swell, as if readying for Gard's mouth. Gard twitched as if someone had poked her with a cattle prod. When she groaned softly, Jenna laughed a satisfied laugh.

"Cut it out," Gard said through gritted teeth.

"Or what?" Jenna stepped into the pants and took her time pulling them up, her brazen expression daring Gard to look, to touch, to take.

"If you don't cut it out, you're going to get a lot more than a new set of clothes at the Agway."

"Is that right?" Jenna laughed and hopped up onto the seat, her feet clad only in her socks, and dug around in the bags. She came out with the new boots. "And what would that be, exactly?"

While Jenna was busy with the laces on the new shitkickers, Gard took advantage of her distraction and slipped an arm behind her shoulders. She leaned over the gearshift and kissed Jenna on the neck.

Jenna jumped. "Gard!"

Gard caught Jenna's head with a hand on her neck and took her mouth in a hard kiss. Jenna's lips parted, warm and welcoming, and Gard deepened the kiss. Then Jenna's fingers were in her hair and Jenna's breasts were pressed to her chest and their tongues were searching, delving, demanding. Jenna hadn't zipped her jeans and when Gard reached around her to hold her more tightly, her fingers grazed bare skin and the top of silk panties and Jenna jerked away.

"We'll get arrested," Jenna gasped, her pupils huge and deep as night. "One more second of kissing you like that and I'm going to have to have you inside me."

Gard's chest exploded as if she'd been shot. "Jesus Christ, Jenna."

"Don't tell me you can't tell."

"I can't even think when all my blood and half my brains are headed between my legs." Gard heaved herself back into her seat and scanned out the window. No one around. She rubbed both hands over her face. Her mind was mush and all she wanted was to touch her again—good sense, consequences, and lookie-loos be damned. "You're making me nuts."

"Stay over there while I put these damn boots on." Jenna

jammed her feet into the ankle-high work boots, quickly laced them up, and jumped out of the truck. She pushed the tails of her pale yellow cotton shirt into her jeans, zipped and buttoned them. "Safe now."

Gard rolled her head on the seat and studied her. Her cheeks and neck were flushed, her eyes bright, her lips swollen. She let her gaze drop lower. The faint outline of Jenna's nipples, hard and round, pressed outward beneath her shirt. Jenna's breathing grew faster the longer Gard looked. "You're a long way from safe. You like teasing me, don't you?"

Jenna rested her arms on the roof of the truck cab and leaned in, her crotch riding against the seat, her breasts pushing forward. She rocked her hips back and forth. "I haven't even started to tease you yet."

"Get in the truck."

"In a hurry for lunch?"

"If you keep it up, we're gonna have to get takeout." Gard gripped the steering wheel in both hands. "There's no way I can sit across from you in a restaurant without everybody knowing exactly what I'm thinking. And what I'm thinking is private."

"Is that right." Jenna got in, closed the door, and put her hand on Gard's thigh. She dragged her nails along the seam inside Gard's thigh, up and down, up and down, until Gard's hips lifted off the seat. "Then let's have a picnic."

❖

"Where are we exactly?" Jenna peered out at the small turnaround where Gard parked. The road ended in a rutted trail narrowed by creeping undergrowth at the base of a mountainside thick with evergreens.

"Right on the Vermont–New York border." Gard cut the engine and came around to Jenna's door. "Go ahead and pass me the food. There's a blanket behind your seat too."

Jenna handed out two bags filled with sandwiches, takeout containers of coleslaw and rice pudding, a nice bottle of white wine, and a faded olive-green blanket. They'd stopped at a little place in a strip mall incongruously called the Epicurean Café, and it had lived up to its name. According to the newspaper reviews tacked up inside, the owner, a well-known French chef, had wanted out of the rat race of competitive big-city restaurants and had retired to the countryside, where he still cooked as if he were in a five-star establishment.

"I don't see any tables." Jenna made a three-sixty. Nothing but more trees.

"This way." Gard held out her hand and Jenna took it as if it were the most natural thing in the world for her to do. The calluses on Gard's palm rubbed lightly against hers, and the little bit of friction was as exciting as a kiss. She wasn't certain how she was going to get through a picnic when she couldn't think of anything except Gard touching her, caressing her, filling her.

"Jenna," Gard said in a dangerous tone.

"Sorry. Sorry." Gard led her to a second trail that hadn't been immediately visible—a rocky, pine-needle-covered path just wide enough for two people to walk abreast. Almost immediately they started to climb, and she was happy for the purchase of her new boots. Sneakers would not have been sturdy enough. "How can you tell the second I get turned on?"

"Your mouth gets soft," Gard murmured. "Your lips darken a shade and you swallow a little bit, as if waiting for me to slip inside."

Jenna caught her breath. "You can't know what you do to me."

"Oh, I know." Gard's voice was rough, frustrated. "Because you do the same to me. I feel like I'm going to explode."

"Good. I hate to suffer alone."

Gard laughed. "You have nothing to worry about, then."

After ten minutes of vigorous uphill hiking, the trail dwindled into a twisting, brush-encroached path. Jenna was about to ask if Gard really knew where she was going when all of a sudden the forest opened up into a small grassy clearing on the edge of the mountain. The deep green carpet of grass was dotted with granite boulders that resembled blocks tossed down by a bored child. Below them stretched a valley completely untouched by human habitation. Mist swirled from its depths and floated on the air like the breath of lovers on a cool fall night.

"God, it's so beautiful." Jenna glanced at Gard who was looking at her, her eyes dark storm clouds. "What?"

"It's all I can do to keep my hands off you."

"Then let's distract you for a while."

"Why?" Gard's voice was gravelly, her mouth a tight line.

Jenna smiled. "Because I like waiting. I like feeling you want me."

"Jesus."

"Come on." Jenna spread out the blanket and stretched out on her side, propping her head up in the palm of her hand. "Bring the food down here."

Gard knelt and put the bags next to the blanket. She found the corkscrew and opened the wine. Handing Jenna the package of plastic cups, she said, "Would you?"

Jenna got out two and held them while Gard poured the white Burgundy. They toasted each other and drank. Jenna loved the way Gard's eyes never left her face. When she skimmed the tip of her tongue over her lips, catching the last drops of wine, Gard's gaze followed. Jenna leaned forward and kissed her, but drew away before Gard could hold her in place.

"Sandwiches?"

Gard stared at her for long seconds and Jenna wondered if Gard's tight reins were finally going to snap. She thrilled at making her lose control. *She* was still in control, and that was good. Essential.

Gard removed the wax paper from one of the sandwiches and spread it out between them. She picked up half and held it out to Jenna. "Bite."

Jenna wet her lips again, watching Gard's eyes narrow dangerously, and, getting to her knees, took a corner of the sandwich into her mouth. She slowly bit down and tugged off a small section. She chewed, murmured her approval. Took another bite. After she swallowed, she said, "Now you."

Gard ate a little and brushed the back of her hand over her mouth. Her fingers trembled and Jenna throbbed.

"Coleslaw?" Jenna asked. Her voice was husky.

Grinning, Gard found the container and took the top off. She set it down, hunted some more, and came up with a plastic fork. She dug into the slaw and held out the fork. "Open."

Jenna stuck out her tongue and laughed when a strand of cabbage dropped into her lap. She licked the tart sauce off her lip, took the plastic container, and fed some to Gard.

They took turns feeding each other. When they were done, Jenna grabbed Gard's wrist and slowly licked her fingers, one after the other, twirling her tongue around the tips, sucking lightly. By the time she got to Gard's thumb and rolled her tongue over the pad, Gard's jaw was so tight it looked as if it might shatter.

"More wine?" Jenna asked.

"I'm good. I'm driving."

Jenna bit lightly and when Gard grunted—her expression flickering between intense arousal and something close to pain—Jenna got terribly wet. She was losing control of her own game and quickly drew back, willing her body to calm.

"Maybe we should get back," Jenna said. "Your office—"

"I called while you were trying on clothes," Gard said. "I didn't have anything critical. My vet tech is handling things."

"So you're free."

Gard nodded. "Completely."

Jenna edged closer on the blanket until her knees touched Gard's and draped her arms over Gard's shoulders. She kissed her, light and quick. Her breasts brushed against Gard's and she tightened everywhere. "How likely are we to be disturbed?"

"This time of day, middle of the week? Way out here? Not likely." Gard caressed Jenna's sides, her thumbs brushing along the outer edges of Jenna's breasts.

"Getting naked is probably not a good idea, though."

Gard smiled. "Not recommended."

"We should probably go, then. Because I want you to get me naked."

"Is that right?" Gard slid her hand around Jenna's nape and clasped her firmly, drawing her closer until their mouths met. She kissed her as if she were still hungry, exploring the inside of her mouth with long, probing strokes, cradling Jenna's breast in her other hand, her thumb sliding back and forth over her nipple.

Jenna's thighs softened and she leaned into Gard, not caring any longer who led and who followed. All she wanted was more. More of Gard touching her, kissing her, setting her on fire. She moaned and caressed Gard's shoulders through her shirt, and it wasn't enough. She yanked up on the shirt and drove a hand underneath, finding her skin, massaging the hard muscles of her back. Gard held her captive with one hand gripping her neck, the other roaming over her body, squeezing her ass, caressing her breasts, stroking her stomach. Still she needed more. She needed to be naked. She needed Gard everywhere, over her and inside her.

Jenna pulled back, gasping. "Oh God. Bad idea. Bad idea."

"Oh no. Very good idea. Amazing." Gard slid her mouth down Jenna's throat and licked the moisture that had pooled in the hollow. She expected salt but got clear cool water. She raised her head and felt raindrops on her face. The sun shone brightly overhead as a summer shower descended on them. "We're going to get drenched."

Laughing, Jenna fisted her hands in Gard's hair. "I don't care."

Gard kissed her again, the heat of Jenna's mouth a searing counterpoint to the rain soaking her. She teased Jenna's damp shirt free of her jeans, dancing her fingertips over the slick, smooth skin of her lower back. Jenna's hands roamed under her shirt. Nails etched lines of fire over her skin, teeth nibbled at her lip. She blinked water from her eyes and focused on the blue sky between the mountaintops. "Jenna. Look."

"Oh God, don't stop kissing me," Jenna moaned.

"Wait." Taking Jenna's shoulders in both hands, Gard turned her on the blanket until Jenna's back was against her chest. A huge double rainbow arched over the mountains, sparkling in crystal hues. Jenna's head fell back against her shoulder, her hands restless on Gard's thighs.

"It's beautiful."

"Yes." Gard held Jenna close with one arm wrapped around her middle and opened the top buttons of Jenna's shirt. She slipped her hand inside and cradled Jenna's breast beneath the flimsy, damp material of her bra. Jenna's nipple was a hard stone against her palm. She squeezed lightly and Jenna rolled her head on her shoulder, whimpering softly. She put her mouth against Jenna's ear. "You like that."

"Oh yes, yes."

Gard fondled Jenna's breasts beneath her blouse and popped the button on her jeans. "Watch the rainbow, Jenna."

Jenna gripped her wrist weakly. "If you touch me, I'm afraid I'll—"

"Shh, I know." Gard skimmed her fingertips beneath smooth silk, caressing the satiny flesh between Jenna's legs. Jenna's clitoris was so hard she'd come very quickly, and Gard had never wanted anything more. She swirled her fingertips over the firm prominence and Jenna trembled in her arms. She kissed Jenna's temple and sheltered her from the downpour in the curve of her body, afraid to break the spell that held them suspended in the arch of color flaming above them.

Trembling, Jenna pressed her mouth to Gard's throat. "You're going to make me come."

"Let me." Gard's chest was so tight she couldn't get enough air. Her head spun but she struggled to go slow, wanting to please Jenna more than she wanted her next breath. She dipped lower, slipped inside, cradled Jenna in her palm as she cradled her against her body. Jenna tightened around her. "You're so close, baby. Let me."

"Yes." Jenna whimpered, her lip between her teeth, her lids almost closed. Her voice thinned to a whisper. "Please. You feel so good. I have to."

Gard kissed her softly, filling her mouth, filling her body, holding her gently and stroking her over and over and over until the rainbow shattered with her cries.

CHAPTER TWENTY

Jenna was torn between opening her eyes, needing to see Gard's face, and never opening her eyes again, wanting to drift forever in the incredible haven of Gard's arms. Still cradled against Gard's chest, she couldn't move, but she felt wonderful. Intensely satisfied. Incredibly pleasured. Inexplicably cherished. Terrifyingly vulnerable. She'd always considered an orgasm just an orgasm—never bad, always enjoyable—and she'd just experienced the most fabulous one of her life. But the amazing climax wasn't what had shattered her into a million pieces. No. That was Gard. All Gard. The way she touched her, held her, knew her. Knew what she needed, what she wanted, what she longed for even when she had refused to admit it. Gard made her feel treasured, and realizing just how much that mattered scared her down to her toes.

"Are you all right?" Gard's breath was a warm wind teasing over her neck.

"Anything I say is going to sound ridiculous." Jenna forced her eyes open, willing her spaghetti-limp arms and legs into action. Bracing her hands on Gard's thighs, she pushed herself upright and swiveled to face her. Oh God. Her heart couldn't take much more. Gard's hair lay in dark wet strands over her forehead and clung to her neck in curling tendrils. Rain ran in rivulets over her cheeks and dripped from the edge of her jaw. Her lips were parted, her breath coming fast, her eyes wild as the midnight hunt. Jenna framed her face, brushing away the clear crystal drops clinging to her lashes with her thumbs. "You're so beautiful my heart hurts."

Gard clasped Jenna's waist. Her throat rippled but no sound came out. Naked need rode hard in her eyes.

"Oh," Jenna whispered, kissing her softly. "No more teasing. I want to take care of you, gorgeous. Right now." She kissed her again and fumbled for the button on Gard's fly, her fingers still clumsy in the aftermath of her off-the-Richter-scale orgasm.

"We can wait," Gard said hoarsely. "I'm—"

"Oh, don't even try that line on me." Jenna caressed Gard's cheek. "I can't tell you how much I want you—you probably wouldn't believe me. But I can show you, and I know you need it."

Jenna got Gard's fly open, worked her hand inside, and clasped her gently, one fingertip gliding firmly down over her clitoris and almost into her. Gard stiffened and her eyes rolled before she seemed to focus on Jenna's face.

"Jenna, I—" She choked, her hips jerking when Jenna squeezed slowly.

"The next time," Jenna nipped Gard's lip and pushed a little deeper, "I'm going to make you wait for a long, long time. But not today. You can't wait today, can you?"

Jenna stroked and Gard shuddered, gripping Jenna's shoulders, fingers digging in as if she were trying to hold herself up.

"Oh no, you can't wait," Jenna whispered, enthralled by the sight of Gard slowly coming apart right in front of her. She teased her a little, then stroked harder, fingers gliding out and then dipping back inside, each pass making her clitoris jump. "You're going to come all over me in about two seconds, aren't you?"

Gard panted, her hands opening and closing convulsively. "Jen…You'll make me…Oh fu—"

Jenna kissed her, filled her, massaged her in her palm until her clitoris grew impossibly hard, pulsed rapidly, and exploded. Gard jerked and tried to pull away but Jenna held her fast with a fist in her hair, kissing her as Gard groaned into her mouth. When Gard finally sagged forward, Jenna clasped her tightly, one arm around her shoulders, her fingers still inside her. She kissed her damp forehead, her eyelids, her mouth. Gard—normally so contained, so defended—looked so exposed Jenna would have killed to protect her at that moment. "I've got you. I've got you."

Gard pressed her forehead to Jenna's shoulder, her breath coming hard. She contracted around Jenna's fingers and, with a helpless whine, pushed down hard into Jenna's hand. "Oh, no... Jenna, God..."

"Oh yes, sweetheart." Jenna watched, rapt, as the pleasure rained down Gard's face. "Yes."

Gard struggled to keep her eyes open, Jenna's fierce expression making her come even harder. She came so fast and so hard it was almost painful. Almost. When the climax finally relented, she was lying on her side, her head pillowed between Jenna's breasts. She didn't remember falling or being caught. Totally wasted, stunned by how easily Jenna had taken her, she rubbed her cheek against the soft skin exposed by Jenna's open blouse. She wanted to laugh and cry and do it again.

"Better?" Jenna whispered.

"Am I still alive?"

Jenna played her fingers through Gard's hair. "I certainly hope so. That was just an appetizer."

Gard chuckled and kissed Jenna's throat. "I'm not sure whether that's a threat or a promise."

"I guess we'll see, won't we."

Jenna sounded pensive, a little distant. Gard tensed, wondering if what she heard was regret. "I'm sorry I was a little quick off the mark. I'm not usually—"

"Oh, shut up," Jenna said lightly. "You ought to know how sexy it is to get a woman so excited she comes the second you touch her. Considering that's what you did to me."

"That's different."

Jenna tugged on Gard's hair, forcing her to tilt her head back until their eyes met. "Don't even think of going there with me. I like to be in charge in bed—which means everything goes both ways."

"In charge, huh?" Gard grinned. "Those sound like fighting words."

"You can always try."

Gard kissed her. The flirtatious note in Jenna's voice didn't bother her. After the intensity of what they'd just shared, she understood needing to back off a little. Hell, part of her wanted to run for the hills. What bothered her was the worry Jenna was trying, and failing, to hide. "Challenge accepted. In fact—"

A sharp ring fractured the steamy stillness of the glade and they both jerked. When the sound came again, Gard grabbed the phone off her belt, sat up, and stared at the readout.

"Damn it. Sorry. It's Rob—my tech. He wouldn't call me unless—"

"It's okay." Jenna stood and arranged her clothes, her expression suddenly remote. "We ought to be getting back anyhow."

"Hello? Hold on for a second, Rob." Gard grasped Jenna's hand. "Is something wrong?"

"No, of course not."

Jenna hurriedly gathered up the remains of the picnic, rushing as if she couldn't wait to leave. Gard knelt on the blanket, her shirt out, her pants open, her body and soul even more naked. What the hell had just happened?

❖

Jenna edged over to the far side of her seat as Gard headed down the mountain into Vermont, hating the distance she had put between them every bit as much as she needed it. Up there, in that secret, beautiful, out-of-time place she had ventured far from her safety zone. She hadn't just lost control, she'd surrendered every protective instinct she'd ever had, physically and emotionally. She had wanted Gard so damn much. She hadn't been able to feel her enough, couldn't get her close enough. If she'd had a way to pull Gard inside her skin, she would have done it. She'd never in her life wanted to be that connected to another soul, to be joined. To be one. Now, when some small bit of rationality had returned, she couldn't absorb wanting her that way, not when all she'd ever wanted, all she'd fought for, was to stand alone and never to be dependent on anyone. Never to rely on someone who might leave her, betray her, use her. She knew somewhere deep inside that Gard was not that kind of person, but knowing and feeling were two different things. Right at this moment she was just plain scared.

"You want to tell me what's going on?" Gard said quietly.

"Nothing," Jenna said quickly. "I'm just a little—" She laughed, hearing the tremor in her voice. "I'm a little done in. You're pretty powerful, Dr. Davis."

Gard looked away from the road, giving Jenna a searching glance. "You're flattering me. Don't insult me, not after what just happened."

"You're wrong about the flattery part. I know what happened up there. How…it was."

Gard nodded slowly. "Intense." A grin flashed across her face and quickly disappeared. "Pretty damn amazing."

She reached across the seat to take Jenna's hand, but Jenna folded her hands in her lap, pretending not to notice. She couldn't touch her, not without losing her mind. Maybe losing herself. "I don't want you to think it was anything less than spectacular for me. You were—you *are*—wonderful."

"I hear a *but* coming."

"No. No buts." Jenna struggled to get everything back on solid, safe ground. Back to where they were before. "Not at all. I love being with you. The company is splendid. The sex outstanding. What more could anyone want?"

"Not a thing."

Gard *sounded* agreeable, but when Jenna sneaked a look at her out of the corner of her eye, Gard's hand was clenched on her thigh, the knuckles white, and the edge of her jaw so sharp Jenna could have bled on it.

"Good," Jenna said, ignoring the stab of guilt and disappointment. Damn it, she was doing this all wrong and she couldn't for the life of her figure out where she'd gotten so off track. She had to keep going, though, no matter how much of a mess she was making. If she didn't, they would both end up getting hurt. "Then we're still on the same page about what this is. Right?"

"Absolutely. After all, we both know how this is going to end. In another couple of weeks, you'll be back in New York."

"Yes," Jenna said softly. "I will."

❖

Gard turned onto the drive at Jenna's a little before five in the afternoon. The thirty-mile return trip was a blur. They'd made casual conversation, light and easy and totally meaningless. As if nothing had happened an hour before under the cover of sunshine and rain. Jenna had said all the right things, and probably meant them too. The sex had been great. Hell, a whole lot better than great. Her heart still hadn't settled after the crazy, mind-blowing orgasm. No wait, two orgasms. That never happened to her. Jenna was right. The sex was spectacular. If she could just get the incredible scent of Jenna off her skin, out of her mind, she might be able to get her head back on straight. And now she was lying to herself.

She wasn't turned around about great sex. She was turned around about Jenna. The way Jenna opened for her, yielded for her, let herself be touched. Just thinking about it made her head swim and her belly tighten. God damn it. She wanted her again, right now.

"Sorry I had to cut things short," Gard said. "Katie said Windstorm isn't looking so good. I need to check him."

Jenna opened the door but didn't get out. "Katie. She's the blonde with the big black stallion. We saw him this morning, right? That testicular torsion?"

"That's right. I thought he was mending, but she told Rob he's off his feed now. Chronic pain and anxiety can disrupt the intestinal function and horses can colic. When that happens, they can go quickly. I don't want to lose him."

"Of course. I hope he's going to be all right." Jenna smiled faintly at Gard. "You do realize she has a thing for you."

Gard frowned. "A thing. Katie? No, I don't think so."

Jenna's brows rose.

"Okay, maybe a little interest, but it's nothing serious."

Jenna climbed out and leaned her forearm against the cab roof, gazing in at Gard. "Nothing serious. Like us, you mean."

"Don't put words in my mouth, Jenna," Gard said. "There's nothing casual about what happened up there on that mountainside."

Jenna sighed. "I know. And I didn't mean to imply otherwise."

"Do you want to do field calls with me again tomorrow? I start at five."

Jenna shook her head. "I don't think so, thanks. I've got a lot of writing to do and with everything I've seen today, I'm anxious to get at it. I usually write at least six hours a day, sometimes more. A whole day away and I'm off my schedule."

"I understand. I'm glad it was helpful."

"Gard…"

"It's okay." Gard tapped her fingers on the steering wheel. Saying good-bye felt so final. She had to go—Katie and Windstorm were waiting. But she had a sick feeling that if she drove out of the driveway, she was never going to see Jenna again. "I don't want to say thanks for today, because that's not what I mean. But…" Gard took a deep breath. "I want to thank you for what you made me feel. I haven't felt anything like that in a long time. And I'm not talking about the sex."

Jenna closed her eyes. "I know. Me too."

"I'll see you, then."

"Yes," Jenna said.

Gard pulled away, knowing they were both pretending everything was all right. When she looked back, Jenna stood on the porch, watching her go. Leaving her made her want to howl in protest. She wanted to slam the truck around, gun it back there, and take her right where she stood. Driving away hurt so much, she was surprised she wasn't leaving a trail of blood on the road.

CHAPTER TWENTY-ONE

Jenna ignored the insistent tapping as long as she dared. Finally she couldn't pretend she didn't hear the knocking any longer and swiveled in the desk chair, squinting in the murky half-light cast by her computer screen at Alice, standing in the doorway of her new office. Dressed in casual stone gray pants, a pale blue boatneck sweater, and docksiders, with her hair caught back in a loose ponytail, she looked for all the world like a New England native.

"Hi," Jenna said. "You look terrific."

"I discovered the true lifeblood of the economy in these parts." Alice came in and sat on the end of the sofa facing Jenna. "Outlet malls. I may have lost a little control in J.Crew. Or maybe it was Calvin Klein. I had to buy another suitcase."

"That look on you works." She checked the time on her monitor. After midnight. The last time she'd noticed had been shortly before seven. "Been out on a date?"

"Hardly. I did have a serious case of cabin fever, though, and visited Ye Olde Tavern on the other side of town."

Jenna laughed despite the ache in her heart. "Is it really called that?"

"No. I think it's called something ingenious, like Joe's or Charlie's or Bill's Beer Joint."

"God, Alice. You probably shouldn't be wandering around by yourself out in the wilds."

Alice snorted and pulled the tie from her hair. When she

shook her head to loosen the waves, her breasts swayed beneath the almost-tight cotton sweater. The motion was wholly unconscious and completely sensual. Her full lips, luscious body, and earthy magnetism promised passionate pleasures.

"I'm serious. A woman like you, without an escort? Dangerous." Jenna smiled, conscious of Alice's charms and just as aware she didn't feel the slightest spark. Whatever attraction she'd entertained before…before Gard had evaporated.

"Dangerous? For whom?" Alice grinned. "Really, everyone was completely civilized. I was, however, the only unattached woman there who didn't seem to be angling for someone to take her home. And I have to tell you, the pickings were slim."

"Were you the only lesbian?"

Alice rolled her eyes. "Probably within a thousand miles."

"Well, we know that isn't true. There's the lovely sheriff, don't forget. And *I'm* here."

"Yes." Alice's expression grew solemn. "And that's what *I'm* here about. You've been holed up in this office for three days. Have you even been to bed?"

"Yes. Every night."

"When?"

Jenna looked sideways, wondering how far she could stretch the truth. "I'm getting enough sleep."

"And that's avoidance. Which generally means the opposite of what you're saying." Alice propped her elbows on her knees and cupped her chin in her hands. "What's going on?"

Jenna gestured to the computer in self-defense. "You can see what I'm doing. I'm twenty-five thousand words in and about getting to the end of the first act. This is always the hardest part for me, you know that."

"I know you think it's always the hardest part. You always lay a perfect foundation for everything that comes later on in the book, you just don't believe it until you're done."

"Well, none of that helps me when I'm in the middle of it." Jenna probably sounded petulant but she couldn't help it. She was tired, her nerves were a wreck, and the only time she had any peace was when she was actively working. The second her concentration lapsed and she surfaced from the fictional world she was creating, she hurt all over. She couldn't stop thinking about the interlude on the mountainside with Gard. How wonderful she'd felt and how hard it was not to see her. Gard hadn't called and she hadn't called her. She didn't blame Gard for staying away. She'd driven her away, knowingly, intentionally. All the same, she hurt.

"What?" Jenna asked, drifting again.

"I said, this sabbatical thing isn't going to work if all you're going to do is behave exactly the same way here as you do in the city." Alice pointed a finger at her. "You can't work twenty hours a day."

"Writing is not work for me."

"Tell that to your body. Remember why you're here?" Alice's frown softened. "I think you should come back to Manhattan as soon as you can. What more do you have to do here, anyhow?"

"I haven't made any real provisions for Elizabeth's property," Jenna pointed out. She'd intentionally been stalling and hadn't contacted the realtor. Elizabeth had been buried in the family plot per her instructions. Also according to her wishes, friends and neighbors had been asked to make a donation to the local farm preservation association in lieu of flowers or a service. All that remained was for Jenna to secure the paintings and put the house on the market. She hadn't done anything about either, because when she did, she'd have to decide whether to go or stay. And she didn't want to make the obvious choice. Her life awaited her in New York City. Little Falls was a detour, a pleasant side road, and she had no reason to linger. The pain lodged deep in her breast throbbed.

"I know you've got the book on your mind and don't want to be bothered with details, so I talked to my friend Diane," Alice said. "She's the gallery owner I told you about. She's going to drive up Friday night and look at the paintings Saturday morning. She'll give us an appraisal and then you can decide if you want to sell them, store them, or donate them to a local museum."

Friday—the day after tomorrow. By early next week she could have all the arrangements made and be gone. Five or six more days of torturing herself, wanting to call Gard but resisting. Once she was back in New York, her life would be all Cassandra again. She'd be too busy to think about any kind of serious romantic involvement. If she wanted company, she knew how to get it. Another week and all of her problems would be gone, because she would be gone.

"All right, I'll call the attorney tomorrow and have him set up an appointment for me to meet with a realtor. After the appraisal, I'll decide about the art, and then I'll come home."

Alice nodded briskly. "Good. Whatever's happening up here is making you unhappy. That's reason enough to leave."

Jenna didn't argue. She saw no point in explaining to Alice that what had happened up here made her happy, and that's what she didn't know how to handle.

With a sigh, she turned back to her computer. This was what she knew. This was what she was good at. This was where she and Cassandra became one. Her world righted itself.

❖

Jenna jerked awake, searching the darkened room in confusion. The computer glowed on the desk in front of her, the cursor jumping at the end of the last words she'd typed. The house was silent, the night outside dark. Something had awakened her, perhaps the dream that still flirted at the edges of her consciousness. The simmering tension in her middle told her the fragmented images of a dark-haired woman ghosting through her mind were surely Gard. God, she couldn't stop thinking of her while awake, and now she was dreaming about her too. She hadn't been this derailed by a woman since her first crush, when she'd thought herself madly in love the way only a sixteen-year-old could be. She was certain she'd outgrown those tumultuous hormonal upheavals, but apparently not. Her nerves were shattered, she couldn't eat, and a dull persistent throbbing in her depths hounded her for relief. She hadn't even tried. No self-induced orgasm was going to give her a tenth of the pleasure as those few insane moments wrapped in Gard's arms. She wondered if another woman could drive out the memories. Maybe, if she could manage to keep Gard out of her mind. That didn't seem likely, and the idea of trying, of being with another woman held less than no appeal. Time to stop kidding herself on that score. No one was going to do for her, *to* her, what Gard had done. No one could touch her that way, down deep, beneath everything.

Rising, she stretched her back and winced at the kinks along her spine from the long hours in the chair. Of course, falling asleep over her keyboard hadn't helped her sore muscles. She loved working in the sewing room she'd converted into her office, but sleeping in it wasn't a great idea.

A knock sounded from the direction of the front door and she leaned down to squint at the digital readout on the screen. 3:15 a.m. The knocking must have awakened her. Spinning around, she hurried to the front door. She twitched the lace curtain aside and stared out, able only to see a silhouette backlit by starlight. She didn't need to turn on the porch light. The shape was unmistakable. Her heart literally fluttered, which she hadn't thought possible anywhere outside of her novels. She grasped the cut-glass doorknob and pulled open the heavy oak door.

"Gard?"

"There's something you need to see," Gard said.

"Is everything all right?" Jenna asked.

"Yes, but we need to hurry."

Jenna looked down at herself. She'd worked all day in threadbare jeans ripped out at the knees from years of wear and not fashion, a black T-shirt with FLETC stenciled across the chest—a gift from a reader in federal law enforcement, and sneakers without socks. Her writing uniform. She was a mess. "I'm not really dressed—"

"You're great. You're always great."

Ordinarily, she would never rush out into the night without knowing who, where, why, what for…and maybe not even then. But this was Gard. She'd been able to stay away from her when only Gard's image haunted her every moment—awake or asleep—but she couldn't turn away from her in the flesh. She grabbed her denim jacket off a peg next to the door and bolted outside.

"Come on." Gard palmed Jenna's elbow and hurried her down

the stairs and across the yard to her truck. Jenna climbed in while Gard shot around and got behind the wheel. Gard gunned the truck around the circular drive and down the lane.

Jenna didn't ask where they were going and Gard didn't volunteer. In another time, another life, she would have questioned her. Tonight, she didn't care where they were going. She was with Gard and the night, the dark, the uncertain destination did not frighten her.

She breathed easily for the first time in days. Wherever they were headed, she trusted Gard to lead her there.

❖

Jenna estimated they'd driven ten miles in under ten minutes when Gard turned off the paved road onto a bumpy gravel lane only a little bit wider than her truck. Gard was driving fast and Jenna could barely make out cornfields encroaching on either side. She'd forgotten how dark it could be when there were no streetlights. The only illumination came from the hazy swath of the Milky Way and their headlights casting ghostly shadows as the truck bumped along.

They rounded a curve and the silhouettes of a jumble of buildings appeared. Windows on the first floor of a rambling farmhouse were aglow, but no one seemed to be moving inside. Weak yellow light spilled out through the open doors of an enormous three-story barn.

"This is Dan Carmichael's place," Gard said.

"What's happening?" Jenna asked.

"Dan called me forty-five minutes ago. He's got a mare about to foal. She had trouble the first time and we lost the foal. He wanted me to be here, and I wasn't sure you'd get another chance to see this."

"Oh!" Jenna squeezed Gard's arm. She wasn't sure what was more exciting—seeing a foal born or just seeing Gard again. It didn't really matter. She was sharing part of Gard's life and the night was suddenly perfect. "Thank you."

Gard stopped the truck in front of the barn. "I would've called, but I didn't have much time and I thought—"

"No. You did exactly right. Exactly."

"Okay. Good." Gard nodded briskly. "I won't be able to talk very much until I see how things are going, and I'll need you to stay back in case the mare gets twitchy."

"Whatever you say. You just put me where you want me and I won't move."

Gard grinned and pushed open her door. "I'll remember you told me that."

"Smart-ass," Jenna muttered. She caught up to Gard on the way to the barn and was about to take her hand when a man dressed in tan canvas pants and a sweat-stained T-shirt appeared in the open doorway. He had a three-day growth of beard and a thatch of brown hair in need of a trim. He looked to be about forty, big and rough-boned. When he called to them, his voice was surprisingly gentle. "Thanks for getting here so quickly. She's moving right along. Her water just broke."

"Stage two," Gard murmured. "Dan, this is Jenna."

"Hello. She's down here." He turned and led the way into the barn as if it were the most natural thing in the world for a stranger to show up at his place in the middle of the night. Jenna stayed a little bit behind Gard, not wanting to get underfoot. The huge barn held stalls on either side of a wide central passageway. Stacks of hay filled an overhead loft and pieces of tack hung from posts and draped stall doors. Most of the stalls contained horses, who stuck their heads over the doors and whinnied as they passed. Light from a hanging bulb shone at the far end of the building and when they drew near, she saw a tan mare with hugely swollen sides pacing restlessly inside an enclosure. Her flanks were sweat soaked and her nostrils flared with every breath.

"God, she looks so uncomfortable," Jenna said, feeling a little bit of sympathetic nausea just looking at the laboring mare. "Why doesn't she lie down?"

"She might when she gets closer to delivering," Gard said quietly. "Although some horses deliver standing. In the wild, it all happens fast so the mother and baby can keep pace with the herd, where they're safe."

"What do you need to do?"

"Nothing right now. The best thing is just to let her do what she was born to do naturally. I'm only the backup." Gard stripped off her shirt, revealing a tight black T-shirt underneath, and strode to a utility sink opposite the enclosure. After soaking her arms, she lathered up to her elbows with a bar of industrial soap. She shook her arms to get most of the water off and, turning to Jenna, dried off with a cloth she grabbed from a stack on a shelf over the sink. "If she gets into trouble, then we may need to give her a little help."

Dan leaned against the stall, turning a faded John Deere cap around and around in his big hands. "Last time the foal got backed around and we couldn't get him out fast enough."

Jenna moved up next to him and rested her forearms on top of the chest-high gated door. The mare snorted and paced. "Is there any way to tell about this one?"

"We'll know soon enough. She doesn't seem to be in any trouble, but I didn't want to take any chances. That's why I called Gard."

Jenna swelled with pride, thinking of the vital role Gard played in the lives of the people in this small town. Gard was important to their livelihood, to their lives. She belonged here.

The mare lay down and almost immediately got up again. She circled around some more. Then she lay down, sides heaving, and she did not get up.

"Here we go." Gard eased close to Jenna. Faint traces of water still glistened on her skin, and she smelled of soap. She looked steady and strong and confident. She was the most beautiful woman Jenna'd ever seen.

"There's a foot," Dan said.

"Good," Gard said softly. "And there's foot number two."

"That's good, right?" Jenna couldn't keep quiet. She was too captivated, too thrilled. The night closed in around her, the only sounds the gentle whinnies of the rest of the horses and the grunts of the mare who worked so hard to give life to the creature inside her.

They might have been anywhere in the world, at any time—or no time at all. All that mattered was right here in this moment, no past and no future. Just the exquisite beauty of what was happening right before her very eyes. She hadn't realized she'd grasped Gard's hand until she felt warm, strong fingers squeeze her own. Gard leaned close.

"It's okay. See the nose peeking out between the feet? Mama's doing fine." Gard rubbed Jenna's back. "She's beautiful, isn't she?"

"Oh, yes." Jenna blinked back tears. *Just like you.*

CHAPTER TWENTY-TWO

Thirty-five minutes later, the foal staggered to her feet and stood on wobbly legs, wet and scrawny and the most incredible creature Jenna had ever seen. Gard eased into the stall and knelt in the straw next to the baby, slowly and gently examining her. They were both gorgeous—woman and horse—unique and special and breathtaking. Jenna wished she was a photographer or a painter instead of a writer, because she couldn't think of any words perfect enough to describe the picture. After a few minutes, Gard checked the mother, then turned to Jenna.

"You want to come see her?"

"Is it all right?"

"Mama won't want us in here for long, but a minute or two should be okay. Just approach slowly and don't make any sudden noises."

Jenna tiptoed into the stall and halted next to Gard, a few feet from the foal. The baby, a darker brown than her mother with a white blaze on her chest and white socks on her forelegs, endured a tongue washing from her mother, barely able to stay upright under the maternal onslaught. "When will she nurse?"

"Soon. We'll stay until she does. Once that happens, we're home free."

Just at that moment, the foal stumbled over to Jenna and nudged her hand. Her nose was wet and warm and soft beyond description. Velvet came to mind, but that wasn't quite right. Even velvet had some texture, but this baby's nose was far smoother. Jenna caught her breath and stood absolutely still as the inquisitive little being explored her fingertips. Gard slid her arm around Jenna's waist and squeezed lightly.

"Worth getting up for in the middle of the night?" Gard whispered.

"Oh yes," Jenna said as they backed out of the stall and the foal, encouraged with a few nudges from her mother, finally found the appropriate target and began to nurse.

Jenna caught a hint of sweet hay and soap, the scents she associated with Gard, and knew the odors would forever be associated with this woman and this exquisite, perfect moment. She leaned her head against Gard's shoulder. "Worth getting up for every night."

Gard chuckled and stroked her hair. "You say that now. After fifty or so, you might change your mind. About eighty percent of the births occur in the middle of the night."

"Have you gotten used to it?" Jenna already knew the answer—it was written in the soft, peaceful contours of Gard's face and the slow easy timbre of her voice. She was at home here. Content. Jenna had never strived for contentment, never even thought she wanted it. Success yes, satisfaction in her work. Yes. Satisfaction in bed now and then. Sure. But contentment? That peace of the heart that comes only from being exactly where you belong, doing exactly what you were meant to do, living the life that completely suited you—no. She hadn't wanted that. Until now.

Dan cleared his throat beside them. "I guess I dragged you out here for nothing, Gard. I'm sorry."

"Hey," Gard said. "I wish every call ended this way. Glad to do it."

"Besides," Jenna added. "This is my first time."

Dan laughed and tugged his John Deere cap down over his unruly hair. "It never gets old."

"No," she said softly. "I don't suppose it does. What are you going to name her?"

Dan looked puzzled. "Hadn't thought on it."

"Jenna's a writer," Gard called from the sink where she had gone to wash up. "She might have an idea."

"Go ahead," Dan said. "Do the honors."

"You're sure?" Jenna glanced from Dan to Gard, who grinned at her. When Dan nodded she watched the foal nurse, its wide brown eyes soft with contentment. Calmness, warmth, and an astonishing sense of peace coursed through her. "Harmony."

"Pretty," Dan said.

"Perfect," Gard murmured.

Gard's gaze was so warm, so intimate, Jenna's eyes filled. Everything *was* perfect. She turned quickly away—hormones, that's all. Totally out-of-control hormones.

"Thank you," she told Dan and once outside, hooked her arm through Gard's. "That was amazing. I can't thank you enou—"

"No thanks needed." Gard's voice was raspy and when they'd settled in the cab, she sat for a moment in silence as if making a decision. "I don't suppose you're hungry?"

Jenna laughed. "Somehow, I think we've been here before."

Gard grinned and reached for the keys. "Yeah. My repertoire is a little thin, I guess."

Jenna rested her hand on Gard's wrist. "I'm famished. Oscar's?"

"You sure?"

"Very sure."

Gard glanced over at her. "Why did you come tonight? I wasn't sure you would."

"I knew when I saw you at the door something important was happening." Jenna didn't add she would have gone with her for any reason, needing to be careful that the beauty of the night and all that had happened didn't carry her away. She'd never felt anything as right as sitting in the front seat of Gard's truck in the middle of the silent countryside, watching starlight flicker over Gard's face and waiting for dawn. She could so easily lose herself here, and yet, despite the risks, she couldn't bring herself to deny her feelings. "And…I missed you."

"I missed you too." Gard heaved a sigh and turned on the truck. "I kept thinking you might leave."

"Alice has arranged for an art dealer to come up this weekend. Once the paintings are taken care of, I can show the house. I'll probably meet with the realtor next week."

Gard's shoulders tightened. "Then you won't have any reason to stay, will you?"

"I never intended to stay very long."

"It must be nice to have life go according to plan."

Jenna laughed humorlessly. "Oh, it must be. But I wouldn't know."

Gard pulled into the parking lot at Oscar's. It might've been noon judging from the jammed lot, although on closer inspection almost all the vehicles were eighteen-wheelers. The farmers in their pickups wouldn't show up for another couple of hours. Gard turned off the engine and jiggled the keys between her fingers. "What do you mean?"

"I'm not quite the country girl you think." Jenna shifted around until her back was against the door. "I grew up in the country, but not on a farm—at a truck stop just off the turnpike. My father died in a motorcycle crash when I was three. My birth mother was never in the picture and his second wife, Darlene, kept me. She was a diner waitress, and later so was I. That's what I was raised to be. Not that there's anything wrong with that, but unfortunately, Darlene tended to supplement her tips with some after-hours work. Work that she brought home with her. A trailer is a small place, and when I got older, it started to look like I might be on the menu soon."

"Jesus, Jenna." Gard's eyes flashed darkly in the light from the diner's glowing white neon sign.

"Oh, things never progressed that far, but Darlene definitely considered me bait for the kind of game she was hunting. That's when I got out."

"How old were you?"

"Seventeen."

"You were on your own?"

"Yes. For the first few years. I managed to get some education, got into the city college, and turned what had always been my passion into something I could make a living at. I got lucky and met

Alice when I was just getting started. She gave me a chance. She gave me a lot."

"You love her."

"Yes, I do," Jenna said. "We're not lovers. We never have been. It's not right for us. I don't love her that way."

Gard's brows drew down. "What way?"

"Desperately. Passionately. All-consumingly."

"That's how you see love?"

"Don't you?"

Gard shook her head. "Once. Not anymore."

"Are you ever going to tell me about her?"

"It's an old story. I thought she loved me. She didn't." Gard yanked open her door and jumped down. "Let's get breakfast."

Jenna followed, absurdly pleased that Gard hadn't said *I loved her* when she spoke about the woman who had obviously hurt her. Silly to be jealous. She'd never been jealous over a woman in her life. Of course, she hardly recognized half of what she was feeling these days. When had she become a stranger to herself? She nearly stumbled when she considered that the stranger might be the woman she'd been *before* arriving in Little Falls.

"Jen, you okay?" Gard grasped her hand.

"Yes," Jenna said, instantly centered by Gard's warm strength. "Yes. I'm just glad to be here."

Gard rested her fingertips on Jenna's cheek and lightly kissed her. "So am I."

Jenna swayed toward her as naturally as the tide surging to the moon's pull. She wanted another minute alone with her, under the stars, She wanted another kiss. "We should go inside."

"I know."

Gard slid an arm around Jenna's waist and when they walked into Oscar's, someone called, "Whoo-ee!" Jenna smiled.

❖

Gard demolished her eggs, biscuits, and sausage automatically, much more interested in drinking Jenna in than what was on her plate. Making easy small talk—catching up on Jenna's progress with her book, answering her excited questions about the foal's future, telling her about the farmers market set up outside of town every Saturday morning—made the stone she'd been carrying around in the pit of her stomach disappear. Beneath the pleasure, though, she was always aware of time passing.

"Sun's coming up," Gard said as she and Jenna strolled back to the truck. "Tired?"

"Pleasantly." Jenna flopped into the seat and dropped her head back against the seat. She looked relaxed, happy.

Gard had a hard time believing she was sitting across from Jenna at five o'clock in the morning when twenty-four hours before she'd pretty much convinced herself she was never going to see her again. Not the way they'd been together up on the mountainside. Not when Jenna had pulled back the minute she'd had a chance to think about what they'd done.

She was certain Jenna hadn't been running from the sex—the sex had been incredible and they'd both pretty much said so. But Jenna had been clear about wanting simple and no strings. Maybe to her that meant one-time sex. Or hell, maybe she just wanted to spend her last few weeks in the country writing without the distraction of an affair. Whatever had put that wall up between them, she'd resigned herself to it. Or tried to.

The idea of never seeing Jenna again had been eating holes in her insides.

Then Dan had called and she knew, she just knew, that Jenna had to see the birth. All she'd been able to show her when she'd taken her around on field calls had been the dirty end of the job— hard work and sweat and suffering animals. She'd wanted to show her the beauty of her work too. And she just plain *had* to see her. It was crazy. Sure. But if she was going to hurt, why not hurt because of what she wanted, instead of what she wouldn't let herself have? A few more hours with Jenna was all she was likely to get. So yeah, the hollow ache in the center of her chest when Jenna left for good was coming. But worth it all the same.

Gard started up the truck and headed out. "It sounds like you'll have things squared away out at Birch Hill pretty soon. I guess you'll be happy to go home."

"Wait." Jenna suddenly straightened.

Gard braked at the edge of the parking lot, her left blinker on, ready to head in the direction of Jenna's house. "What's wrong?"

"Nothing. Everything. I'm not really sure." Jenna slid over and stroked Gard's jaw with the backs of her fingers. "I should've stayed away from you in the first place, but I didn't want to. I shouldn't have gone out with you last night, either, but the minute I saw you on the porch, the only place I wanted to be was with you."

Gard caught Jenna's hand and kissed her palm. "Then we both wanted the same thing. Maybe we should just leave it at that for now."

"And next week? Next month—whenever I go?"

"Won't be any worse than the way things have been. I couldn't get you off my mind." Gard pushed a hand through her hair. "I was glad for the night work because I couldn't sleep anyways. We're both adults. We both know the score."

"What are you saying?"

"I feel good when I'm with you."

"Oh God," Jenna whispered. "So do I."

Gard relaxed and pressed Jenna's hand to her thigh. "So what do you say to a date Friday night?"

"A date." Jenna laughed. "That sounds so old-fashioned. In a really nice way."

"I guess it is. The Simpsons are having a barn-raising on Friday afternoon, followed by a barbecue and a barn dance. I got roped into going because Ida Simpson is my tech's sister, and I promised Rob I'd go if he covered my hours this morning."

"A barn dance. Is there actual dancing?"

Gard laughed. "There might be."

Jenna stroked Gard's leg, enjoying the way she laughed, the pleasure in her eyes. "And if we danced? Would there be a riot?"

"They survived us at Oscar's just now. You'll just need to behave."

"Me? What about you?"

Gard gave her an innocent look. "I'm always the picture of decorum."

"I don't remember that being the case up on the mountain."

"I had to have you or die." Gard's gaze raked down Jenna's body.

Instantly breathless, Jenna quickened. "And now that you've had me, you're not hungry anymore?"

"No," Gard said, her voice low and rough. "Now I'm starving."

"Are you." Jenna refused to think about what she was doing. She *always* thought about what she was doing—about what she would wear, what she would read, how she would answer questions, what she would write and why. Her life had never been spontaneous, because uncertainty equaled danger. Her only comfort had been knowing exactly what each hour would bring. Whenever she was with Gard, she was never certain what she would say or do or feel. A terrifying feeling, but strangely freeing too. Gard pushed her to say more, do more, feel more than she wanted to, but she also made her feel safe, even when she was so exposed. "What should we do about that?"

"You know what I want," Gard muttered, her teeth clenched. "What do you want?"

Jenna rubbed her thumb in the palm of Gard's hand, pressing into the firm flesh, running her nail over the calluses. "I really don't want you to take me home right now."

Gard flicked her blinker up to signal a right turn and rocketed the truck out onto the highway. "Then I won't."

Chapter Twenty-three

Jenna was content to let the drive pass in silence, watching the countryside awaken as Gard drove through the dawn. A herd of deer raised their heads in the midst of a field of belly-high corn, ears flickering with curiosity as they passed. A spotted fawn nestled close to its mother, heartbreakingly beautiful in its fragile innocence. The green fields glistened with dew under the bright yellow sun, so fresh and untarnished Jenna was reminded of a time long ago when she had imagined her life as a similar sea of endless possibility. When had those possibilities become defined by the next deadline, the next book launch, the next award? She'd replaced personal happiness with professional success, and wondered if they really were mutually exclusive. As the melancholy stole in around the edges of her consciousness, she concentrated on the hard heat of Gard's thigh under her palm and rubbed her hand along the seam of Gard's pants until Gard grasped her wrist.

"Take it easy," Gard said, her voice deep and mellow. "I'm driving here."

"Am I bothering you?"

Gard shot her a look, her eyes smoky. "Oh yeah."

Jenna smiled. "Sorry."

"Bull."

"Okay. Not sorry."

"Are you all right?"

"Yes, why?"

"You look a little sad."

"No," Jenna said quickly, "far from it." She hesitated, knowing she was on dangerous ground. She'd been the one wanting their pasts to stay in the past, but the more time she spent with Gard, the more she wanted to know her. Even more terrifying, the more she wanted to be known. "Have you ever wanted to go back? Back before everything changed, back before you stopped believing in happy endings?"

"Jenna," Gard said softly, fitting their fingers together and rubbing the back of Jenna's hand against her middle. "Until just a little while ago, happy didn't figure into anything I ever thought I was going to be."

"And now?"

Gard lifted their hands and kissed Jenna's knuckles. "Right this minute I'm very happy."

"So am I." Happier than she dared think about. She'd loved sitting with Gard in the diner, sharing a private moment in the midst of all the activity. She never would've imagined that a simple meal could be so intimate. By the time they'd left the diner she was wet.

Jenna went back to stroking Gard's thigh.

"You're doing the distracting thing again," Gard said.

"I think you're tough enough to handle it."

Gard laughed and slowed for a tractor pulling a hay wagon across the road. A mile or two farther on, Gard turned off the highway onto the dirt lane leading to her house. An ocean of corn seemed to have sprung up out of nowhere and extended as far as Jenna could see on either side.

"Do you farm this?" Jenna asked.

"I'd like to, but I don't have the time. I lease it." Gard pulled up in front of the house, put the truck in neutral, and turned in her seat. Beam raced around the side of the house, barking ecstatically. "Are you sure about this?"

"Quite sure." Jenna turned off the ignition, pulled out the keys, and dropped them in Gard's lap. Without waiting for Gard, she jumped out of the truck, scratched Beam's ears, and ambled up the walkway to the house. Gard caught up to her and together they climbed onto the porch. She remembered talking to Rina out here, thinking at the time she'd only be passing through. So much had changed for her since then, more than she could ever have imagined. Gard watched her with a worried expression and she took her hand. "Remember last night when you wanted me to promise that I would stand exactly where you wanted me and not move?"

"I remember," Gard said with a note of caution.

"Turnabout is fair play. Now you promise."

Gard's eyebrows went up. "All right."

"Come inside then."

Jenna opened the screen door, turned the brass knob on the heavy walnut door, and found it unlocked. She tugged Gard's arm and they went inside. She didn't hesitate but headed down the hall and directly up the stairs, only pausing when she reached the top. To the left was Gard's bedroom, to the right the guest room where she had stayed. "Right or left?"

"Left," Gard said instantly.

Jenna continued on, pleased with Gard's choice. She wanted to be in Gard's bedroom. In her bed. She didn't want casual, she didn't want quick or easy. She wanted to get inside Gard's skin the way Gard was inside hers. Gard had seduced her on the mountainside, intentionally or not. She'd surrendered completely up there, and as much as she'd loved not being in charge, she regretted not showing Gard just exactly how much she'd wanted her. Now she intended to make that message very clear.

Gard's bedroom was like the rest of the house, spacious and elegant. High beaten-tin ceilings, a huge four-poster bed, Craftsman dressers and armoire, floor-to-ceiling windows with sheer white curtains. The covers were pulled down on the bed, but there was no dent in the pillow, no wrinkles in the sheets. No one had slept in it and Jenna liked that too. She pulled Gard over to the side of the bed and then backed away from her.

"Watch," she whispered. Reaching down, she grasped the hem of her T-shirt and slowly pulled it up and over her head. She let it drop behind her, smiling as Gard's eyes widened, feeling her color rise as Gard's gaze dropped from her face down her body. Her nipples rose and tightened. She unbuttoned her jeans, pushed down the zipper, and stepped out of them, getting rid of her shoes at the same time. She hadn't worn any underwear while she'd been working at home and now she was naked. Gard sucked in a breath and Jenna's belly quivered. At the touch of Gard's hands on her waist, she nearly relented and gave up her plan of command. The slightest brush of Gard's fingers made her wetter, and she wanted to collapse onto her back and pull Gard down on top of her. She wanted Gard over her, Gard's fingers inside her, Gard's mouth tormenting her nipples. She wanted to come for her. For her.

"No touching," Jenna said.

"Jesus Christ." Gard slid both hands up Jenna's sides and tried to cradle her breasts, but Jenna pushed her arms away.

"I mean it."

"You let me see you naked for the first time and I can't touch?"

Gard made a very uncivilized sound and Jenna laughed. "You promised to stay where I put you and not move."

"You tricked me."

"You'll live." Jenna unbuttoned Gard's shirt, one slow button at a time, and worked it down her shoulders. She bunched the cotton T-shirt underneath in her hands, jerked it free of Gard's pants, and pulled it up and off. "Boots."

Gard obeyed, toeing off her work boots and leaning down to yank off her socks. When she straightened, naked except for her jeans, Jenna clenched inside. "I get so wet just looking at you."

"Let me have you," Gard demanded.

"Be patient." Jenna ran her hands over Gard's chest and cupped her small breasts. She lightly rubbed the pale tan nipples, her breath hitching when Gard's stomach tightened, the squares of taut muscle popping between the etched furrows. Oh God, she wasn't going to be able to wait. Had to taste her. Had to be in her heat. She pressed her breasts to Gard's and kissed her.

The instant their tongues touched, Gard groaned and jerked Jenna close. Their bodies fused from breast to thigh and the rough cotton of Gard's pants rubbed against the soft skin of Jenna's belly.

Jenna spread her legs to let Gard slide one thigh between her legs. She rolled her sex against Gard's hard muscle until her clitoris pulsed on the edge of explosion. Dragging herself away from Gard's mouth, she knelt on the thick Persian rug and gripped Gard's ass to hold her in place. She'd left a wet spot on Gard's pants. She liked that. She wanted to rub herself against Gard's stomach and leave her scent everywhere. She brushed her mouth over Gard's stomach instead, circling Gard's navel with the tip of her tongue. Gard tried to open her fly, but Jenna quickly caught her hands.

"No." She tugged the rim of Gard's belly button with her teeth and licked downward until she reached the waistband of her jeans. She opened the top button, slid the zipper down partway, and worked her tongue lower.

"Come on, Jenna," Gard whispered.

Smiling, Jenna shook her head. She sucked lightly on the satin-soft skin exposed by the vee of Gard's open fly until Gard's ass tightened and her hips jerked against Jenna's mouth. Jenna's thighs grew damp and her clitoris twitched and she was seconds away from begging Gard to slide her fingers inside her. Mustering her willpower, she stood and pressed her palms against Gard's chest. Gard backed up, hit the bed, and fell backwards.

Instantly, Jenna straddled her, pinning her to the bed with both hands on her shoulders. "You weren't supposed to move."

"You pushed me." Gard bucked her hips, forcing her crotch into Jenna's swollen center. The pressure was exquisite and Jenna had to bite her lip not to cry out. She squeezed Gard's shoulders harder.

"Stop that."

"You can't expect me not to—"

Jenna silenced her with a kiss, sliding her tongue inside, taking her in a deep, deep kiss that had Gard arching off the bed. While she played in Gard's mouth, she rocked in the cradle of Gard's pelvis, teasing herself as her tender clitoris rubbed back and forth on the cotton fabric of Gard's half-open pants. Gard clasped her hips, increasing the pressure between them, and she moaned, rubbing her breasts over Gard's. She wanted to come. She really, really wanted to come. If she could just come, she could get control again. Make things last, make Gard wait. Make it good for her—

"Oh." Jenna trembled, the orgasm coiling between her thighs. Almost there now, and so so good. No, no, not yet. With a sharp cry, she pushed upward, easing the exquisite tension in her pelvis.

"What are you doing?" Gard's grip on Jenna's hips tightened. "You want to come." She tried to pull Jenna up the bed. "Let me make you come in my mouth."

Jenna planted her hand between Gard's breasts, preventing her from dragging her up. She'd come in a second if Gard took her that way. "Get your pants off."

"Damn it, Jenna."

Jenna leaned away from Gard and caressed her own breasts with both hands, catching her nipples between her thumbs and forefingers, tugging them. The shock made her clitoris jump. "Do it or I'll make myself come."

Gard cursed and half sat up, pushing at the waistband of her pants. The rippling muscles in her chest and abdomen bore stark witness to her need and Jenna had to fight not to just give in and fall on her. She skimmed her fingers down the center of her abdomen and pressed the base of her clitoris with two fingers. Her hips lifted and she caught her lower lip between her teeth. Oh God, she was close.

"Go ahead," Gard said, her attention focused on Jenna's fingers. "Make yourself come."

"I might." Jenna gasped as pleasure filled her throat. She fondled herself until she knew she had to stop or surrender. "In a little while."

Gard reached for her but she pushed away, sliding down the bed until she was lying between Gard's spread thighs. She kissed the base of Gard's belly and rubbed her cheek over the soft skein of hair at the apex of her thighs. "But I've got something else in mind first."

Gard drove her fingers into Jenna's hair, trapping her head between her hands. "Go slow."

"I'll go any way I want to." Still, she *did* take her slowly, wanting to savor each heartbeat against her lips, each thrust and shivered breath as she kissed and licked and sucked. She knew how to keep Gard on the edge and she did, slowing her strokes, softening the suction when Gard tried to press harder into her mouth. She toyed with her, teasing and rubbing and dipping inside with her fingertips.

"I need to come." Gard sounded so matter-of-fact, her voice so flat and hollow, Jenna knew she was right on the brink.

Jenna pulled back and covered her with swift, light kisses.

Gard's legs shook. "I need to come."

Jenna trapped Gard's clitoris between her fingers and watched it pulse, licking with a rhythm too uneven to bring her over.

"I need to come." Gard groaned, seeming to turn to stone, every muscle so tight Jenna feared she might splinter. She wasn't sure Gard was breathing anymore, and she had to give her what she needed now. She sucked her gently and swirled her tongue and Gard's breath shot out and she came in a series of hard thrusts.

Jenna smiled around Gard's throbbing flesh. Her lips would be bruised—the idea pleased her very much.

"Now." Gard reared up before she was even done coming, catching Jenna by surprise.

"What—" Jenna gasped.

"Damn it, Jen, come here." Gard pulled Jenna upward, unable to wait any longer to sink into her. She kissed her, the last of her orgasm roiling in her belly. Racing a hand over Jenna's breasts, down her body, and between her legs, she cupped her and squeezed. Jenna cried out and Gard slid her fingers inside her, her thumb working Jenna's clitoris back and forth.

Jenna jerked, her eyes wide and stunned. "Oh my God."

"You coming, baby?"

Nodding helplessly, Jenna fell into Gard's arms, flooding Gard's hand with hot release. Holding her breath, Gard rolled onto her side, keeping Jenna securely in her arms. She kissed her, needing to be inside her everywhere. Needing, in that infinite moment, nothing more.

CHAPTER TWENTY-FOUR

Jenna kissed Gard's throat. Salty sweet, fragrant as fresh-cut hay. The sun streamed through the window onto her bare back. With her cheek pillowed against Gard's shoulder, she might have been lying on a grassy slope on a lazy summer afternoon with nothing on her mind except the clouds flickering by overhead. She burrowed a little closer, absorbing all that was Gard. The bold, steady beat of her heart. Slow breaths flowing in and out, as soothing as the wind in the trees. The oh-so-seductive rasp of Gard's slightly rough fingertips up and down her spine. The wondrous panorama of Gard's body—tanned shoulders, pale breasts and belly. Hard muscle. Soft skin. Sweet, sweet taste.

She hadn't realized she was rocking her hips until Gard gave a satisfied rumble and cupped her ass, drawing her center hard against Gard's thigh. She caught her breath at the sudden swell of desire.

Gard murmured, "Whatever you're thinking, I like it."

"You do wonderful things to me."

Gard's chuckle was a deep powerful vibration beneath Jenna's ear. A breeze brushed the hair at her temple. Gard's mouth skimmed over her ear.

"I want to do all kinds of things to you," Gard said.

Jenna teased herself, rolling her pelvis in slow circles on Gard's leg. She was wet, and certain Gard could tell. Her clitoris tingled and very soon she would want to come. "Don't you think you should give me time to catch my breath?"

"You sound plenty rested to me. Feel that way too."

Laughing, Jenna pulled Gard's nipple into her mouth. Instantly, Gard arched, a soft moan quivering in her throat. Jenna wanted to purr with satisfaction. Turning Gard on was more exciting than her own excitement. "And I can't get enough of you."

Gard rolled onto her back and pulled Jenna over her, scissoring their legs together. "I can't get enough of what you *do* to me. Just waking up next to you makes me want to come."

"Oh God." Jenna tented her lip between her teeth. Gard's eyes were so dark, her need so undisguised, Jenna's heart ached. How could anyone be so trusting, how could anyone be so damn brave? She wanted so much to cherish that trust, to take away the last lingering shadows of pain in her eyes, she could barely swallow around the lump in her throat. And then Gard kissed her, so tenderly, so gently, that every single bit of control she'd ever had crumbled. She wasn't sure she could hold off her own climax long enough to bring Gard to orgasm, but she was damn well going to try. She pushed up on both arms and settled her hips between Gard's legs.

"Jen," Gard groaned.

"Want to come, do you? Let's see what we can do about that." Jenna kissed her and thrust with the rhythm she knew Gard liked. Gard moaned and she bore down harder, ignoring the ache between her thighs. Her breath was short, her words a whisper. "You like that?"

"Just…like that."

Gard was so hard and so wet, her eyes so hot—black swirling wildly through the gray, a volcano boiling over. Jenna wanted her so much. So much, too much…too much to hold. "Oh God, I'm sorry," Jenna gasped. "I'm going to come."

"Please," Gard whispered, her leg tensing between Jenna's, giving her just the extra pressure she needed. "I want to feel you."

Jenna exploded. The orgasm shook her so hard she fell into Gard's arms, moaning open-mouthed against Gard's shoulder. Tears leaked from her eyes.

"You're beautiful, Jenna." Gard brushed the moisture away and kissed her.

"Damn, damn, I didn't mean for that to happen," Jenna said weakly.

"I love when you come for me. Makes me so hot I just want you all over again."

"I want you to have me." Jenna closed her eyes, her strength draining away with the last tremors. She couldn't move, which was fine, since she never intended to move. The night had been perfect, the morning exquisite. She'd never been so connected to another human being. Gard touched her, inside and out. Being known, being united so intimately, was terrifying and exhilarating and wonderful. Gard was the most incredible woman she'd ever met.

And oh, what was she thinking? What was she saying?

Jenna pushed herself up on her arms and looked down the length of their bodies tangled together on the bed. They fit perfectly, breast to breast, belly to belly, center to center. Oh God. She was in love with her, wasn't she? That couldn't be. She couldn't let that be. What would she do? She'd never made space for that in her life. She'd never planned on needing anyone, counting on anyone. Wanting anyone this much. Her chest tightened and she couldn't catch her breath.

"Hey. Hey." Gard caressed Jenna's cheek with the backs of her fingers. "Baby, what is it? Did something hurt you?"

"No," Jenna said. "I'm fine. Everything is fine."

"You sure? For a second there, you looked scared."

Jenna forced a smile. "How could I be? I'm here with you and you make me feel wonderful."

Gard wasn't convinced, but she wouldn't press Jenna to talk about something she wasn't ready to share. She rubbed her cheek over Jenna's breasts and kissed each one, letting her lips skate over Jenna's erect nipples. She wanted to make her come again, wanted to feel her lose control, wanted to feel her open the gates and let her in. "I want you again."

"No way." Jenna feebly slapped Gard's shoulder. "I might not even be able to walk after this."

"Did I hurt you?" Gard sat up quickly, shifting around so Jenna was lying in her arms. "Did I?"

"No, no." Jenna kissed her, stroked her hair, kissed her again. "God, no. You just make me come so hard I'm totally exhausted."

"That good, huh?"

Jenna rolled her eyes. "Oh my God. I've forgotten who I was talking to. Yes, it was quite satisfactory, thank you."

Laughing, Gard settled back, wrapped Jenna in her arms, and pulled the sheet up over them. "Get some sleep. You'll feel better when you wake up."

"What about you?" Jenna skimmed her hand down Gard's stomach and between her legs. She was hot, her clitoris swollen and throbbing. "I'm not going to go to sleep with you like this."

"I'm okay. When you come, I feel satisfied. Better than that. You're...there's never been anyone like you."

Jenna pressed her fingers to Gard's mouth. "Shut up. Shut up, shut up. Don't say things like that."

"Even if they're true?"

Jenna wished she knew some way to make the truth less painful. "Especially if they're true. I'm sor—"

Gard kissed her. "Go to sleep, Jenna. We'll figure it all out."

❖

Gard didn't sleep. Holding Jenna was all she needed, except for wanting desperately to imprint every memory so she'd never forget a single sensation. She'd slept with women before, but never like this. Never as if her very life depended on being with Jenna, holding her, protecting her, being hers. Most of all, being hers.

We'll figure it out.

The words kept playing through Gard's head. What was there to figure out, really? Before long, Jenna would go back to New York, and their affair would be over. Maybe that's why she'd let herself feel so much with Jenna—she'd known any connection would end before her past surfaced and destroyed what was between them. Because sooner or later, the past would catch up to her.

There's never been anyone like you.

She'd thought she'd been in love, been loved, only to have it all come apart when she'd made a devil's bargain. She'd walked away from her life, but Jenna couldn't—Cassandra Hart couldn't. Cassandra was a public figure. Cassandra wasn't invisible, couldn't be a ghost, as Gard had become. She might have constructed a life where nothing mattered before her arrival in Little Falls, but Jenna had created a very different life. If Jenna didn't just turn around and walk out on her when she learned the truth, she'd ultimately be hurt by a relationship with her. Gard couldn't let that happen.

I want you to have me, Jenna had said. But would she, if she knew the truth? Would she ever trust her?

Gard held Jenna closer, stroking her hair, the curve of her shoulder, the hollow above her hips. So beautiful. So incredibly warm and giving. Jenna was far braver than her. She'd shared the story of her life. How calmly she had spoken of what she'd been through, as if it were an everyday occurrence for a teenager to strike out on her own and find a way not only to survive, but to be incredibly successful. Jenna was special. Far, far too special for her. She couldn't contaminate Jenna's life, and thankfully, she wouldn't have the opportunity.

Closing her eyes, she kissed Jenna's forehead, her temple, her mouth. She wanted her again so much, she forced herself to be nothing but gentle.

Jenna stirred and caressed Gard's breast. "You're all tense. Something's bothering you. What is it?"

Gard shook her head. "Nothing, go back to sleep."

"I can't. If I sleep, I'll miss something, and I don't want to miss a second of being with you."

"I don't suppose anyone's ever mentioned how stubborn you are."

"Never once." Jenna lightly bit Gard's shoulder then soothed the spot with a kiss. "Want to tell me what's wrong?"

Gard brushed stray strands of sun-kissed hair from Jenna's cheek. "I'm gonna have to go to work soon."

Jenna groaned. "What time is it?"

"About noon."

"I need to get back too," Jenna said, although she wasn't ready to get up. Something was bothering Gard and she wanted to know what. She didn't believe Gard regretted their lovemaking. Gard wouldn't have given herself so completely, so openly, if there hadn't been something special between them. If Gard hadn't felt something for her. She blamed herself for insisting they leave the past in the past. At the time, she'd thought she'd been protecting herself and sparing Gard the pain and embarrassment of reliving something she obviously did not want to talk about. Now she wondered if she hadn't been a coward, and Gard was suffering for her decision. She sat up and draped the sheet around her waist. "There's nothing you can tell me that will change anything between us."

Gard's face instantly shuttered closed. Her withdrawal hurt more than Jenna had believed possible. What was she doing? Jenna pleated the sheet between her fingers, searching for words. "I'm sorry. I know you don't want to talk about whatever it is that's bothering you. I'm not even sure why I'm trying to get you to talk about it."

Abruptly, Gard rose and searched around on the floor for her pants. She pulled her jeans on and zipped them partway, not bothering to close the top button. She stalked to the other side of the room and braced an arm on either side of the window. From where Jenna sat, all she could see was the sunlight splintering around Gard's head and dusting her shoulders, leaving the stark planes of her back in shadow. She was so beautiful.

Jenna threw the sheet aside and went after her. She wrapped her arms around Gard's middle and rested her cheek between her shoulder blades. "Gard?"

When Gard didn't answer, Jenna caressed the tight muscles in Gard's stomach and kissed her back. "I don't care, Gard. What matters to me is this moment with you. The moments that we've shared. I'm sorry I asked for more."

Gard covered Jenna's hand and held it hard against her stomach. "You didn't ask for anything unreasonable. I just…I'm not used to talking about things."

"And you don't have to." Jenna held her more tightly. This was better, to leave the secrets where they belonged. They had the now, they had this.

"Are you still going to come to the barn dance tomorrow night?" Gard asked.

"Of course I'm going to come." Jenna gave Gard a little shake. "First of all, we have a date, and I don't take kindly to being stood up."

Gard chuckled and Jenna's heart eased.

"Furthermore," Jenna said, "you promised me a dance."

"I'll dance with you." Gard turned and cupped Jenna's face in her hands. "I'll do anything you want."

Jenna brushed her fingers through Gard's hair and caressed her until the shadows left her her eyes. "What I want is this." She kissed her. "And I'd like very much to see you smile."

"Jenna," Gard murmured, kissing her back. When she drew away, she smiled.

Jenna nodded, satisfied. Enough. Enough for now.

CHAPTER TWENTY-FIVE

Y ou want to explain to me again exactly why you're going to spend the night in a non-air-conditioned barn filled with scratchy hay and smelling like horse poop?" Alice stood with hands on hips in the middle of Jenna's bedroom.

"I already told you—twice." Jenna turned slowly in front of the full-length, wood-framed mirror hanging on the inside of the cedar closet door, trying to get a view of her ass in the new jeans she'd picked up that morning. "It's a community thing. People get together and help put up a barn, and then they party. The barn's brand new, so it's not likely to be filled with hay or poop."

"Just sweating people. And your ass looks fine." Alice plopped onto the end of the bed and leaned back on her elbows. "Remember, Diane is coming tonight."

"Bring her to the dance. You don't have a date."

"You've got to be kidding." Alice snorted. "First of all, she's completely not my type. Second of all, she owns an art gallery in Soho and a condo off Central Park. A barn dance?"

Jenna pulled a sleeveless white shirt from the closet and turned to Alice. "You can't really be this much of a snob. You *are* kidding, right?"

"Mostly. Although, really. You know how hot it's going to be in there tonight?" Alice grinned. "Do you think the sheriff will be there?"

Jenna buttoned the cotton shirt and tucked it in. "Undoubtedly."

"In that case, I suppose I could live with the heat. Your nipples show through that shirt."

Jenna looked down at herself. "A lot or just enough?"

Alice pursed her lips. "Just enough to drive a certain someone crazy if she happens to be looking. Is that what you want?"

"Of course that's what I want. I'm sleeping with her, aren't I?"

"About that." Alice plucked at the pink chenille bedspread as if the small cotton nubs peppering the surface were the most fascinating items she'd ever seen. "Where are you going with it?"

"Why do I have to be going somewhere?" Jenna eyed the cowboy boots she'd purchased on a whim. Maybe her feet would get sore if she tried to dance in them all night, but damn, they were sharp. Glossy black, slightly pointed toes, chunky heels. She felt a little wild and sexy wearing them. What the hell, a few blisters were a small price to pay for looking, and *feeling*, hot. She sat on the window bench to pull them on.

"I'm just not used to seeing you so...into someone," Alice said.

"Meaning you think I'm loose?"

"No, I just don't think of you as getting attached."

Attached. Jenna considered that word. Attached was what you got to a close friend, maybe even a fuck buddy. Attached was not the word for what she felt about Gard. "I'm not attached."

"Then what are you?"

Jenna paused, one boot on, the other in her hands. Confession time. "I'm in love with her."

Alice threw up her hands. "That's completely impossible. That plotline is not going to fly. You'll have to rework the entire sentence and whatever paragraph came before it. Possibly the entire chapter."

Jenna smiled. "I'm afraid this is one story I can't massage into anything else."

"For God's sake, Jenna! She lives in Vermont. She's a vet. You live in Manhattan. You're something of a star, and you spend half your life traveling. Not to mention the rest of your time working. And God damn it, she's got a sordid past."

"You don't know what that's about. And what does that matter anyhow? I never heard of her before. Probably no one else has either."

"I Googled her the other day," Alice said. "About five hundred hits came up, and some of them are recent. It's pretty easy to find the story."

"You…" Jenna's whole body flared hot. "You *Googled* her? Do you want to look through her underwear drawer too? Jesus, Alice. Whatever happened to privacy?"

"There is no such thing as privacy anymore, that's what I've been trying to tell you. Do you think your readers won't be curious about your lover? That they won't do the same thing I did and find the same stories? Do you really want to field questions at book readings about your lover's illicit past? And don't even get me started on the publicity department." Alice waved an arm dramatically. "We are not talking about a traffic ticket here, she—"

"No! You do not tell me anything." Jenna tried to sit on her temper, but she hated Gard being attacked, even by someone trying to protect *her.* "Do you think I don't know how to do an Internet search? If I'd wanted to look her up, I would have."

Alice stared. "You're just going to pretend this is a non-issue?"

"When Gard is ready, she'll tell me. I know what I need to know. She's a wonderful woman. People around here like and respect her. She's…she's gorgeous and funny and strong and…" Jenna closed her eyes. "And oh God, when she touches me I feel like the most precious thing in her life. Do you know what that feels like?"

The silence grew so heavy, Jenna half expected to open her eyes and find Alice gone. Instead, she was shocked by Alice's stricken expression. "Oh, damn, Alice. I'm sorry. I didn't mean to go off—"

"Hell, no, don't apologize. I didn't realize you didn't know how special you are. How precious you are to me. You're an amazing woman with incredible talent. And I'm probably going to kick myself for the rest of my life for not trying to seduce you before you ran into James Dean of the Cornfields."

Jenna laughed. "She's not like that."

"I bet you five hundred dollars she picks you up tonight in her big ole truck, wearing dusty boots and faded jeans and a tight white T-shirt."

"Oh God, I hope so."

"What are you going to do?"

"I don't have any idea. But I don't think I'll be leaving right away. I just want to be with her right now. Can't that be enough?"

"I don't know, Jenna. How long can you put the rest of your life on hold?"

Jenna ducked her head, pretending to be busy pulling on the second shiny black boot. How long indeed.

❖

Gard swung her truck up the drive to Jenna's a little before eight. She hopped out and hurried onto the porch, but before she could knock, the screen door opened and Jenna was there, framed in the soft yellow light from inside. The day and a half since she'd last seen her felt like years. The second Jenna'd left the house she'd started missing her, and the missing wasn't just from wondering if she'd ever see her again. She missed the way Jenna's gaze made her feel centered and focused and a million other things she never thought she wanted or needed. Hell, when Jenna smiled at her she was instantly taller than tall, brave and bold, and so swamped with tenderness she wanted to cry. Jenna turned her inside out and she liked it. Liked it an awful lot. In the hours they'd been apart, she'd half convinced herself Jenna was only a wonderful dream. She traced her fingertips over Jenna's face. Jenna was solid and real and smiling at her right now—and the churning in her stomach settled. She kissed her.

"Hi."

"Hi, you." Jenna slid her arms around Gard's waist and kissed her back, long and slow and deep.

Awash with peace and excitement, Gard never wanted the kiss to end. She pulled Jenna onto the porch and walked her backwards into the shadows until Jenna bumped into the wall. Bracing her forearms on the clapboards, Gard spread her legs and boxed Jenna in between her thighs. She pinned her with her body and kissed her, hot and hungry.

Jenna gasped and clutched Gard's shoulders, suddenly famished, her cool resolve of the last two days burning away at the first taste of Gard's heat. She'd been so pleased with herself since she'd left Gard's bed—keeping her head on straight, not letting the constant memories of being with Gard derail her. Oh, she got wet every time she thought about her, which was about a hundred times a day, so she walked around half turned on pretty much all the time, but that was all about good sex. Sex with Gard was great. So the horniness was a given. Normal. And she dreamt about her, or at least woke up with Gard on her mind, and started to call her cell twice for no reason at all, but she'd been cool. Really cool. Until right now, when she was incinerating. She yanked Gard's tight white T-shirt out of her jeans. A second later she drove her hand down the back of Gard's pants and palmed her tight, firm ass. Gard rewarded her with a low growl. Jenna feasted on her for a few more seconds, until she edged way too close to the cliff. She dragged her mouth away. "Stop. Stop it right now."

"Fuck no," Gard muttered and tried to kiss her again.

Jenna got a hand between them and pushed on Gard's chest. "We're going to the dance. You promised. No more kissing."

"Jenna," Gard said dangerously.

"Really, sweetheart, I can't. I've wanted you to make me come since yesterday, and I really won't be responsible if you kiss me again."

"God damn it." Gard's throat worked convulsively and the muscles stood out like iron bands beneath the taut skin.

"Mmm," she murmured, caressing Gard's neck. She loved knowing she made Gard want her this much. She'd never enjoyed turning on a woman this way before. She kissed Gard's throat. "Please? Dance?"

"You're killing me, you know that, right?"

Jenna nipped Gard's chin. "Oh, I certainly hope so."

"I surrender." Gard had to put some space between them or she was going to drag Jenna off into some dark corner and take her. She was so damned stoked her clit was jumping in her jeans.

Stepping back, Gard grabbed Jenna's hands and pulled her into the light that shone down on the porch steps. Moths as big as silver dollars fluttered around the uncovered bulb. At the edge of the yard, fireflies flickered in the gathering dusk. Diamonds danced in Jenna's eyes. "You look great."

"So do you. Thank God Alice was right." Jenna smoothed a hand over the tight white T-shirt clinging to Gard's chest.

"Huh?"

"Never mind." Jenna smoothed both hands over Gard's shoulders and down her bare arms, her thumbs tracing the swell of her biceps.

Gard's nipples hardened and her throat went dry. Her stomach tightened painfully. "Jesus, Jen, have a heart. I don't know how much I can take."

"Don't be a baby." Jenna smiled, the smile of a woman who knew her lover wanted her. "Besides, I like it when you want me."

"Then you ought to be happy pretty much all the time."

Jenna's expression became suddenly solemn. "You know? I am."

"Good." Gard lifted Jenna's hand and kissed her knuckles. "Hot boots, by the way."

Jenna looked down and made a pleased sound. "You think?"

"I do. If I knew you were getting duded up, I would've changed mine. I've got some pretty fancy tooled leather boots."

"Next time."

Gard feathered her fingertips through Jenna's hair, wondering how many next times they would have. She tried not to think about the future, just as she never thought about the past, at least not before Jenna came into her life. And she wasn't going to think about lies, and betrayal, and broken trust now either. Tonight was about Jenna, and tonight they would dance.

"Let's go to a party." Gard scooped Jenna into her arms, turning in a wide circle before kissing her. Jenna's arms came naturally around her neck.

"What was that for?" Jenna asked quietly, resting her head on Gard's shoulder.

"That was for happy." Gard sucked in a hard breath when Jenna licked her neck.

"Mmm, you taste nice." Jenna tilted her head back. "Are you? Are you happy?"

Gard buried her face in Jenna's hair. Sweet dahlias and spice. "Whenever I'm with you."

"Gard, I…"

"What?" Gard steeled herself. So soon? She couldn't be saying good-bye so soon. "What, Jenna?"

Jenna's answer was interrupted by the sound of an approaching car. Gard carefully let Jenna down to the porch and peered down the drive. A silver Jag sports coupe cut through the twilight, pulled in behind Gard's truck, and a blonde climbed out.

"Hi. Is Alice Smith here?" the woman called. "Or am I completely lost?"

Behind them, the screen banged open and Alice bounded out. "Diane! You're in the right place. Come up."

The svelte blonde with elegant, sculpted features joined them on the porch. Even dressed in plain navy pants, flats, and a loose silk tee, she screamed New York society. Gard's jaws clenched so hard her teeth ached.

The newcomer waved to Alice before holding out her hand to Jenna. "Hello. I recognize you from your book jackets, Cassandra. Wonderful to meet you. I'm Diane Bleeker."

"Call me Jenna," Jenna said.

Alice threw her arms around Diane. "God, you look amazing. Tell me her name."

Even in the near dark, Diane's blush was evident. Gard found the woman's undisguised pleasure disarming. She'd never seen Susannah light up like that at the mention of her.

"Valerie."

"Well," Alice said, "she's doing something right."

"Yes," Diane said softly.

Jenna wrapped her arm around Gard's waist. "Thank you so much for coming up on such short notice, Diane. This is—"

"Gard," Gard interrupted. "Nice to meet you."

"You also," Diane said.

Alice grabbed Diane's hand. "Come inside and catch me up with all the news. We'll get your bags later."

Diane nodded to Jenna and Gard. "It was nice meeting you both. I'll talk to you tomorrow, Cass—Jenna."

"Yes. Thank you."

When Alice and Diane disappeared inside, Gard took Jenna's hand. "Still want to go?"

"Absolutely." As they crossed the yard to Gard's truck, Jenna said, "Diane is an art dealer and gallery owner. She's here to look at Elizabeth's paintings."

"I remember you telling me someone was coming. That's great."

Jenna stopped, leaned against the front fender, and pulled Gard over to her by the waistband of Gard's jeans. "Are you all right?"

"I'm great." Gard wanted Jenna to have a good time. She wanted every minute they had left to them to be lived free of past regrets or future fears. "No stalling. You owe me a dance."

"I think you have that backwards." Jenna brushed her mouth over Gard's. "Just the same, I intend to give you a dance like you've never had before."

CHAPTER TWENTY-SIX

Looks like the whole county is here," Jenna said as Gard parked atop a grassy slope at the end of a long line of pickup trucks, station wagons, and the occasional motorcycle.

"Might be before the night is over." Gard pocketed her keys and jumped out.

Jenna hopped down and met her in front of the truck. Below them, an enormous blood red barn with a gambrel roof, three cupolas, and an iron weather vane loomed over a cluster of ramshackle outbuildings. Light spilled out through the wide-open double doors, illuminating people milling about with bottles of beer and plastic cups. The low roar of voices and the strains of a band playing country western tunes floated on a breeze fragrant with honeysuckle.

"Ready for this?" Gard clasped Jenna's hand.

"Oh yes." Jenna swung their joined hands in a long easy arc, astonished at her own excitement. Nothing could be further from her usual night out—an evening with a woman dressed for success, dinner in a chic restaurant, ending the night in a five-star hotel having urgent sex with someone who was looking for nothing more than she was—a moment's connection and the physical proof of being alive. She wanted to make love with Gard at the end of this night, too, but not to prove anything. To celebrate something. And that difference changed everything. When she was with Gard, she was more than just happy. More even than just whole. When she was with Gard, she was more herself than she had been since the night she'd left home. Somewhere in the process of falling in love, she had found herself.

She tugged Gard's hand until Gard slowed, a question in her eyes. A crescent moon rode the clouds overhead, silvering the sharp planes of Gard's face with haunting beauty.

"Second thoughts?" Gard asked.

"No, none," Jenna said. Walking beneath a summer sky ablaze with starlight, her fingers entwined with those of a woman who knew her and a lover she trusted, she was completely certain of everything that mattered. "I love you."

"Jenna," Gard whispered, her hand trembling in Jenna's.

"No response is required." Jenna cupped Gard's jaw and trailed her fingers along the bunched muscles beneath the smooth skin. "I just wanted to say it. Now let's go dance."

"In a minute. Give me a minute. You can't just say that and keep walking." Gard framed Jenna's face, her thumbs lightly brushing the corners of Jenna's mouth. "You honor me, and I don't deserve it. I don't deserve you. I—"

"Don't say that." Jenna kissed Gard's palm. "It's not about deserving. It's about how you make me feel—which is pretty damn wonderful." Jenna threaded her arm around Gard's waist, sensing her worry, her fear. Wanting to soothe her, she teased, "I'm going to have a hard time tonight if I can't touch you pretty much all the time."

Gard grasped Jenna's shoulder and held her tightly. "You can touch me anyplace, anytime. I...I pretty much love it when you do that."

"You're in trouble now." Jenna laughed, wondering how she'd never noticed she'd been living half a life before. Now the incredible sensation of being whole lit up her soul. Her past, her present, and hopefully her future were finally connected. The thread of her life ran straight and true, and even the pain was part of her happiness. She rested her cheek against Gard's shoulder. "Loving you makes me so happy."

"We're either going inside now," Gard muttered, "or we're

going back to the truck so I can take you home and make love to you."

"Well now, there's a difficult choice." Jenna released her grip on Gard's waist and squeezed her ass. "But you know, I'm in the mood for foreplay, and I don't think there's any better kind than dancing. Let's go inside."

"Anything you want." Gard pulled her close. "Anything."

❖

Anything you want.

Gard only wished she could keep that promise, but if Jenna didn't come to her senses, she didn't see how she could. She guided Jenna through the crowd, stopping every few feet to return greetings and introduce Jenna. Her mind was only half on the fragmented conversations—she was still reeling from the words *I love you.* Nothing she'd ever imagined hearing again, and not from Jenna. Not now, not when every waking moment she'd been preparing herself for Jenna to leave. Waiting for the awful barrenness of heart to swallow her when Jenna went home. She hadn't expected love. And she knew damn well she couldn't have it. But for tonight, for these few hours, she'd have Jenna. She never let go of Jenna's hand and no one seemed to notice, or if they did, they didn't care.

"There's Rina," Jenna said.

Rina, wearing civilian clothes—black jeans, a white shirt, and black motorcycle boots—stood by a long trestle table covered with a bright red and white checkered tablecloth talking to a buxom brunette in a shiny black vinyl skirt. A big aluminum tub of crushed ice with beer bottles standing out like fence posts in a winter field squatted on the table next to platters overflowing with sliced ham, turkey, and roast beef, and baskets of bread.

"Feel like a sandwich?" Gard asked.

"I don't think so. But I'd love something to drink." Jenna brushed the sweat off her cheeks with her fingers. "Alice was right. It's hot in here."

"Wait until later."

Gard plucked two dripping longnecks out of the tub, handed one to Jenna, and left a ten in a pile of bills on the table. She twisted off the cap and took a long pull just as Rina skirted the crowd and slipped in next to them.

"Not working tonight?" Gard asked.

Rina's gaze dropped to Gard and Jenna's linked hands, then rose back to Gard's. "Believe it or not, I'm completely off duty. Good to see you both."

"Hi, Rina," Jenna said.

"Your houseguest still with you?" Rina asked.

"Alice? Yes. I tried to talk her into coming tonight, but I'm not sure I sold her—"

"Appears that you did." Rina tilted her chin in the direction of the door. "She just walked in. With a date, it looks like."

Jenna checked over her shoulder and waved until Alice saw her. "Not a date, a friend and business associate."

"Huh," Rina said, tracking Alice through the crowd. "How are things coming along out at the house?"

"Fine," Jenna said. "I love the place."

Rina gave her a long look. "It's a damn fine farm."

"Yes, it is." At that moment, Alice and Diane, both in jeans, T-shirts, and boots with heels quite a bit higher than Jenna's, arrived. Jenna made introductions.

"Pleased to meet you, Ms. Bleeker," Rina said, shaking Diane's hand. She grinned at Alice. "I was hoping you'd make it tonight."

"Really," Alice said with a speculative smile. "You'll have to tell me why, later."

"I'll do that."

Alice grasped Jenna's elbow. "Diane took a quick look at a few of Elizabeth's paintings. She thinks my idea for a book signing and art exhibit is a good way to judge local interest. I'll make some calls in the morning, but I think I can set something up in Bennington almost anytime."

"Thanks. It'll be good promo for my new release." Jenna said to Rina, "Diane is an art dealer. She came up to look at Elizabeth's paintings."

"Really? Paintings." Rina frowned. "I didn't know she did that."

"Apparently, no one did."

"Well, if you do a book signing, be sure to let me know." Rina grinned. "I'm a fan, remember? I know quite a lot of folks who are."

"I'll see to your invitation personally," Alice cut in.

"Counting on that," Rina said.

"Save me a dance tonight," Alice said with a last look at Rina before hooking her arm through Diane's. "And now, let's go hunt up something to drink."

The music provided by two guitar players, a fiddler, and a drummer switched to a slow ballad and couples, young and old, congregated in front of the makeshift stage to dance. Jenna glanced at Gard and lifted her brow. "Well?"

Gard gave a little bow. "Would you care to dance?"

"I most certainly would, thank you."

Gard made yet another path through the laughing, jostling people to the dance floor and swung Jenna into her arms. Jenna's arms came around her neck and Gard clasped her waist. Their legs slid together as naturally as their fingers interlocked when they held hands. Gard rested her cheek against Jenna's temple and led her into a slow, easy waltz.

"You're a good dancer," Jenna whispered against Gard's throat.

"A bit out of practice," Gard said, stealing a quick kiss. She stroked Jenna's back as they swayed in the crowded space. Holding Jenna made it practically impossible to think about anything, not when blood rushed through her head and her loins with equal intensity. Just the same, despite the haze of arousal, she kept hearing Rina saying she wanted to go to Jenna's book signing. A public event. Cassandra Hart in a local appearance. Jenna had said she loved her. Jenna was willing to risk her heart and maybe her career.

Jenna had never pressed about her past, hadn't asked for anything at all, not even if Gard had any feelings for her. Jenna had taken all the chances, and what had Gard given her? Nothing. She'd taken what she shouldn't have, because like always, she was selfish. She skimmed her hand over the back of Jenna's neck and into her hair, cradling her head as she kissed her again. The lights were low in the barn, but anyone watching could have seen them.

Jenna moaned softly and pulled away. "Sweetheart, I can't resist you, and this might not be the place…"

"I know," Gard said, her throat tight. "I just need you. Jenna, I need you."

"Oh," Jenna whispered, brushing away a stray lock of hair that had fallen over Gard's forehead. Her fingers were trembling. "You need only ask."

"You don't know what you're offering."

"Don't I?"

"No, but you should. I'm not who you think I am, Jenna. I can't tell you what it means to me that you love me. It means…everything. But…" Gard took a breath and wondered if she could make up for the past by doing the right thing now. "My life and yours, they're worlds apart. And I've done things, things I'm not proud of. Things that could hurt you."

The music ended and dancers dispersed. The overhead lights dimmed further, and Gard welcomed the camouflage of near darkness. Maybe Jenna wouldn't be able to read the uncertainty in her eyes. She kept her voice steady and sure. "I thought we agreed we'd keep this simple and uncomplicated. Temporary."

"I haven't asked for anything else." Jenna sounded calm but her pulse raced in her throat.

"No, you haven't. And that's good, because there can't be anything else." Gard let her arms drop away until she was no longer holding Jenna. The loss of the connection was as painful as an amputation, and her stomach cramped so hard she nearly winced. "I think we need to slow things down. I'm sorry."

"For what?" Jenna spoke softly, her eyes unwavering, and unaccusing.

Gard hated herself for what she'd done. Then. Now. "I knew going in I couldn't give you…"

"I already told you, I'm not asking."

"But you should be. Just not with me." Gard saw the hurt Jenna tried to hide and it killed her to know she was hurting her. The self-loathing she usually kept at bay washed through her with such force she felt wrong just standing there. Just being anywhere near Jenna.

"Jenna, I have to go."

"Gard? Gard, don't do this."

Gard swung around so abruptly she nearly stumbled into Alice.

"Hey? Get an emergency call?" Alice asked, lifting her plastic cup of wine out of Gard's path.

"You should get her to go home, Alice. Away from here. Away from me."

"What?" Alice looked from Gard to Jenna, her forehead creasing.

"Gard, damn it." Jenna grabbed for Gard's hand but Gard slipped away. She lost sight of her almost instantly in the crowd, and pain exploded in her chest.

"Jenna?" Alice asked. "What the hell was that all about? What happened?"

"I might have made a tactical error," Jenna said softly, the color draining from the room along with the lost joy in her heart.

"Translation?"

"I told her I loved her." The elation of that moment was bittersweet now.

"Oh. Well. I can see where that might have changed the game a little."

"Apparently, it ended it."

Alice squeezed Jenna's shoulder. "You know, maybe it's for the bes—"

"Don't say that." Jenna didn't understand what had just happened, but she knew her own heart. "Just don't say that."

"Okay, okay." Alice's eyes softened. "You really mean it, don't you? About loving her?"

"I do."

Alice took her hand. "Then what—"

"I'm not going to let her run away. Not before I know why. Then, if she wants to go—" Jenna fought back the tears. Not now. There would be plenty of time for those later. She drew a breath, steadied herself. "If she doesn't want me—doesn't love me, all the way—then none of the rest of it matters."

"Maybe she just needs a little time. Why don't we get out of here? You can call her tomorr—"

"No." Jenna knew she'd never sleep, wondering where Gard was. Knowing she was hurting. "Give me fifteen minutes. If I'm not back by then, don't wait."

"Take care of your heart, you hear?" Alice said.

"I don't think that's up to me any longer." Jenna kissed Alice's cheek, then took the biggest risk of her life.

CHAPTER TWENTY-SEVEN

The crowd outside was even thicker and noisier than when Jenna had arrived. She twisted around clots of laughing people, desperate to reach the road. Finally she broke through onto the dirt lane and ran, chest heaving and lungs burning, up the long slope to the ridge where the truck had been parked. There. There! A dark silhouette up on the knoll, blocking out a patch of sky. Gard's truck. Still there. Gard was still here.

The vise-like constriction in Jenna's chest eased and she gulped cool night air. She tasted sweet clover and the tang of fresh-plowed earth, and beneath that, hope. Gard hadn't left. It wouldn't have mattered if she had, Jenna would have found her. Followed her home, to the clinic, to the farms—anywhere, everywhere. She wasn't letting her go until she had answers. If Gard didn't love her, didn't want her, she would have no choice but to walk away. She'd hurt, oh God, how she'd hurt, but they would at least have the truth, and not secrets, between them when they parted. She deserved that. Gard deserved that too.

As the truck slowly took form, emerging from the night shadows, Jenna saw Gard leaning with her arms braced against the hood, her head bowed. Alone in the dark, Gard looked broken, defeated. Seeing her in pain pierced her like a knife, tearing at her heart even more than Gard walking away from her. If her love was making Gard this unhappy, she'd find a way to live without her. She'd never be able to deny loving her, never be able to bury her feelings as she had in the past, but she'd live with the loss. Somehow. She'd have to endure the agony of letting her go, if that's what Gard needed.

Jenna slowly crossed the damp grass and rested her backside against the truck a few inches away from Gard. She stroked Gard's back, once, and then slipped her hands into her pockets. She couldn't be this close to her without touching her. "Are you all right?"

"I don't think so," Gard said, her voice husky and strained.

"I know you don't want to, but you need to talk to me. I deserve it," Jenna said. "We deserve it."

"I know. I just don't think I can. If you end up hating me—" Gard touched Jenna's cheek. "If the light goes out in your eyes when you look at me—that will kill me."

Jenna's throat closed with tears. "Oh, sweetheart. What have they done to you?"

Gard turned her face away and was swallowed by the night. "It was me, Jenna. No one is responsible except me."

"Take me home." Jenna clasped Gard's hand. "Take me home and tell me what happened. Please."

Gard sighed. "All right, Jenna. All right."

❖

Jenna kept her hand on Gard's arm all the way back to Gard's house. Even while Gard shifted gears, she curled her fingers over hers, unable to tolerate any more separation. The heavy silence in the truck was already unbearable, but she didn't want Gard to start talking until there was no chance she could stop. They walked together, side by side, up the flagstone path and sat in the rockers. Only then did she release Gard's hand, but she turned her chair so their knees brushed. The moonlight provided just enough light to see Gard's face.

"I'm here," Jenna said.

"Do you know, no matter how dark the night is, I can always see the starlight in your eyes," Gard said. "It's never dark when I'm with you."

"And it never will be, I promise."

"You don't know that," Gard said.

"I do. And I need for you to know it too. Please, give me a chance to show you."

"I love you, Jenna. I love you so much." Gard's voice cracked.

"Then trust me." Jenna caressed Gard's leg. "I'm here. I love you."

"I've tried not to love you, not to let you love *me*. Losing you is going to take everything I have left."

"How can you love me and still believe I could be so weak as to let you go because of something you did before we even met?"

"I don't think you're weak, just the opposite. And that's why you'll hate me."

"Damn it, Gard," Jenna snapped, "if you don't tell me what's going on, I'm going to get really pissed off at you."

Gard sighed. "I forgot how tough you can be."

"Well, I haven't forgotten what a pain in the ass you can be. Now, Gard. It's time."

"I destroyed my family, Jenna. I nearly killed my father. I drove away everyone I ever loved."

"How?" Jenna asked gently. "How?"

"You said you were going to fashion the hero in your new book after me." Gard rubbed her face with both hands. "You should have cast me as the villain."

"What did you do?"

"I grew up privileged. Rich. Very rich. Spoiled, indulged. I didn't really think about it at the time, but that's the truth of it."

Jenna waited, letting Gard start wherever she needed to. She didn't care how long it took—she'd never hear a more important story.

"I never really thought much about where the money came from," Gard went on, her voice flat and disconnected. "When it's always there, you don't think about it. All my friends came from wealthy families. Their lives were just like mine—private schools, exclusive camps in the summer, trips to Europe. It was just the way things were."

"Why should you question the life you were born into?" Jenna asked.

"Not at first, maybe. But later. Later, I should have." Gard rose abruptly and paced to the edge of the porch. "Right after I got to college I met a girl, Susannah. My first real relationship. My first love. I'd known for a long time I was a lesbian, but I hadn't done much more than steal a few kisses until then. I thought I loved her, I thought she loved me. My parents loved her. Her parents loved me—we were the golden couple. I'd go into the family business, she'd have our children and do whatever made her happy. Life was turning out great. Just the way it should."

Gard wrapped one arm around the porch column, her back to Jenna. "My family made their money in real estate, mostly. Everyone in the family went into the business. My older brother was already a VP. I didn't think about my career any more than I really thought about the money. I'd always wanted to be a vet, but I never really considered it a serious possibility. It didn't fit in with my family's expectations, or even my own."

"Somehow," Jenna said softly when Gard fell silent, "I can't see you in a three-piece suit and a corner office."

"No, neither can I now. I think eventually I would've realized I wasn't going to fit in the family mold. I might not have had the guts to break away, but as things turned out, I never had a chance to find out."

"What happened?"

"One morning I was in a coffee shop in Harvard Square. A woman sat down beside me. Young, attractive. She knew my name. She told me a story, a story I didn't believe at first."

Jenna's heart beat faster. Gard sounded so resigned, as if her guilt were leaching the life out of her. As if she already believed Jenna was gone. Jenna wanted so badly to touch her, to hold her, to reassure her. But she couldn't do any of those things until Gard finished the story. Until the truth lay bare between them.

"What did she tell you?" Jenna asked.

"It seems that I come from a long line of criminals," Gard said. "The money came from illegal real estate deals, fraudulent mergers, a laundry list of white-collar crimes going back generations. There are nicer names for it, but *crooks* kind of sums it up and I was right in line to carry on the family legacy. I even worked summers in the business, so I was already involved."

"Who was the woman in the coffee shop?"

"A federal agent. They'd been after my family for a long time. I didn't believe her at first, but after several meetings where she showed me some of the evidence, I couldn't keep denying it. The federal case was strong, probably strong enough to indict most of my family, including me."

"But you didn't know," Jenna protested. "You were what, twenty years old?"

"Almost twenty-one, and no, I didn't know. Although maybe if I'd questioned some of the things I'd seen, or even questioned how it was the family was so successful when most of the country was in a decline, I might have known. But I never bothered to ask. I never questioned."

"You're awfully hard on yourself."

"You haven't heard it all."

Jenna went to stand beside her and gripped the railing. "All right. Finish the story."

"They offered me a deal. I took it. I provided the evidence that the feds hadn't been able to get. No one in my family suspected I was gathering reports, chasing paper trails, uncovering double sets of accounting files. I testified in a closed hearing to the grand jury. I gave the federal prosecutors everything they needed to sew up their case." Gard shuddered. "I betrayed my family, Jenna, and after I testified, my father tried to kill himself."

"What aren't you telling me?" Jenna said.

"What makes you think there's more?" Gard asked, her tone a bitter rain of acid regrets.

"Because I know there is. Because I know you wouldn't have sacrificed your family, not to save yourself. That's not who you are Gard, I know it. I've seen you work—the way you care. I've felt the way you love me. You're not selfish, and you're no coward. If you made a deal, it wasn't to make things easier on yourself."

"The reasons don't matter." Gard caught Jenna's hands and kissed her fingers, then rested her cheek against Jenna's palm. "The result is still the same. My family was ruined, my father imprisoned, my brother too. I lost them all."

"What about Susannah? What about your lover?"

"Oh, she was the first to leave me." Gard laughed bitterly. "She couldn't get away from me fast enough. I'd ruined my family's social standing, as well as my own, and she didn't want to be tarred with the same brush. She never even asked me why I'd done it. She just told me she never wanted to see me again."

"*I* want to know why. Tell me why. What did you get in return for your testimony?"

"They promised they'd reduce the charges against my father and brother and not go after anyone else in the family if I helped them secure the case. If I didn't help, my father would have been looking at the rest of his life in prison."

"Does your family know what you did to *help* them? Does Susannah?"

"No."

"So you sacrificed everything you had—your reputation, your lover, your family—to make things easier for your father and brother, is that what you're telling me?"

"That's a nice way of putting it."

Jenna shook Gard's shoulders. "That's the only way to put it. Because that's what you're telling me happened."

"They hate me, Jen."

"Oh, sweetheart," Jenna murmured. "I love you."

Gard's shoulders shook, her tears rending Jenna's soul. Jenna pressed Gard's face to her neck and Gard clutched her as if she were the only solid thing in a shifting landscape. "You're not guilty. You didn't betray them. You sacrificed everything for them."

"Please don't leave me," Gard whispered.

"Oh, baby, I won't. Don't cry, sweetheart. Don't cry." Jenna kissed Gard's temple, her tears mingling with Gard's. "I love you. I love you so much."

CHAPTER TWENTY-EIGHT

Jenna guided Gard upstairs to the bedroom, undressed her, and quickly shed her own clothes. She climbed into bed and held out her arms. "Come here."

Gard curled around her, one leg over Jenna's thighs, her head on Jenna's shoulder, and sighed wearily. An instant later, she was asleep.

As tired as she was, Jenna couldn't sleep. She kept hearing Gard's despair. Gard, strong kind gentle Gard, had sounded so empty and lost and broken. Jenna pulled her closer, cradling Gard's head against her breast. How could anyone who loved her believe she would betray them? If she could get her hands on any of those people—Gard's parents, her lover…not that she deserved to be called *that*…the federal agents—she'd cheerfully strangle them all.

She must have slept because the next thing she knew gray ribbons rippled through the inky black outside the window, announcing the day. She kissed Gard's forehead and Gard murmured something incoherent and nuzzled her neck. Smiling, she combed her fingers through Gard's hair. Lying with Gard in her arms as dawn broke and the morning erupted with the chatter of birds and the distant crow of a cock, she felt so alive. Despite the long night and the broken sleep and the tears she'd shed, she was happy. Gard was so strong and so tender. And so in need of being cared for. Holding her, loving her, made Jenna feel stronger than she'd ever felt in her life.

Jenna's heart hammered and she stirred inside. Turning onto her side, she pressed against Gard and kissed her on the mouth.

Gard's eyes opened and flickered from puzzlement to desire in a heartbeat. "Mmm. Hi."

"I'm sorry I woke you," Jenna murmured. "You just felt so good in my arms. I got excited. I'm sorry."

Gard cupped Jenna's breast and stroked her nipple into hardness. "And you're apologizing, why?"

"You were sleeping so deeply."

"You think I'd rather be sleeping than doing this?" Gard kissed her, long, slow, deep strokes of her tongue, while she gently squeezed Jenna's breast. Jenna whimpered and slid her leg over the curve of Gard's hip, pressing her center against Gard's thigh. She was wet, open, and Gard's flesh was so hot. She moaned.

"I love you," Gard whispered.

The words shot to Jenna's core and she dug her fingers into the thick muscles along Gard's spine, her hips rolling up and down Gard's leg. So damn good. "I love you too. I'm going to come."

"You do that." Gard skimmed the tip of her tongue over Jenna's lower lip, nibbled on her. "You come on me, baby."

Jenna arched, the glorious pressure building until she overflowed. Just as her orgasm peaked, Gard sucked her nipple and she came again, harder. She cried out, reaching blindly for Gard.

"Here, baby. Right here." Gard pushed Jenna onto her back and covered her, bearing down hard between her legs. Jenna opened for her and wrapped both legs around the back of Gard's thighs, lifting to her.

"Now you," Jenna demanded.

Gard groaned and rocked between Jenna's legs. Jenna clutched Gard's ass, rising to meet her downward thrusts, giving her the pressure she needed.

"Oh God, Jenna," Gard gasped. "You feel so good."

"I love you. I love you." Jenna kissed Gard's throat and bit low on her neck. As she left her mark, Gard's hips jerked and she came in hard, frantic thrusts. Then, spent, she shuddered in Jenna's arms.

"That's right," Jenna crooned. "I've got you."

❖

Gard awakened with sunlight on her eyelids and squeezed them closed, wanting a few more seconds with Jenna. Her cheek was pillowed on Jenna's breast and Jenna's hand cradled her neck. Jenna breathed rhythmically, deeply asleep. Gard smiled to herself, thinking that she had put Jenna to sleep. She'd loved her. Satisfied her. Carefully, she kissed Jenna's breast.

"Don't start," Jenna murmured.

Gard laughed. "Why not?"

"You already wore me out."

"I hope not. What will we do for the next fifty years, then?"

Jenna went completely still and Gard's heart plummeted.

"I'm sorry," Gard said quickly. "I'm getting a little ahead of things, aren't I?" She started to move away and Jenna's hand clamped onto the back of her neck, keeping her from escaping.

"No," Jenna said, "you're not getting ahead of anything. Except I don't remember hearing a proposal of any kind from you."

"Proposal, as in—uh—offering a plan?"

"Not exactly."

"A proposition?"

Jenna laughed. "Not exactly."

Gard propped herself up on her elbow so she could read Jenna's face. Jenna's eyes were trusting, completely undefended. Jesus, she was brave. Gard traced the curve of Jenna's brow, the arch of her cheek, the gentle line of her jaw. She kissed her mouth, tenderly.

"I love you," Gard said. "I want us to spend the rest of our lives together. I want to be yours, and I want you to be mine. Is that what you mean?"

"Yes, exactly that," Jenna said. "And the answer is yes."

"What about New York?"

Jenna smiled. "Is it going somewhere?"

"Are you?"

Jenna brushed her fingers through Gard's hair. "Now and then, I suppose I will. You know I travel a lot. I need to do that for my work. But I'm never leaving you."

Gard nodded, waiting.

"I'll keep my place in Manhattan. It's convenient and a lot of events take place there."

"People know me there, Jenna. We were big news. Maybe not me personally, but my family—"

"I don't care about that," Jenna said.

"I care. I'm willing to bet *Alice* cares." Gard saw instantly she was right, even though Jenna tried to hide it. "She told you to stay away from me, didn't she?"

"Alice worries too much."

Gard started to sit up and Jenna grabbed her and yanked her down until they were lying face-to-face again.

"Don't you dare pull away from me now," Jenna said, but there was no heat in her voice. Only tenderness. "Alice was concerned at first, you're right. But she cares about me and she knows I love you. She'll be on our side."

"I want her to worry about you." Gard caressed her cheek. "Don't tell me my past, my reputation, isn't going to hurt your career."

"My personal life is my own business. And I am nothing except proud of you." Jenna's eyes flashed. "My career is very important to me, but you're much more than that. You're everything to me. If there's trouble—any kind of trouble—tomorrow, next year, fifty years from now—we'll handle it together."

"Oh Jesus, I love you," Gard whispered. "The only thing I need is for you to love me. No one, nothing means more."

"And all I need is for you to trust me. Trust me to always believe in you. Because I do."

"You don't have to tell anyone about me," Gard said.

Jenna frowned and storm clouds rolled through her eyes. "Now you're pissing me off. Besides insulting me. I love you. I want everyone to know—well, maybe not everyone." Jenna kissed her. "I love you. Don't be an idiot."

"That will take some doing."

"I know. But we've got time to work on it."

"What about Birch Hill?"

"Where do you want to live?" Jenna asked.

"At Birch Hill. I'll sell this place. It's a great house, but that farm is your home."

"You're sure?"

"Absolutely. It's the Hardy homestead. That's where we belong."

"We'll live there." Jenna drew Gard's hand to her heart, placed her palm over Gard's, and kissed her. "But here is where we belong."

About the Author

Radclyffe has published over thirty-five romance and romantic intrigue novels as well as dozens of short stories, has edited numerous romance and erotica anthologies, and, writing as L.L. Raand, has authored a paranormal romance series, The Midnight Hunters.

She is a seven-time Lambda Literary Award finalist in romance, mystery, and erotica—winning in both romance (*Distant Shores, Silent Thunder*) and erotica (*Erotic Interludes 2: Stolen Moments* edited with Stacia Seaman, and *In Deep Waters 2: Cruising the Strip* written with Karin Kallmaker) and a 2010 Prism award winner for *Secrets in the Stone*. She is a member of the Saints and Sinners Literary Hall of Fame, an Alice B. Readers' award winner, a Benjamin Franklin Award finalist (*The Lonely Hearts Club*), and a ForeWord Review Book of the Year Finalist (*Night Call* in 2009; *Justice for All*, *Secrets in the Stone*, and *Romantic Interludes 2: Secrets* in 2010). Two of her titles (*Returning Tides* and *Secrets in the Stone*) are 2010 Heart Of Excellence Readers' Choice finalists.

Writing as L.L. Raand she released the first Midnight Hunters novel, *The Midnight Hunt*, in March 2010. *Blood Hunt* is due for release March 2011. Her next First Responders novel, *Firestorm*, is due in July 2011.

Visit her Web sites at www.llraand.com and www.radfic.com.

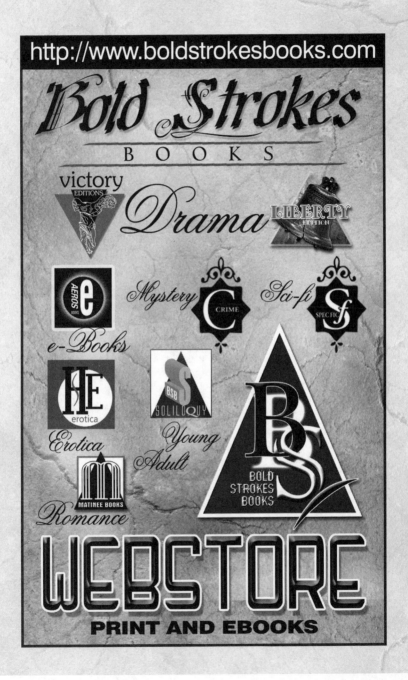